Start Without Me

ALSO BY JOSHUA MAX FELDMAN

The Book of Jonah

Start Without Me

A Novel

Joshua Max Feldman

HARPER LUXE

An Imprint of HarperCollins*Publishers*

HarperCollins
PUBLISHERS
Since 1817

This is a work of fiction. Names, characters, places, and incidents are products of the author's imagination or are used fictitiously and are not to be construed as real. Any resemblance to actual events, locales, organizations, or persons, living or dead, is entirely coincidental.

HarperCollins books may be purchased for educational, business, or sales promotional use. For information please e-mail the Special Markets Department at SPsales@harpercollins.com.

FIRST HARPERLUXE EDITION

ISBN:978-0-06-274333-6

HarperLuxe™ is a trademark of HarperCollins Publishers.

Library of Congress Cataloging-in-Publication Data is available upon request.

17 18 19 20 21 ID/LSC 10 9 8 7 6 5 4 3 2 1

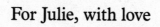

For Julie, with love

Anyone can save you
Anybody could
A touch of their hand would be enough
If they only would

—KISS AND KILL,
   "Any Given Sunday"

I
Strangers

[1]
The Warshaws'

Adam looked up at the basement ceiling, not sure how long he'd been awake. There was no clock in the basement—never had been, for as long as he could remember. He pushed himself up on his elbows. Weak gray light filled the line of slender windows at the top of the wall. He'd been dreaming; something had woken him up. Then he heard the gurgle of a toilet flushing.

A child appeared in the doorway in a corner across from the couch: a boy, five or six, in blue underpants and a SpiderMan T-shirt, dark hair matted on one side, a sour, suspicious look on his face. "Who are you?" the boy demanded.

"I'm Adam," Adam said. "*Uncle* Adam," he clarified.

The boy shook his head solemnly. "My uncle's Travis. He lives in Texas."

"I'm your other uncle. Your dad's brother."

"Why are you on the couch?"

"Kristen's—your cousins are sleeping in my room. My old room. What used to be my room." The boy scowled, as though none of this added up, and Adam had to admit it didn't sound very convincing. "Uncle Adam," he repeated. "You don't remember me?"

The boy's eyes narrowed. "Are you the uncle who smashed the piñata?"

"Jesus, that's what you remember?" Did he actually owe apologies to the kids, too?

"The candy went all in the—"

"It was a piñata, it was meant to get smashed. And if they didn't want me to smash it, they shouldn't have given me a turn."

The boy made a slow movement of his thumb beneath his chin, which, in the mental squint of just waking, looked to Adam downright menacing, like a mafioso's throat-slitting gesture. "Nobody's allowed to download mods on my dad's computer," the boy intoned.

This nonsense alerted Adam to the absurdity of the conversation: The kid didn't even know he was awake. "It's okay, man, go back to sleep," he said—would have preferred to use something more personal than "man," but he wasn't entirely, entirely sure whether this was Toby or Sam. Still, the child wordlessly obliged. He leaned his shoulder against the wall, padded back into the bedroom, leaving the door open—a gesture Adam found unreasonably touching, as though it were proof the boy didn't hate him, didn't fear him, after all.

He lay back down and stared up at the pocked tiles above him. The basement had a lurking, familiar odor: plaster and lavender air freshener locked in combat with something vaguely musty. He remembered what he'd been dreaming of: Music. Playing. Some sense of the sound still filled the corners of his memory—taut, sharp notes, like from a harpsichord, tripping down a thrumming baseline: a half song, half-remembered. Once upon a time, he'd have made the effort to recall it, tried to reach into the cracks between sleep and waking to pull the chimerical sound out—sing it into a voicemail, the way you fixed a butterfly to a board with a pin. Occasionally, what he'd listen to an hour or so later wasn't even half-bad. More often, though, what he heard was nonsense, and even before he stopped playing he'd concluded that it was a waste of time. He wasn't actually dreaming of music, he was only dreaming of playing it: the texture and resistance of the keys under his fingertips, the beer residue in the metal mesh of the mic on his lips, the bass rumble from the stage through his torso, and more and more lately that rarest feeling, of getting picked up and carried by the music itself: no more distinction between him and the keyboard, between him and those he played with, between crowd and band, all of them racing along with the same roar—the communion of that, the freedom.

The paisley sheet his mother had made up the couch with had gotten tangled around his thighs in the night. He yanked it up toward his chin, but without much hope of getting back to sleep. The stillness of the house was deafening somehow—like all the sleeping people were vibrating at a frequency only he could hear: his family, ringing in his ears.

He kicked off the sheet and sat up, grabbed his jeans, crumpled on top of his duffel bag, and took out a sweatshirt. He climbed the carpeted stairs as he pushed his arms through the sleeves. Above the rail to his right were taped a dozen or more crayon drawings on white paper: houses and suns, oceans and triangle-sailed boats, violent inchoate swirls that resembled things he'd seen when he dropped acid in the Mall of America before a show in St. Paul. "The fridge just isn't big enough when we all get together!" his mother had exclaimed as she'd led him down the night before—as though he were some kind of stranger, as though she were a tour guide, explaining to a foreigner what it was like when "they" were together. But he reminded himself: If he'd been absent for so long, he had only himself to blame. Fixed on the door at the top of the stairs was more kid art: brown, hand-shaped cutouts of different sizes, with glued-on elaborations (yellow feet, red-orange wattles, plastic googly eyes) to establish that these were turkeys. "Happy Thanksgiving!" one of his nieces or nephews had written in careful elementary school cursive on a piece of construction paper, masking taped above the doorknob. For some reason, it struck him like an ultimatum.

He opened the door a crack, listened: more tinnitus quiet, no one else was up. He moved as softly as he could down the corridor toward the front hall. When he was a teenager he'd snuck out so often, and apparently so needfully, he'd been able to make this trip without turning on a single light: the twelve stairs up from the basement, left and down this hall to the front door, his hand reaching the knob in the dark by pure muscle memory. Then he'd get into his father's car, put it in neutral, and roll down to the end of the driveway, only then turning on the engine. And from there it was off to some friend's or to some agreed-upon clearing in the woods, bottle caps and butts littering the ground like pine needles, or if there was nothing going on he and his friends would drive around the campus of the local state college, hoping to stumble on a party, smoking weed and listening to cassettes of Mudhoney, Guster, Pearl Jam, NWA. He knew he shouldn't look back on those nights quite so fondly. But he couldn't help it. Yes, it was drugs-and-alcohol-laden fun—but it was still fun.

He carefully opened the coat closet; the old ski jacket that his mother had pulled from somewhere was hanging next to the blue peacoat he'd worn from San Francisco. Within sixty seconds of his walking in, his mother had declared the peacoat "too nice" for the game of touch football planned for the following afternoon, and bustled around upstairs until she produced the ancient jacket. He'd tried to tell her he'd bought the peacoat for forty bucks at a thrift store almost a decade ago, and anyway, there was no reason to find an alternative at eleven o'clock at night. But she ignored him, and when she held out the ski jacket, of course he took it, of course he tried it on, and though the synthetic fabric was so stiff with age it was almost sharp, he declared that it was perfect, and thanked her, and thanked her some more. Why? Because he wanted to be agreeable—amenable, he thought as he took his cigarettes from the pocket of the peacoat, zipped up the ski jacket to his throat.

His pair of ratty Converse was on the drip tray amid

a double line of neatly ordered Velcros and snow boots. He tied his laces and pulled open the door. And the instant the door parted from the jamb, the cat appeared out of nowhere and slid outside. "Fuck!" Adam said, making a flailing attempt to grab the animal by its tail as it darted out. He lost his balance and fell on his hip, knocking over the drip tray, one arm stuck outside.

He sat there for a moment, waiting for the whole house to wake up: doors flying open, shouts of alarm. As the quiet continued, he tried to assess what key of crisis, major or minor, this cat situation represented. Was it an outdoor cat or an indoor cat? Had it ever been to the house before? If so, was it allowed to roam the yard? It was Kristen's family's cat. Adam could imagine her twin daughters wailing when they heard; he imagined spending the whole day searching the neighborhood for the animal, only to discover its bloody corpse fresh from the maw of some displaced mountain lion or overzealous rottweiler or whatever. In short, the day ruined, and all his fault.

The open door was letting the cold air in; that had to be against the rules. He pulled himself up, went outside and shut the door behind him. With what the cigarette had cost him, he figured he might as well smoke it. And as he lit it and sat down on the top step, there was the cat—perched erect and expectant at his feet, swishing its tail, regarding him as though it were on to him, too: He didn't know what he was doing. He didn't know how to be an uncle or a son or a brother—not here, not anymore. Not without a drink. The cat sauntered up the steps; Adam opened the door and it vanished inside. "Asshole," Adam muttered after it.

And then he smiled, because it was funny he'd called the cat an asshole. The whole thing was kind of funny, if you looked at it the right way: Uncle Adam, freaking out about the cat getting out, but the cat spent lots of time outside! It knew when to go out and come back in. Maybe proving he belonged wasn't so much a matter of mastering every last rule for who slept where, when the cat was allowed to go out, what to do with the surplus crayon drawings, but rather knowing what it was okay to laugh about. "You'll never believe what happened with me and that fucking cat!" he could tell them over breakfast.

He took another pull on the cigarette, blew the smoke upward to try to warm the tip of his nose. The spruce trees at the end of the yard, planted by his parents when he was a kid to block the sight of Parr Street and the McReedys' garage, were so still in the cold they appeared frozen solid. A bright layer of frost had settled over the grass of the lawn and over the slope of blacktop where the cars were parked: Kristen and her husband Dan's minivan; Jack and his wife Lizzy's Tahoe; and last in line the cobalt blue Chevy Adam had rented in Hartford, because he hadn't wanted anybody to have to come and get him from the airport. They'd offered, everybody'd offered; but again, he'd been try-ing to be amenable—so amenable they'd hardly notice he was there.

He smacked his fingers against his palms, finally fixed the cigarette at the corner of his mouth and stuck his hands under his armpits. Smoking without your hands was one of the easier things you could learn to do at a piano. He should've found a pair of gloves in the closet, though. Even when they weren't squeezed in his armpits on a freezing New England November morning, the joints of his fingers ached when he first woke up. He'd met an older jazz guy in Miami who'd had to stop playing altogether because of the arthritis. All things considered, though, you had to have a pretty lucky career for arthritis to force you out, and not the mile-below-the-poverty-line money, or the burnout from the road, or the booze and the bars, not to men-tion all the harder stuff you could get with as little as a mutter to the right promoter, hanger-on, somebody-on-the-bill's girlfriend. He remembered at a party after a Kiss and Kill show in New Orleans, in some swel-tering shotgun crash-house, he'd wandered into a back room and stumbled on a shirtless, comically mulleted guy poking at the thighs of a glassy-eyed redhead, her jeans around her ankles. It took Adam a moment to register the syringe clasped between the dude's teeth. He looked up at Adam and grinned around the syringe like the fucking Cheshire cat. "What about you, amigo?" he asked, taking the syringe from his mouth. "You're in the band, you want one on the house?" Earlier in the night, he'd introduced himself as a friend of Johanna's. And maybe he was. You could never guess who her friends would be—where they came from, what they wanted.

Adam couldn't say whether he'd been too smart, or too scared, or simply plain lucky to have refused that offer—that and the thousand others like it, escaped all those choices even worse than the ones he'd made to make it back here: the steps of his parents' house, on Thanksgiving morning. The juxtaposition of the two moments—heroin in the back room, the sleepy home on Thanksgiving day—somehow made both of them seem ridiculous, maybe made him seem ridiculous, too, with the clumsily stitched-together persona he'd carried on with for so many years: the rock keyboardist, the nice suburban kid from western Massachusetts.

But what did he care if he'd turned out to be ridiculous? He ought to be thrilled to be nothing worse than ridiculous! And he wished he could explain something like that to Jack, or to his dad, or to any of them—that he was grateful, grateful almost to tears, to be here: sober for nine months and four days (as of this morning), invited back for a family holiday.

From the moment they closed the door behind him, though, it'd been awkward. His mother giggled painfully after she asked him if he wanted anything to drink. His father kept announcing how glad he was to see Adam while clasping his hands together and shaking them in front of his chest, like a politician pleading for racial harmony. The only other person who'd waited up was Jack, and Adam couldn't help wondering whether his older brother had stayed up on the chance Adam would show up blotto, and they'd need to throw him out. When Adam said after five minutes he was exhausted and just wanted to get some sleep, he could tell they were all relieved.

He put the cigarette out on the bottom of his shoe, slid the butt into the pocket of his jeans. As he opened the door, he saw above it was hammered a strip of sanded wood with the words "The Warshaws" painted in blocky purple letters. The loneliness he felt looking at that sign was at once so predictable and so unaccountable all he could do was stand there. Then he went back inside.

He took off his sneakers, righted the drip tray and the scattered shoes, hung up the ski jacket, and went into the kitchen. The table was already set up as the children's table: orange paper tablecloth, paper plates with cartoon Pilgrims, the centerpiece a fan-tailed, leering paper turkey. He surveyed the family photos on the shelves above the sink, images spanning from his and his siblings' childhoods to the birth of Kristen's twins. There were a few photos of him playing: a recital when he was six, looking freakishly tiny at the keys of a six-foot grand; the time Kiss and Kill played *Late Night* in the Conan era. (His mother must have cut the photo to leave Johanna out; pretty tactful, he had to admit.) The most recent photo of him was maybe five years old, some solo show he'd done: his back bent, his face down near the keys, eyes shut, lips curled in concentration: the Artist at Work, or trying to look that way. He'd lost weight since then—his face at thirty-five narrower, the angles of chin and cheek sharper. He had an impulse to hide his pictures behind the others, but his mother being his mother would notice, and he'd have to explain what he'd done. Why should he feel humiliated? she'd want to know. She had the pictures out because they were *proud* of him (which, of course, was the most humiliating part of all).

He dropped the cigarette butt into the trash can

under the sink, and shook the can so the butt jiggled under a banana peel. He pulled opened the refrigerator, looking for he wasn't sure what. The shelves were stacked with casseroles and tin-foil-covered pots, ready to be reheated. A couple green glass bottles sat wedged in the door: sparkling cider, he saw from the labels. He had a hunch they'd even gotten rid of the cough syrup.

He imagined making himself useful—tidying up, putting away. But everything was spotless: the countertops wiped down, the cereal boxes on top of the fridge lined in descending order. A piece of yellow legal paper was taped to the handle of the dishwasher, on which one of the kids had written "Clean!" Adam lifted the paper. On the back was "Dirty!" with some comically grubby plates and glasses, flies buzzing around them in the air. He smiled again. He loved these kids. He didn't know which one had made the sign, so he felt his love for all of them collectively—felt it as a form of relief. He switched the sign over to "Dirty!" and opened the dishwasher. But as he took out the first pair of clean plates, he realized he didn't know where anything went. There was a coffeepot in the top rack; the coffee maker was plugged in on the counter. Okay, this he could do. He could make them coffee. He could fill the house with the smell of freshly brewed coffee in the morning. Who could object to that?

He took the glass coffeepot from the dishwasher and set it on the counter by the coffee maker, took out the plastic lid and the filter basket. He opened some cupboards, got lucky and found the filters. The coffee was right there in the freezer, like he'd guessed. So far, so good. He slid the filter in the basket, spooned in the coffee grounds, snapped the basket into the coffee maker, and poured in the water. He even imagined himself doing it all with a certain finesse—the practiced grace of his hands. And maybe this idea made him careless, or maybe it was something else, but as he tried to snap the pegs of the lid into the holes of the pot, the pot slipped from his hands. It made a balletic turn on the counter and spun off the edge.

He didn't even bother to watch whether it broke, only listened, with hope that bordered on prayer. Silence followed the shattering sound. Then he heard from somewhere in the house, "Dad!" And then the same voice, more desperately, "Moooom!" And he heard doors opening.

He knew he ought to pick up the larger pieces of glass, find a broom and a dustpan, be there to warn anyone who appeared about the shards and apologize for depriving them all of coffee on a holiday morning. He ought to do a thousand things that real members of a family would do without thinking. But he found he lacked the will to do any of them. He went back to the closet, put on his peacoat, and went outside.

Sunlight was slanting through the needles of the spruce trees. Maybe he should go out and get coffee—that would make up for all of it. "Don't worry, Uncle Adam got coffee from town!" Someone would clean up the glass; surely, no barefooted child would step on the pile of glass, need stitches—shit, for all he knew, lose the foot.

This was called catastrophic thinking, he'd been taught at Stone Manor, the Maine rehab he'd been through at the beginning of the year: His mind had a compulsion to seek out the worst possible outcomes. Why did it do that? Harder to say. But the point was, he shouldn't trust his fear that breaking the coffeepot would lead to one of his nephews losing a foot. He could have another cigarette, and in a minute he'd go back inside and clean up the glass—and explain.

But that was the part he couldn't summon the energy for: the explanations. Having to say, over and over and over—to Jack and his mother and father and Kristen and Dan and Lizzy and Emma and Carrie and Toby and Sam and the baby whose name he forgot, and hell, to the cat while he was at it—tell them all about his meager hopes of making them coffee, and how with his graceful hands, he'd fucked it up. No, he couldn't do it. Not after one cigarette, not after a hundred. Not sober.

He dug in the pockets of his peacoat and found the keys to his rental car. He walked across the lawn and got in, put the car in neutral, rolled down the drive, stopped at the bottom of the hill, and started the engine.

[2]

Breakfast at Dunks

Adam felt terrific as he drove. Turning along the curves of Burnette Road, he plugged his iPhone into the car stereo and put on a Wu-Tang mix he'd made. A second later, bass thumped so loud he imagined the glass of the windows bowing. The tree-pocked lawns and driveways up to boxy colonials—white siding, painted shutters—looked distant and remote, like he was staring down at them from the window of an airplane. He blew the stop sign at the end of the road and made a right onto the straight arrow of Parr Street, pressed the gas pedal to the floor and watched as the speedometer climbed all the way to eighty, the feeling of freedom swelling in his chest with each little number the arm of the speedometer glided past. He recalled the dream he'd been having: playing when it was at its best, when the boundaries broke down and everything was swept up in a single roar. You'd forget all about yourself—you didn't have to *be* yourself.

He came to a red light where Parr Street met Rector and was alarmed to feel the tumble of the antilock brakes before the car came to a halt. There must have been black ice on the road; he should take it easy. The good news was, he didn't want a drink. On the road, you drank to come down from that feeling, to come down after any night onstage, good or bad, and then later to get up onstage in the first place, and finally to find the courage to look at the keys at all. But now, no, he didn't want a drink, he told himself. He didn't want one at all.

The succession of driveways ended abruptly at Rector. On the corner was a gas station with a minimart, beyond that tracts of fallow farmland, a handwritten sign stuck into the soil by the road: Acreage for Sale. Adam was humming these words to the tune of "Address Unknown" when it occurred to him he didn't know where he was going. A sign on the corner had an arrow to the right for I-91 North and South. He should go to New York City! He hadn't been there for years, but he still had friends there, they wouldn't all have moved. Then again—it was Thanksgiving morning.

Even assuming anybody was home, how happy would they be to find him at their apartment doors today? He tried to avoid thinking about it, but he was pretty sure if he did, he'd remember a lot of reasons his welcome in New York might be less than whole-hearted. He had the vague sense of owing a lot of people in the city money.

A car honked behind him; he hadn't noticed that the light had changed. Ahead on Parr was nothing but more farmland—fields, he remembered, in which he and his friends had once gone cow tipping, in the ex-hilaration of polishing off their very first keg. Adam raised his hand apologetically to the car behind; the slouched silhouette of the driver only honked again. He turned right, toward the highway.

Okay, New York was a bad idea. Where, then? He was approaching the roundabout where Rector met Route 32. On the opposite side of the road he spotted a Dunkin' Donuts, its pink-and-orange logo like a flashy grin against the building's asphalt roof. He made a U-turn across the double yellow and pulled into the parking lot.

The sun had risen in an empty blue sky. If anything, though, the sweeping brightness as he got out of the car only made the morning seem colder—as if the sunlight carried its own form of chill. He banged his hands together, blew on his knuckles as he hurried across the lot, and pushed open the door of the Dunks.

He was struck pleasantly in the face with heated air, tinged with the smell of sugared pastry. The surfaces beneath the florescent lights were all clean and bright pastels; "Sleigh Ride" by the Ronettes was playing.

A short, doe-eyed young woman stood behind the counter, wearing a black headscarf topped with a pink Dunkin' Donuts visor. She smiled as Adam approached.

"Welcome to Dunkin' Donuts," she said. "What can I get you?"

He'd skipped dinner the night before, and surveying the Willy Wonka racks of donuts, he found he was starving. "I'll take a chocolate bow tie, a dozen jelly munchkins, and a large coffee with two creams," he said. It was his high school order. He paid with his debit card, and the woman began loading his breakfast into a paper bag with a pair of plastic tongs. "Happy Thanksgiving," she said as she handed him the bag and the great Styrofoam cup of coffee.

"Thanks," he answered. "You just working today?"

"I'm going over to my cousin's tonight."

"Cool. Well, enjoy it. Happy Thanksgiving."

"Thanks for visiting Dunkin' Donuts," she answered.

He sat at a table by the window, watched the occasional car turning on or off the roundabout up the street. He could probably drive all the way to Chicago and back without hitting any traffic—anyone with somewhere to be was already there by now. Nat King Cole's "Frosty the Snowman" started playing, which was pretty painful if you knew the jazz piano stuff Cole did earlier in his career. But that was just pretentious music nerd griping, Adam thought as he took a swig of the scalding coffee, and anyway, you did what you needed to do to get over. He sure as shit had.

He plucked off one end of the bow tie, put it in his mouth. He was losing some of the ecstatic momentum of his initial flight. They'd probably be awake at the house by now; they'd notice he was missing. He imagined them standing in a circle around the shards of the coffeepot like a forensics team, trying to reconstruct what had happened from the pattern of shattered glass. Soon they'd start to worry. Jesus, was he really going to do that to them again? But then it occurred to him—he could still put it all back together. He was at the Dunkin' Donuts. He could get one of those big paper cartons of coffee, like that had been the plan all along, set it triumphantly on the kitchen counter, and then . . .

But they wouldn't believe that he'd just gone out to get them coffee. They wouldn't believe it, because it wouldn't be true. Yet they'd spend the whole day pretending they believed it, and he'd pretend he believed they believed it, and then the day would still be ruined, only no one would be allowed to admit it. No, better to let them have their Thanksgiving. They were used to his absence by now. They could talk shit behind his back if they wanted, they could feel sorry for him if they wanted. Either way, it'd be easier for everyone if he wasn't there.

He pulled his phone out of his pocket. He wasn't sure which one of them to text, though. Once, Kristen would have been the obvious choice. He'd always had that bond with his older sister, an innate sympathy that was the yin to the yang of mutual antagonism that seemed to have existed between him and Jack since Adam was in diapers. But Kristen was different since she'd gotten married. Her husband, Dan, worked in finance, traded Asian currencies or something like that. The upshot was he was rich, and hence Kristen was rich, and she'd started acting like it, like somebody's rich wife. She lived in Westport, she rode horses, she had a sailboat and an au pair, and she was always posting pictures of that shit on Instagram. Not that there was anything criminal about it. It was just that once, she and Adam would have laughed at people who lived in Westport, owned horses and sailboats. Growing up,

Adam believed his older sister was the coolest person in the world: wry, tough, worldly (by the standards of suburban Roxwood, anyway), with a nose ring and an oversize green army coat she wore every day of high school and shoulder-length hair streaked with blonde. She used to give him drags off the cigarettes she'd sneak in the backyard. And when he was eleven, she gave him a cassette that changed his life, a mixtape of all her favorite bands, with the songs an eleven-year-old had hope of liking, too: "Psycho Killer" by the Talking Heads, "Heart of Gold" by Neil Young, "Battle of Evermore" by Led Zeppelin, "Casey Jones" by the Grateful Dead. None of this music was on the radio in the early nineties, and more to the point, at eleven, music to Adam was études and impromptus and Vladimir Horowitz. He even had a poster of Vladimir Horowitz on his wall! Listening to that tape was like stepping through the wardrobe into fucking Narnia. The music was simple, sure, but it was the simplicity that let it reach into your chest and drag you around by the heart.

But now Kristen had abandoned him—set him on a path and then disappeared along the journey. Somewhere in his mind, jangly acoustic rockabilly started up, and a sardonic, untrustworthy singer: "Yer So Bad" by Tom Petty. On some shelf in his head was a sort of radio that broadcast his emotional background noise as songs he'd heard too often, or occasionally (painfully) written. He couldn't open a credit card bill without the accompaniment of the galloping tremolo of Schubert's Erlkönig; he heard a choral melisma he'd written for a Kiss and Kill album whenever he was about to come.

When he was still playing, he could take this as a kind of affirmation: that he was doing with his life what his brain was wired to do. Lately, though, he identified a mocking quality to it—as though something in his mind was making fun of him.

He didn't remember the specific lyrics to "Yer So Bad"—he knew there was a sister in there, but lyrics were never his thing. In whatever band he was in, they were always someone else's job. He remembered the sense of the song well enough, though: to hell with the squares, we've got each other.

He didn't need Tom Petty to tell him that he was angry at Kristen. At Stone Manor, he'd been led to the realization that he was angry at all of them. The problem was he had no right to be.

He texted Jack because it would only confirm everything Jack already thought about him, and so it would be like a gift.

Couldn't do it. Had to go. Tell everybody sorry.

Then he hit SEND. The phone answered with a *bhwoop.*

It took him to the sixth Munchkin to realize how fucking stupid that text had been—that it could only ratchet up the alarm over his disappearance. He picked up his phone again. No missed calls, no texts back. Maybe they hadn't seen the text, hadn't yet noticed he was gone; or maybe they'd expected it, and didn't need an explanation. He began another text to Jack.

I'm cool, I just

But then he didn't know what to add, and hit SEND by mistake.

Wasn't done with that text

But once again, he couldn't think of what else to say. As he stared at the screen, a wheel of spinning bars appeared, and in the next instant, the screen was entirely black. "Aw fuck," he said aloud.

He looked around the Dunkin' Donuts, as if a phone charger might be found lying around one of the tables.

"Hey, do you have an iPhone charger?" he asked the woman at the counter.

"Sorry," she said. "Mine's a Galaxy."

"These things die so quickly," he said to her. "It's like as soon as you unplug them, the countdown starts." She smiled a little and shrugged.

Just my luck, he thought as he shoved the phone back in his pocket. But no, he corrected himself, that was the dumbest, the most dangerous way to think: That it was bad luck; that he was its victim; that he was a victim at all. Self-pity was toxic to recovery. It was the vortex that pulled in all your resolve, all your good intentions, all your promises to yourself, until there was nothing left to do but drink, smoke, snort, fuck, whatever— because what other choice had life ever given you? No, he was the one who'd run out on his family. He was the one who'd written dumb, cryptic, alarming texts. He was the one who'd left his charger—all of his shit, for that matter—back at the house. It wasn't bad luck. It was him: Adam being Adam.

And it was obvious where he should go next. He should go back to San Francisco. That's where his life was now: his job, his apartment, his stuff. So his attempt to spend the holiday with his family had flamed out. It happened. You dealt with it, sober, and you moved on to the next thing: the next flame out, the next triumph, disaster, challenge, whatever. You kept on moving, forward. That's what recovery was—that's what *life* was, if you were any good at it. Progress. One foot in front of the other, one day at a time.

He was doing good in San Francisco, too. He'd chosen to live there after getting out of rehab because it seemed far from all the places he'd fucked up, all the people he'd fucked over; plus, he happened never to have played a Kiss and Kill show there, so none of it was overlaid with memories of Johanna. And it'd turned out to be a pretty cool place: low-key, good-natured, scruffy in a mild way, like your buddy's dog or something. He had his job at the bank, had even gotten promoted recently, to General Accounts Manager, now got to help people open checking accounts and rent safe deposit boxes. It was the least exciting, least surprising, least *rock* job imaginable—he wore khakis and a tie every day, for Christ's sake. But that's exactly what he'd wanted: no surprises, no music. And while he hadn't really made any friends in the months he'd been out there, he didn't think of himself as lonely, exactly. At any rate, he was rarely alone. He shot the shit with guys at work, talked basketball, Netflix. And most Fridays and Saturdays, he was out on dates.

He'd put a profile up on a couple sites—it wasn't

hard to find someone to have dinner with. Dating—
"putting himself out there"—seemed to him another
component of a rightly directed life. Granted, if he
was honest, his heart wasn't really in it, and often he
sensed the women's hearts weren't in it, either. There
was a predictability to the interactions that was stul-
tifying, like they had the choreography of a Japanese
tea ceremony or something: meeting; ordering from
the menu; exchanging amusing anecdotes and snippets
of biography; waiting for the check; paying the check;
either having sex, or not. The sex was fun, sure, but it
seemed to make another date less likely, as if it resolved
the encounter in a way that made further meetings
superfluous. But he'd come to suspect that everything
beyond the act of the date itself was superfluous. The
point was you were trying.

"Last Christmas" by Wham! had started playing.
The synths were pretty cool, though the Dunks' speak-
ers weren't exactly doing them justice. Anyway, he
figured he ought to get moving—what with the coffee
situation, it wasn't impossible his father would pull into
the parking lot next. That would be a fun conversation:
"Hey, Dad, no, I was just leaving, y'know, it turns out
you guys are all sort of terrifying, and by the way, did
any of the kids step on that pile of glass and lose a foot?
Anyway, happy Thanksgiving!"

He stood, picking up his coffee. "Take it easy," he said to the woman at the counter.

"You, too," she answered brightly.

He got back in the car and turned on the heat. It was time to head to the airport. San Francisco, the bank, dating—trying. When would it end? But the point was it wouldn't end—it *couldn't* end, because it was his sobriety, his life. Thinking of it as temporary, as something that would lead to something better, or easier, was just another trap, another way for him to piss it all away. "So do it right for once," he told himself: You won't see Johanna again; you're done with music. You tried, you failed, just like a million other kids with perfect pitch and a good left hand. But you didn't die, and you got sober, and your liver's not even in bad shape, the doctor said, so be grateful for that, and go to the airport. You'll make it to Thanksgiving some other year.

"Okay," he said. "Okay." Through the window of the Dunks, he saw that he'd forgotten the rest of his donuts. He watched as the woman in the headscarf went to the table, picked up the bag, ate one of the Munchkins, threw the bag away. He put on his seat belt and put the car in reverse.

[3]

The Airport Sheraton
in Windsor Locks

Marissa knew she should change out of her uniform before going down to the lobby for breakfast. She should shower without letting her hair get wet, she should iron and put on the sweater she'd crammed into her rollaboard, she should grab a coffee and a muffin in the lobby, and get on the road. It was already past nine. Even assuming there wouldn't be any traffic on a holiday morning, it would take at least an hour to get to Robbie's parents' house in Vermont. She'd never get there by ten, as she'd promised him. And the longer she delayed, the later she'd be.

But as a flight attendant, Marissa labored under the perpetual tyranny of having no time to waste, serving drinks and collecting trash in a workplace in which the most minor jolt to normal procedures (a passenger's bag popping open in the aisle, a lav door spontaneously deciding not to close) could send tremors of inconvenience that might grow to shake the entire system: planes in the air waiting to land, planes on the ground waiting to board, passengers sitting at gates and parked in No Standing zones across the country, if not around the world. In other words, she was always in a rush. And having flown in that morning from Seattle, after having flown to Seattle from New York the previous afternoon, Marissa found it hard to keep on with the rushing when there was no more at stake here than the annoyance of a husband who'd be annoyed with her anyway, the irritation of in-laws she doubted liked her very much to begin with. What she wanted—all she wanted—was to let herself fall facedown on the hotel room bed, close her eyes, and worry about the consequences in ninety minutes or so.

But though she might fantasize about doing this, she wouldn't. The most she allowed herself was to fold her trench coat over her rollaboard in the entryway of the dayroom VentureJet had provided her and Delia before the turnaround to Sea-Tac that night, sit down on the bed, take off her shoes, and rub the arches of her feet through her nylons. The room was not so bad, as these places went: tidy, spacious, neutral smelling. Yet something about looking around it hardened her exhaustion. Maybe it was simply that she'd seen it all before, so many times, if not in this particular hotel, then in the hundred hotels like it: the drab colors of the thin carpeting, the plastic sheaths around the plastic cups by the ice bucket, the flaccid neatness of the made-up bed, with its white bed skirt, white duvet, white pillowcases all bleached and starched to lifelessness. Hotel rooms started to look a lot like hospital rooms, she'd realized: Whatever happened there, the expectation was you would not be staying long.

Thinking of hospitals seemed to make her nauseous. She dropped her foot from her hands and closed her eyes. Don't lie down, she warned herself. Don't lie down, or you'll fall asleep.

She took her phone out of her purse at her feet, and for the first time since getting on the airplane the previous night, turned it on. Robbie had sent her a text at some point.

I'm not angry anymore. Let's enjoy the holiday. I love you.

It took her a few moments to put together what he was talking about. The long-haul flights effected a sort of mental suspended animation, in which the realities of life on the ground fell away, her mind as bare as the cloud cover out the window. It was something she'd learned to like about her job. But everything ignored or forgotten was always there when you landed. The fight before she'd left had been bad, escalating from the usual assurance that "It's not a big deal, but" all the way to screaming and tears. They'd gotten into it this time because he announced he was hurt she was "skipping" the better part of the holiday with his family to work.

Yes, she had agreed to swap onto flights on the holiday, but it was time-and-a-half, and they needed the money. What argument could be more compelling than that?

But he said he didn't understand why she'd become a flight attendant in the first place. And when she answered that it was because she wanted a job with a pension, he rolled his eyes and told her if it ever came to that, they could count on his parents for money.

But she didn't want money from his parents. She wanted to be independent.

Independent from what? You're always leaving! he complained, like always.

I don't have a choice! was all she could ever say back.

They'd been fighting daily lately, like it was a setting in their relationship they didn't know how to turn off. It's just a hard time, he'd tell her in the intervals, when they were okay to hold each other or even just sit beside each other on the couch and talk. It's a hard time, so what could you do? If you fought, you had to make up, over and over and over, as many times as it took. But even the making up required emotional labor it took Marissa another couple minutes to summon. Finally, she texted him.

Got 2 BDL. Hope you & yr parents having a good morning. Be there soon. Love you too.

She sat on the bed, staring at the phone. The little bubbled messages stared back, as unchanging as if they'd been carved in stone. She didn't know what she was waiting for. It didn't mean anything if he didn't write back. He'd been the one who'd sought to make peace, and she'd agreed. This fight was over, officially. But there was still some reassurance she craved, some confirmation that wherever he was, that whatever they'd put each other through most recently, Robbie still loved her, right then. She had no right to this re-assurance anymore. But God, she craved it. She felt a pang of something that was either visceral need for him or more nausea, she couldn't tell the difference.

The phone didn't beep or ping or vibrate in her

hand. Through the wall behind her, she could hear the permanently delighted chatter of a TV morning show. She put the phone down on the bed, stood up. The curtains in the room were drawn, which meant there wasn't much to see behind them, but sunlight would help her feel more alert. A few flight attendants she'd flown with popped Adderall in the lav during red-eyes; she understood the appeal, but even if she'd been open to messing around with prescription pills (and she wasn't), her feeling was that at thirty-one, she ought to be able to stay on her feet without pharmaceutical assistance.

She pulled the curtains apart: Half the view was filled by the concrete wall of the adjacent parking garage; in the other half of the window, she could see the stubby cream buildings of an office park, casting rectangular shadows across an empty lot. It had an abandoned, failed sort of look, but of course this was only because everybody who worked there was home for Thanksgiving. Thinking of the holiday filled her nostrils with the smells of stacked turkey slices and gobs of mashed potatoes, and now the nausea clenched her stomach and wouldn't let go. She raced into the bathroom, knocking over her rollaboard, flung up the toilet seat, and vomited stomach acid and orange juice into the bowl. Then she dry heaved for several minutes, at last slumped against the wall, leaned her temple against the cold tile.

She never threw up. Saint Marissa, her friends in college used to call her, because she wouldn't have more than one beer at a party, and so they could count on her to rub their backs, hold their hair, talk them through whatever they might be crying about when they were in this position; by the time she graduated, anything a Syracuse undergrad had to sob into a toilet bowl, she'd heard it before.

Marissa wanted to believe it was the Red Lobster she'd eaten in Hartsfield. That was a week ago, though, and here she was, still puking in the mornings. And then the ominous timeline: four months since Robbie's birthday, the last time they'd had sex; two months since her last period; and six weeks since Brendan. The morning sickness had to confirm it. So what would Saint Marissa do now?

She closed her eyes, leaning further against the wall. She could hear her mother's cackling Boston accent: "The Cavanos aren't lucky people, so you expect the worst." It was maybe the best advice her mother had ever given her. But what was the competition? Don't talk to cops? In the darkness behind her eyes, a scene filled in: tidy rows of houses along thin, placid streets.

It was what she saw out the window during descents. The height made the scenes on the ground—the highway clovers, the shopping malls, the parks with their dirt baseball diamonds—look so benign, toylike, like a still life.

She jerked her head up in a panic—she'd fallen asleep. The shadows of the bathroom seemed to have stretched, darkened. It was nighttime—she'd missed her return. She brought her watch to her face so fast she banged herself on the nose. But no, she'd slept only a couple minutes. "Thank God," she muttered. And she got to her feet.

She retrieved her toiletry bag from her rollaboard, brushed her teeth furiously to clear away the stomach acid taste, arranging her uniform with her free hand: pulled the button-down shirt taut on her shoulders, smoothed the front of the skirt with her palm. She would drive up to Vermont in what she had on, she decided. She could change when she got there, wash the uniform in her in-laws' machine. Then in a few hours, it would be back here to Connecticut, change in the dayroom, catch the shuttle back to Bradley, and—but she knew better than to get ahead of herself. One trip down the aisle at a time, as Delia would say from the other side of the drinks cart, in the hopeless middle of a five-leg day.

She washed her face, rubbed moisturizer from the little amenity bottle on the sink into the pinched corners of her eyes, spread it over her cheeks down to the cleft in her chin. Then she released her hair from the bun she wore for work, letting the black, unruly tendrils fall down her back. It'd be nice to wash it before she saw her mother-in-law—but it'd be nice to do a lot of things she didn't have time for this morning. She retied the knot in the scarf at her throat: down-up, down-twist-up, forming the furrowed triangle that they were supposed to call the "Skyfarer knot" if a passenger ever asked (they never did).

Last, she put on her eyeliner and mascara, and surveyed herself. Better, she thought—then clenched her teeth with furious frustration that threatened to swell over into tears. Because God almighty, who was she kidding? She looked not an inch different from what she was: a woman who'd been up all night, hadn't showered in days, had just vomited, made an attempt to hide it all with mascara and hotel room moisturizer, and was scared shitless she was pregnant.

Well, knowing for sure couldn't make it worse. She went back out to her rollaboard and fished out the pink-and-purple cardboard box Delia had bought her at Sea-Tac. She would have gotten it herself, but under the circumstances, she didn't think she could handle the dirty looks she'd inevitably get from passengers in the airport shop. She hadn't understood these looks until Delia explained them to her: If passengers see you doing anything but going to or from an airplane, they assume you're delaying a flight, and they figure it's probably theirs. She didn't really blame the passengers, either. She agreed that the first priority in any airport was to leave it as soon as possible.

It was a digital test, $39.99 before tax (Delia had given her the change and the receipt). And it would leave no ambiguity: The one-inch screen on the stick would display either "yes" or "no." She opened the flaps—carefully, as though she would need to reseal the box—ripped open the pink plastic sheath, removed the stick's pink cap. All this pink struck her as idiotic. The makers of these devices had to know they were used as often in panic as in girlish delight.

She hiked up her skirt, sat on the toilet, and waited. But she didn't have to pee. Or rather, she did have to pee, she just—wasn't. The image flashed in her mind of a bride at the altar, the groom and the priest and all the guests waiting in awkward silence for her to say the words "I do."

"C'mon, c'mon," she said. She looked at her watch again—it was almost nine thirty. On top of everything, she didn't have time for this.

There was only one thing she could think of that had never once failed to make her need the bathroom. She went out to the minibar, took out a Bud Light, and returned to the toilet. This was a pretty white trash moment, she reflected, taking a long swig, skirt at her thighs, panties at her ankles—but rather than crying about it she laughed. The whole mess was pretty white trash—pretty Cavano, finally, in its tight braiding of stupidity, absurdity, and yes, bad luck. Her mother would have been gratified to have been proven right; might've been proud, even, in her way.

Marissa heard the pee before she felt it—stuck the stick into the stream, held it there for a couple seconds, and put it down on the edge of the sink. She wiped, flushed, threw the three-quarters-full beer bottle in the trash can (and nine dollars with it), and washed her hands twice, an essential survival technique for any flight attendant. On the stick's screen was a flashing message: "Thinking." "Thinking." "Thinking." This time the image that came to mind was a cartoon fuse, burning down toward a stick of TNT.

"If you're not, then you're good," Delia had told her when handing her the box. "And if you are, you get it taken care of and he never has to know."

"He's my husband," she'd said.

"It's a little late for that, honey," Delia answered.

"I'm a Catholic," added Marissa. Delia looked at her as if she'd declared the voices in her head had promised her she would be the mother of the messiah.

The stick was still "Thinking." Each flash seemed a drumbeat of rising dread.

Could she do that to Robbie: lie about where she was for an afternoon, "get it taken care of," and simply never tell him? How would honesty ever be possible between them again? How would anything genuine be possible? Or was it already too late, like Delia suggested? The thought of losing Robbie sent panic shooting up the sides of her head, as if she were falling. He never has to know, she repeated to herself. She'd find a way to bury it and move on. But even if she could manage that, could she do this to—she tried to evade the phrase that came roaring to mind—"her baby."

Her first year out of college, she'd taken Plan B after the condom Robbie was wearing broke. He was practically giddy that a pill was all they'd needed to ensure that they were "safe." But she hadn't been able to shake a sense of foreboding. What if they never got another chance?

"It wasn't a chance," he told her, "it was an accident."

If she was pregnant now, and did the only sensible thing about it, could she expect a second chance, a third chance? Robbie's attitude about having kids had drifted over the course of their marriage from ambivalence to something approaching opposition. In the elevator after meeting the newborn of some friends—who, granted, looked more dead than alive from sleep deprivation—he'd declared, "They are crazy to do that to themselves."

"Thinking." She turned the stick over and shut off the light, left the bathroom. She could just go down to the lobby, leave the test on the sink, not find out for at least a few more hours. But a few more hours wouldn't save her—and she had to stop acting like the kind of girl she had spent her whole life trying not to be. She returned to the bathroom and turned on the light, lifted the stick a quarter inch with her fingernail.

It was as if she felt a blast of heat and the walls shake around her as she read, "Yes."

Christmas music was playing in the lobby. They'd started playing it on the VentureJet planes now, too, as the passengers were shuffling on, lifting their bags into the overheads, grunting, swearing, shoving, farting. She'd stopped hearing the music at some point, the way she no longer heard the engine noise. But as she surveyed the lobby—the clusters of empty, square-armed club chairs, the idle luggage carts, the table arrayed with copies of yesterday's *USA Today*—the threadbare cliché melancholy of "White Christmas" struck her as brand-new, so poignant she had to bite her tongue between her incisors to stop herself from crying.

Christmas was a holiday she felt she'd never gotten right—never *had,* in the fullness Bing Crosby at least used to know. Growing up, Christmas could mean a trip to a church soup kitchen, her mother insisting they take the food and eat it on the bus, in her pride refusing to sit down at the tables. Or, in years when they were faring better, she and Caitlyn might spend the whole day watching the *Grinch* and *Charlie Brown Christmas* on TV in whatever apartment they'd landed in for the winter, while their mother went off and did whatever it was their mother did. The Christmases with Robbie's family in their house in Vermont had many of the conventional yuletide flourishes: a fire in the brick fireplace, stockings hung above, eggnog served without rum, a ceiling-high tree with an Amazon warehouse's worth of presents radiating from its base. But in the six years she'd been married to Robbie, she'd never managed to think of herself as a real member of the Russell family, and she was reasonably certain the Russells didn't think of her that way, either. She was someone they tolerated, for Robbie's sake. As she considered it, her best Christmas was probably the one she and Robbie spent in their first apartment, in Syracuse their senior year—improvised, no family, just the two of them and lights they'd strung around the bedroom door, Chinese delivery and *It's a Wonderful Life* on his laptop. At the time, she felt like they were half-assing it, missing out on something—only now she realized that that Christmas contained everything she'd always been seeking.

She took out her phone and called Robbie. The call went right to voicemail. It didn't mean anything. Maybe his battery was dead; maybe he was driving through somewhere with bad coverage. As she lowered the phone, a pair of Lufthansa flight attendants were rolling their bags by her, chatting happily in German. Marissa pulled her shirt straight again. The international attendants always looked so glamorous, so blond, so put together. One of the two glanced at her, gave her and her uniform a thin smile of recognition. In the high school hierarchy of these things, the Emirates attendants were at the top, followed closely by the Europeans. As for the crews of domestic discount airlines like VentureJet, well, they were the aviation equivalent of the short bus.

Marissa's phone chimed in her hand—but before her hopes could surge she saw that the voicemail wasn't from Robbie, but her younger sister, Caitlyn. She listened: "Hi, Marissa. It's your sister. Hope you're doing okay." The tone was to-the-point, unemotional—typical of Caitlyn. "So I know what you're going to say, but Mom said we could do Thanksgiving this afternoon if we came to her place. And it'd be really nice for Jade if you were there. We won't stay long, but I wanted . . . I don't know, whatever, Thanksgiving. Like I said, it'd be nice for Jade if you were there, and for the record, it'd make my life easier, too. Mom's actually gotten a little mellower lately, if you can believe it. Anyway, I know it's a long shot. But if you want to, call me. I'm working a double but I'll get the message when I finish. Okay, happy Thanksgiving, Marissa."

Marissa sighed as she deleted the message. Notwithstanding a vague curiosity about what "mellower" could mean, one thing she would not be doing that day would be spending a minute with her mother. She'd made up her mind years ago to exclude her from her life—and it was, she believed, among the smartest she'd ever made. She called Caitlyn's cell, left a voicemail. "Hey, Caitlyn. Good to hear from you . . . Um, look, I'd like to help you out, and I'd like to see Jade, but I'm not going to come today. I have to go up to Robbie's, and then I'm flying out to Seattle tonight. But maybe we can figure out a time around Christmas or something. It'd be great to see you, I'm . . ." She had an unexpected urge to blurt out about Brendan and the pregnancy, and what should she do? But she and Caitlyn had never been close, had drifted further since Marissa's estrangement from their mother. "I really am sorry I won't be seeing you and Jade today," she finished. "Happy Thanksgiving, Caitlyn." She hung up, and dropped the phone back in her coat pocket.

Past the check-in desk was a bar/restaurant, cordoned off from the rest of the lobby by red ropes on stanchions. There was the standard urn of free coffee to the left of the *USA Today*s, which would be faster, but the prospect of a few more minutes off her feet before getting in the car proved too enticing. She pulled her rollaboard across the lobby.

At the podium, the only waitress working—a heavyset woman in her late forties, with mottled skin and ink-black hair pulled back in a bun—smiled widely in greeting. "Welcome to Lester's! Just one, sweetie?"

"Just one," Marissa confirmed.

"Okeydokey." The waitress took a menu from under the podium.

"Could I get a table away from the . . ." Marisa made a gesture toward the handful of men seated singly at the bar, looking up at television screens showing sports highlights. The uniform was like honey to flies in these places, she'd learned: louche, horny, lonely flies on business trips. What any man found attractive about a knee-length wool skirt and a white button-down she sweated into ten hours a day was another mystery of the male libido, but apparently there was "something sexy about it," as had been whispered thickly into her ear more than once.

"Oh, I know, honey, believe me, I know," the waitress answered, rolling her eyes in solidarity. She led Marissa to a table on the opposite side of the restaurant. "You fly in this morning?"

"From Seattle."

"You based there?"

"No, New York."

"Oh, New York!" the waitress said brightly. "I bet that's a lot of fun."

"Um . . . sometimes." Marissa had never been much good at small talk, but she detected something sincerely warmhearted in the woman's manner. "Do they give you overtime today?"

"Don't get me started, love," she answered, adding a wink, and she went so far as to pull Marissa's chair out for her. "Now I'll get you coffee. You need anything else to start with?"

"Just the coffee. And some water. Please." The waitress winked again, Marissa wasn't sure in reference to what, and moved off toward the bar.

Looking again at the men on the stools, Marissa

thought maybe she'd been overdoing it with her concern. Uniform or not, she was not the kind of woman men dropped their drinks—or even necessarily turned away from their TV screens—to hit on. The men didn't look threatening, really; more, they looked sad. Two sat on opposite sides of the bar in nearly identical blue shirts and khaki pants, another in a checkered wool coat and a Red Sox hat, all watching sports by themselves on Thanksgiving morning in a shitty hotel restaurant next to the airport in central Connecticut. There was a sort of resignation in their faces that maybe wasn't actually there, but was something she put there—because she was by herself in a shitty hotel restaurant next to the airport in central Connecticut, too.

Enough wallowing in self-pity, she commanded herself. She'd chosen to be here, and she could leave whenever she wanted—get on the road and head to a Hallmark-card Thanksgiving in a lavish house on a hill. And as for the pregnancy, she had only herself to blame there, too, because she'd been stupid, and then stupid some more, and when you piled up that much stupidity . . .

She pressed two fingers to her right temple, like she was poised to massage a headache that hadn't formed yet. As rigorous as she might be in assigning cause and effect, in building back from the test's yes a daisy chain of her dumb choices, she couldn't help noting that even allowing for all her dumbness, the pregnancy had depended on a maddeningly improbable series of events. A freak hail storm canceled an evening's worth of flights and left her stranded for a night in a crash pad in San Antonio; and she managed to forget her birth control pills in the crash pad; and it took her weeks to find time to get to the pharmacy for a refill, and it wasn't like she and Robbie were having any sex, anyway. And it was a few weeks after all of this as she was gesturing in pantomime to the exits on a 757 on the LaGuardia tarmac that her eyes landed on Brendan, in his army fatigues, in the exit row, smiling at her with a sort of wonder. She'd started taking the pill again by then—but evidently it hadn't kicked in yet. "Hadn't kicked in yet"—that was a tough little phrase to hang an entire marriage from, maybe an entire life, too.

Without thinking to, she moved her hands to her stomach. It was important she not think of it as a baby in there. It was just something her body was doing that she didn't want it to. But no hail storm, or getting to the pharmacy a little sooner, or seeing Brendan a little later, or never seeing him again at all: An inch, a glance, a cell or two one way or another, and it never would have happened. It was all so unlikely, you could call it miraculous. Only it was the opposite of a miracle: It was a catastrophe.

The waitress came over to the table, coffee and cream on her tray. Putting the saucer down without looking at Marissa, she whispered, "You just hang in there, sweetheart." Then she straightened, said at normal volume, "You going to want some breakfast? We do French toast that's good, with strawberries and whipped cream. Or the garden omelet. I can tell you watch your figure."

Marissa blinked up at her. Clearly, if she hoped to disguise her roiling inner turmoil from her in-laws and husband, she was going to have to work a little harder. "Just the coffee, I think," she answered. "I need to get going soon."

She poured the cream into the cup; she watched the ivory liquid sink, the black at the lip grow lighter shade by shade, like it was melting, giving way to something. She considered calling Delia. But she already had Delia's advice: Get it taken care of. Forget it ever happened. Marissa thought of herself as unsentimental, but Delia really was unsentimental. And yet she had a great husband, four children she doted on, four children who adored her. Had she ever done what she was telling Marissa to do? Marissa knew better than to ask. They were friends, but work friends—the sort of friendship that depended on its limits.

She watched as the waitress slid some change off a nearby table into her palm. If she caught the woman's eye, maybe she'd order a Bloody Mary. Sure, it was before ten in the morning on a Thursday and she was pregnant and had had some beer already. But if fate was determined to make her a Cavano, she might as well act like one. But she'd never believed in fate—or if she had, only to the extent that she'd spent her whole life pushing against its tide with all her strength. When the waitress straightened up, Marissa looked back into her cup of coffee.

When she looked up, her eyes landed on a skinny guy sitting down at a table beside the stanchions. He had deep-set, gullied eyes, bony and stubble-stained cheeks, greasy black hair and a gaunt frame under an overcoat two sizes too large. He kept glancing anxiously around the lobby, as though looking out for someone, but not sure who. The waitress walked over to him, dropped a menu on his table. He picked it up, immediately pushed it aside without opening it, shoved his hands in his pockets, and leaned back in the chair with his legs extended, the way teenagers in the boarding area did when they wanted to tell the world they'd rather be anywhere else. (Well, who didn't?)

He must have sensed Marissa watching, or maybe again it was some curlicue of chance (Good? Bad? Who can say?), but he turned his head and looked at her. Marissa didn't feel the coursing back and forth of raw sexual interest; there was no antagonism, there was no superficial smiling. He just looked at her, and she looked back, as though they were both surprised to see another person there. "Hi," he mouthed at length.

And after a moment, she mouthed back, "Hi."

Then he stood up and walked toward her table, a stiff-legged, arm-swinging gait. The silent greeting had been a mistake, obviously. Where could this lead that wouldn't be awkward, or worse? He wasn't bad-looking: his thinness sinewy, like a runner's, the lived-in look around his soft brown eyes eliciting an instinctive sympathy, like this guy had been through it. And what did she need in her life less right now than a good-looking stranger, tough and vulnerable all in one face?

"Cool if I sit down?" he asked, with a note of something like desperation, his hands on the back of the chair across from her.

She hesitated, put her left hand on the table, keeping her wedding ring between them. "Yeah, okay."

"Thanks," he answered with relief, and sat down. "I

just figured, I don't know, there's nobody else in here, and it's Thanksgiving . . ."

"Yeah, it's okay."

"So I take it you're a fireman!" he began, grinning. The tips of his smile fell when she didn't smile back. She didn't want to be unfriendly but she heard variations of this joke five times a day. "Sorry," he added. "So, like, you're working on a flight today?"

"I'm flying to Seattle tonight."

"And you're just hanging out here until then?"

"No, I'm . . ." She hesitated. "I don't know," she finally told him.

But he nodded, as though this made sense. "That's pretty much where I'm at, too. Fucking holidays, right?"

The waitress appeared, a soda on her tray. "Are you moving tables, sir?" she asked him.

He looked at Marissa. "If it's all right with you." He had his palms up, as though promising to do no harm. She moved her ring an inch closer toward him on the table, and nodded. The waitress scowled at Marissa as she set the soda down, then stomped away with her tray under her arm.

The stranger said, "I'm Adam."

"Marissa."

He lifted his Diet Coke. "Happy Thanksgiving."

She raised her cup of coffee. "Happy Thanksgiving."

His smile rallied a little, he had a sip from the straw in the glass. "So, you live around here?"

"No, New York."

His face brightened further. "No shit? Where?"

"Astoria."

"You know, I almost was gonna, today—but anyway, I used to live in Williamsburg, right on the water. But that was a while ago, before you needed a trust fund to live in Williamsburg. Astoria's still pretty cool, though."

"It's easy to get to LaGuardia. That's really the best part for me. I'm flying most weekends, so . . ."

"So it's not like you get to seek out the little authentic Syrian bakery or whatever."

"Exactly."

"What airline do you work for?"

"VentureJet."

"Ah, VentureJet!" he said, grinning fully again. "They lost my bag a couple times."

She smiled now, too. "Do you want to yell at me?"

"If you think it'd help." She laughed, allowed herself that. "I work at a bank, believe it or not," he continued, "and we get people coming in all the time, screaming at us because the ATMs won't give out less than twenty bucks. I mean, I get it that it's frustrating sometimes, but it's not like I'm the one programming the ATMs and deciding what denomination of bills to put inside."

"Sometimes when we're delayed on the tarmac, passengers will hit the call button just to tell me it's unacceptable. Passengers love that word, 'unacceptable.' It's like they think if they say it, I'll run up to the cabin and have the pilot call the tower to make the weather change."

"When is it cool to push that call button, though? Like, only if someone's choking?"

"Depends who," she answered, and now he laughed, his mouth opening to expand the breadth of his smile, his brows lifting over his eyes, the watchfulness that seemed etched with their creases easing a little. Laughing made him look younger. The waitress walked behind Marissa and bumped into the back of her chair, and walked away.

"What'd you do to her?" asked Adam.

She shook her head, watching the waitress's back. "God knows . . ."

"Y'know what's weird, though?" he went on. "How on the holidays it's easier to be around strangers than your own family. That's why the night before Thanksgiving is always the biggest night in the bars in New York, have you noticed that? Everyone's relieved they're not at home." He took a sip of soda. "Or, I don't know, they're depressed because they're going home. But it works out to the same thing. It's not as if all your family issues just magically disappear because it's the third Thursday in November."

"Fourth."

"But then you look at a place like this," he continued, ignoring her correction, gesturing around the restaurant, the lobby. "Yeah, it's sterile and corporate, and it's really just a place in between the places people are going. But that's what's so great about it! There are no awkward conversations you need to have, you're not going to disappoint anybody, by, y'know, doing something. We can just sit here and drink our coffee, or soda, or whatever it is. You know what I mean?"

"I guess so," she answered. "There're no expectations, no one you have to answer to."

"Exactly!" he replied, nodding vigorously. "Sure, you wouldn't want to spend your whole life here, and yeah, the waitress seems to hate you. But at least she doesn't have a *reason* for hating you. It's not personal—it's the opposite of personal. In here you're just somebody in a hotel lobby. We might as well be invisible! It's like . . ." His face became still, as if to demonstrate some quality invisibility had; then his eyes widened, he raised his index finger toward the ceiling. "'Christmas Is the Time to Say I Love You,'" he declared.

"What?"

"Billy Squier."

"Who?"

"Listen," he told her, still pointing upward. She heard the song—recognized it, though she had no idea from where. "Christ, I can't remember the last time I heard this. Do you remember this video on MTV? It was like, all the VJs and the production crew and whoever at a Christmas party, and Billy Squier playing acoustic guitar and lip-synching? God, that seems like a million fucking years ago."

He seemed to become engrossed in what he could hear of the song, his face fixed in a look of happy attention. He was right, she thought, there was something easier about being with strangers. And she understood better, too, why he'd wanted to sit down with her. He wasn't seeking what she worried he might be seeking, wasn't hoping they'd end their chat by heading up in the elevator together. The strangely needful look he'd had on his face when he asked to join her was one she recognized from airport boarding areas, from airport bars, from terminals and shuttles and ticketing lines and the planes themselves—from all the sorts of in-between places he'd described, and where she spent so many of her waking hours. It was a desire not for sex, not even for friendship, but rather for something simpler: mere confirmation that you were not entirely by yourself.

When the song ended, he leaned back in his chair, his hands behind his head. "Okay. So what's your story?"

"What do you mean?"

"Not, like, your story starting from birth, just what you're doing here. You've got to fly to Seattle tonight, but in the meantime, you're sitting around drinking coffee? It seems like there's a story there. Not that you have to tell me or anything," he added, leaning forward on his elbows, "but I am pretty curious."

And here was another benefit of the company of strangers: The conversation didn't have to be freighted with the seriousness of your life. Your dilemmas, your bad choices, your multipronged regrets could be kept off to the side, out of frame. "Just . . . working up the courage to see my in-laws."

"You're married?" he answered, surprised. She held up her hand, flapping the ring he'd been meant to notice. But men never noticed these things—not when you wanted them to, at least. "Huh," he said, with something between a nod and a shrug. "So your husband's a pilot?"

"Yeah, he proposed over the PA and everything."

He laughed. "It must happen!"

"It happens. There are girls who maybe want it to

happen when they take the job, but they never last very long. But no, Robbie's not a pilot, he's a filmmaker . . ." Before he might pursue this, she added, "We met in college."

"College sweethearts," Adam replied, thoughtful. "That's cute. I mean, it's pretty smart. I didn't stick around college long enough to meet anybody serious, but that seems like a good way to do it. Finding somebody who is at least compost mentis enough to get to class and write essays and whatever. Marriage is pretty terrifying, in my opinion, but it's probably the right thing to do."

"It's not for everybody."

"No, but most of the people I know who truly have their shit together are married. And that's kind of my priority these days: keeping my shit together."

The waitress walked past their table, dropped the check without stopping, muttered, "Whenever you're ready."

Marissa was giving her a puzzled look when Adam asked, "So? What's he like?"

"Who?"

"Your husband. Who's not a pilot."

"Robbie? He's—he's a really nice guy. He's . . ." She trailed off, glanced back into her cup of coffee—half-gone and lukewarm, but she knew better than to expect a refill. "He's a really nice guy," she repeated. She kept her eyes on the cup, not wanting to see whatever reaction Adam might have to this. It was not that she couldn't think of anything else to say about Robbie; it was rather that everything else that came to mind was so tangled in emotion—guilt or regret or see-saws of gratitude and resentment. Even saying he was nice brought her back to the verge of tears because tepid as the compliment was, it was so central to what she loved about him: his kindness, his patience, his gentleness . . .

When she looked up at last, something frantically apologetic was happening in Adam's face, his hands flapping like he was shaking them dry. "Sorry, I have a real talent for saying the wrong thing. Seriously, I am the Art Tatum of randomly insulting people."

She was crying—felt now the warm liquid leaking down the sides of her nose. She grabbed the napkin, sending the fork and knife inside clattering across the table.

"I was just making conversation, y'know, just vamping, so to speak, and if you don't want to talk about your, um—"

"No, it's not . . . ," Marissa said, wiping her eyes. "Jesus, no, it's not you, it's not that, it must be the . . ."

She was about to say "hormones"—but dear God, could that already be true?

"No, no, I get it," he said encouragingly. "It's just the holidays."

She studied him. "Right," she said.

"Fucking holidays," he affirmed, with a smile.

She asked pointlessly, "What's this song?" He looked up at the ceiling, maybe to listen, maybe to give her the opportunity to pull herself together.

"This is 'Santa Baby,'" he told her as she dabbed with the napkin where she imagined the mascara stains must be. By the time he looked back at her, she felt she'd regained something like self-possession. "I don't know who the vocalist is, but Auto-Tune gets most of the credit. She must be really good looking, put it that way."

"So you're really into music?"

"Not as much as I used to be." He began nodding, as if to encourage himself now. "Actually, I used to be a musician," he continued. "I played keys. Y'know, piano, synth, anything with a keyboard. I can play almost any other instrument, too, but that was really where I made my bones. Playing keys . . ." He chuckled uncomfortably. She was ready to ask something else, happy to keep to topics she considered mutually harmless, when he continued, "Yeah, I first started taking piano lessons when I was a little kid."

"Were you a prodigy?"

If she thought this was harmless, it appeared she was wrong: He winced in a gut-punched way, pushed himself up in his chair. "That's a—that's a loaded word, that's really not, a, so that's not a term you should just throw around, I don't think. I was . . . I had a knack, when I was a kid, that's all."

"Sorry."

He forced another unconvincing chuckle. "That's okay, it's just a weird thing to say about a kid, and I think people should realize that. It's like telling a kid he's a Jedi knight or something."

"Right . . . Sorry."

He settled in the chair, leaning on his left elbow, and it looked like this was going to be the end of it, but then he started talking again. "So yeah, I started out when I was a kid playing classical, but it's a pretty miserable existence, especially for a kid, practicing every second you're not in school, and then the competitions. Anyway, I eventually got into rock, and after I dropped out of college, I joined this band called the Deployers. Our sound was pretty punk, but there was always this push-and-pull with the other guys, because they wanted to do the big, guitars-attack thing, and I wanted to do

more than just play loud. I was listening to a lot of prog
rock then, so, you can see there were going to be problems." Marissa nodded, not really following. "Anyway,
after the Deployers broke up, I sorta bounced around
for a while, and then I started a band with this girl, this
woman, Kiss and Kill. And that was pretty good, we did
some real things." His right hand had gotten to work,
lifting his straw halfway from the soda, dropping it in
again—like a kid at a dinner of adults, she thought, lifting, dropping. "Yeah, Kiss and Kill, we achieved, I'd
say, the minimum level of indie success that can look
like success to the outside world." He'd pulled the straw
from the soda, was bending it into a triangle. "We played
what the label called experimental pop, and I guess
that's not too, too far off. But it was more about meeting
people halfway, musically, without compromising who
you are. That's harder than it sounds. But anyway, Johanna could really play guitar, and I could really play
keys, so—so, yeah, we did some things. We only put
out one record, though, in the end." He'd begun squeezing one end of the straw so it could fit inside the other.
"I think if we'd had a permanent drummer, that might
have helped. Drummers are always the diplomats in a
band. But the truth is, it would've taken a pretty great
fucking drummer to save Kiss and Kill." He laughed,
hoarse, unmerry. "Whatever, long story short, things

fell apart for about a million reasons, then I was sorta at sea. The biggest thing people don't get about playing music is that you don't make one fucking dime doing it, so it's not like I could go sit by my pool in the Hollywood Hills for eighteen months and figure shit out." He started spinning the straw triangle around his pointer finger. "And by then I was having some personal issues, there's no point getting into it, except I—oops." The triangle had spun off his finger onto the floor. He looked at it, appeared uncertain whether he ought to pick it up, didn't, and continued, "I ended up playing at the kind of bar where you're only there so the manager can gouge anybody who comes in for a beer with a cover, and if anyone listens, it's only long enough to shout 'Freebird' at you." Abruptly, he fixed her with his eyes, his face so earnest he had to be kidding, only he wasn't. "We talked before about not hitting the call button on the airplane, and, well, hand to God"—and he went so far as to raise his right hand—"I will never touch that button again. But you have to promise me you'll never, ever shout 'Freebird' at some poor bastard playing 'Rocket Man' for the thousandth time for whatever people put in the fishbowl on top of his piano. You might as well throw rocks at the dancing bears in the circus." He began to smile but gave up halfway through the attempt. "Anyway, that's the back-of-the-milk-carton version of Adam

Warshaw's musical career. I don't play at all anymore, and that was definitely the right decision, I think, and I'd say I'm doing pretty well now. Like I said, I work at that bank, so." He finished off the last watery half sip of soda. "'Freebird,'" he said, putting the glass down. "'Freebird, Freebird, Freebird.'"

"I promise," Marissa said.

"Promise?"

"I won't yell that at anyone."

He snickered, like he'd forgotten what he'd asked. "That's cool of you. Like, sincerely. That means a lot."

"Fucking holidays, right?" she said.

"Yeah," said Adam. "Yeah, fucking holidays."

The waitress walked over, picked up Adam's glass, reached for Marissa's cup of coffee. "I'm still drinking that, thanks," Marissa told her.

She let the saucer drop back onto the table.

Adam sat up in his chair. "Y'know, we're all in this together here."

The waitress bunched her lips into a scowl. "Excuse me?"

"I mean, it is Thanksgiving. And I feel like you're going out of your way to be shitty to our table."

"I don't appreciate cursing. If you're not having anything else, why don't you pay the bill and go?"

"You can see my friend is in the service industry,"

Adam continued. "As it happens, I work in a customer-facing role at a bank myself. So we all know what dicks people can be all the time. We can at least be nice to each other."

The waitress gave him a thin, mean smile. "Oh, sure, I bet she's the type who'd be nice to just about anybody."

Marissa's temper had a velocity such that she only knew she'd lost it about the same time everyone else did. "What the fuck is your problem?" she heard herself demanding.

"I think you better leave," the waitress shot back.

"Yeah, I think I better." Marissa stood up, knocking her chair over, and rather than walking across the restaurant she kicked over the stanchion and tramped across the lobby.

"Man, okay, I think we all got a little heated. Let's all take a beat," she heard Adam saying as she stomped away.

She stopped beside a standee printed with the departure times for the airport shuttle. She resisted the urge to lift this up and slam it against the floor a few times. At least there was no danger of crying again. In these moments, an iciness took hold of her—an alarming detachment that made her capable of just about anything. During a lacrosse game sophomore year of college, after a girl yanked her ponytail for the hundredth time, she threw her stick down and smacked the girl in the face so hard the girl fell on her back. Marissa's teammates were stunned and then laughing as they dragged her away—this was Saint Marissa, after all. But it was such a fucking stupid thing to do. She could have gotten kicked off the team, lost her scholarship. And then where would she be? Back in Boston, waitressing. In the simplest terms, that was the destiny she'd been fighting her whole life, the one her Cavano temper and everything else Cavano in her urged her toward: dead-ended in Dorchester or wherever the fuck.

She looked back over to the restaurant. Adam was still speaking with the waitress, making broad, con-ciliatory gestures. She watched him right the stan-chion; to her astonishment, she watched him and the waitress hug.

"You're hugging that bitch?" she said as Adam ap-proached, pulling her rollaboard behind him.

"She lost her Mom last week," he explained. "She's totally devastated about not spending Thanksgiving with her. That's the only reason she's working. Don't even take it personally."

"She picked the wrong day to call me a skank," Ma-rissa muttered.

"No, no, she was totally shitty. I'm saying I don't

think it had anything to do with you." He put the rolla-board on the floor beside her. "That's the problem, people are hard to figure. You've basically got to for-give them for everything."

She couldn't decide whether this was real insight or if he was maybe not a smart guy. But it occurred to her she'd like to believe what he'd said was true. "Thanks for . . ." She gestured vaguely to the bag.

"No worries."

"I'm pregnant."

He nodded equivocally, watching her face. "Con-gratulations?" he tried.

"This isn't the kind of pregnancy you say congratu-lations about. This is the other kind."

"Oh. Yikes." Then he shrugged. "If it makes you feel better, I just ran out on the first family gathering I got invited to in more than a year."

"Why would that make me feel better?"

"I dunno." He looked troubled that she wasn't more amused. "I guess it's like I was saying, we all make mistakes."

"It just sounds like a waste to me."

For a moment, he appeared on the verge of defen-siveness, or anger, but in the next instant, his features went slack, and he rubbed his cheek with his palm. "Yeah, you're probably right."

"Sorry," she said. "I don't know anything about it. I'm still pissed about . . ."

"Nah, it's cool," he replied, shrugging under the oversize coat.

For several moments, neither of them spoke; he had a distracted look, rubbed the knobs of his knuckles with his thumb. A poppy Christmas song had started playing, something he'd probably recognize, but she didn't feel like asking. And so, Marissa concluded, that's that. They'd shared a cup of coffee and a Diet Coke, and now they'd drift out of each other's lives, the same way they'd drifted in. Maybe that was the final comfort of strangers: It was never too long before you said goodbye.

"So what'll you do now?" she asked.

"San Francisco!" he answered. "Back to San Francisco . . . What about you?"

"I have to drive up to Vermont. They're waiting for me."

"You'll take ninety-one?"

She pushed stray curls of hair behind her ears. "Whatever Google tells me."

"Yeah, you'll take ninety-one, I'm from here, so . . ."

She extended her hand, and they shook, quick, formal; she was not a hugger. His fingers were long and slender, like his limbs. "Good luck!" he told her.

"Good luck," she replied. It was strange to know you'd never see someone again, she thought; but then, it was the most ordinary thing in the world. Most people you saw, you'd never see again.

In a jokey, half-crooning voice, he said, "'And have yourself a very little . . .'" He smiled awkwardly.

"Right," she answered. "Same to you."

She turned and pulled her bag over to the nearby bank of elevators, pressed the down button for the garage. A few seconds later, the doors opened. She got on, the doors closed behind her, and the elevator began a moaning trip downward.

She hadn't even had time to wash her hair.

[4]
Out Front

Adam walked through the revolving doors at the front of the hotel lobby. Wind howled across the sidewalk, seemed to gather beneath the concrete portico over the drive before the hotel, come back at him in rising gusts. There was a metal bench to his left, next to some skimpy box hedges. He sat down, waiting for the shuttle to the airport to appear. Stupidly, he heard a reedy "Leaving on a Jet Plane" in his head.

He was aware there were people who felt great in these moments, who could identify a type of freedom in knowing there were no more backdoors, no more off-ramps or escape hatches, that the only path left was dead ahead. But Adam was not one of those people. He loved escape hatches.

But he'd returned his rental car, absorbing a fifty-dollar "early return fee" plus whatever they'd charge him for not filling up the gas tank. He'd killed time by hopping on a shuttle from the car rental place to this hotel, because sitting around a lobby seemed preferable to wandering around an airport terminal. He'd had a soda he hadn't really wanted, he'd met a flight attendant who was more interesting than he might have expected. Now, though, there were no more ways he could think of to delay the inevitable. There was nowhere else to go but to the airport, to pay whatever he needed to change his ticket, and fly back to where he'd started the day before.

He felt the dull daily ache of missing Johanna, like an indentation at the bottom of his stomach. It'd started during the conversation with Marissa. There was no good reason for it. Marissa didn't look like Johanna, didn't act much like her, except when Marissa exploded with anger and stormed out of the restaurant. But even the most conventional women reminded him of Johanna, sooner or later—because they held their lips an inch apart when they were listening, or didn't; because they covered their whole faces with their hands when they laughed hard, or didn't; because they had the finest gold-blond hair on their lower backs, or didn't. Even now, he could catch himself convinced he saw her pulling the door of a car closed, bending down

for her purse in a coffee shop window. Drinking had
once been his solution to all this. The alcohol would
muddy up his senses enough that he'd stop seeing her
ghost. In the sharpness of sobriety, though, Johanna
was everywhere.

A Gibson in his head now, plus a sharp harmonica
moan: "Visions of Johanna," for fuck's sake. God, he
hated that song. He hated Dylan, too, and no one had
ever been able to badger him into appreciation, either.
The wry smirk in every chord change: What kind of a
spiritual voice-of-the-people was that supposed to be?
"Desire" was pretty cool, though, the Christian stuff
was actually pretty cool, too; at least Dylan seemed to
mean it at the time. Adam had to remind himself that
his opinions about this stuff didn't matter to anyone
anymore.

He pulled his shoulders together, tucked his chin
into his collar against the cold. Now that it was certain he wouldn't be seeing his family, he found he had
the audacity to miss them. But he couldn't help it. He
missed the chaos and kindness of his nieces and nephews; he missed Kristen's dry humor, he missed Jack's
grumbling displays of competence—fitting a dozen
suitcases in a trunk, getting the Reagan-era refrigerator in the garage to work again. And he missed his
parents: his father's winking self-effacement, his un-

breakable good humor apart from unaltering grimness about the bottom of the Red Sox roster; his mother's inevitable "Aw, jeez!" as her carefully laid plans for the day unraveled. They were an unremarkable family, just like every other, but something about their familiarity made them exquisite to him. He wished he could tell them—he'd even planned on it, maybe—that it wasn't their fault he'd gotten so drunk all those times he saw them. It wasn't because he didn't like them, it wasn't because he didn't like being with them. It was more that he got so drunk because he *did* like them, and he couldn't stand it.

And because he was sitting out there all by himself in the cold (no accident, of course; he sought these situations, they taught him at Stone Manor), he indulged the feeling of missing everybody now, anybody: his brother-in-law, Dan, his sister-in-law, Lizzy; Hank and Michael and Bruno, his bandmates in the Deployers; his high school crew, his few college friends; all the characters from the scene in New York; and Marissa, too, because sure, why not? Most randos weren't nearly that cool, and if there was a little crazy mixed in there, all the better.

A taxi pulled up to the curb—a beefy-faced man in a hooded down jacket over a suit got out. He had a neatly trimmed goatee and a red widow's peak, a shoulder bag dangling from one arm and a Bluetooth earpiece in his ear, a wry grin on his lips. ". . . as a witch's tits here," he was saying, presumably to someone via the Bluetooth. "Connecticut, I think . . . Ha! Exactly! . . . Half the time I don't remember until the stewardess says what the weather's like where we're landing." The cabdriver had gotten out, handed the man a receipt, which he tucked into his wallet. "Thanks," the man said, addressing the driver, patting him on the shoulder. "Good talking to ya . . . Yeah, I'll dial in from the business center before my two fifteen . . . No, to meet Cindy and the girls, it'll be two days with her folks, then Disney." He chuckled. "It's called having daughters. I might fly right from Orlando to meet—" He disappeared through the revolving door inside the hotel.

He was the quintessential corporate lemming, but even so, Adam thought, there was something to admire about guys like that: the übercompetent road warriors who always knew where the business centers were, who knew exactly how much time they had before their two fifteen and just how to spend it. It was like they'd gone native in the soulless transitional places he'd described to Marissa. They persisted there, they thrived there. Sure, this guy had Cindy and the girls to meet—but

Adam's guess was that that was the obligation, and the walk from the cab into the airport hotel was where he felt most at home.

Adam wondered if he could learn to do that, master that style of constant motion: the ceaseless flying, riding, chatting, chuckling. Maybe he could get a job taking business trips, selling shit or whatever, and just float across the country, skyway to carport.

He considered this for another second or two—then sneered into the lapels of his coat. He had two years of college toward a music degree. He needed an app to figure out the tip at restaurants. And now he was going to make sales presentations, write on whiteboards, dial in to conference calls or whatever the fuck? Not to mention, a job that had him bouncing unpredictably back and forth across the country would be as dangerous, sobriety-wise, as having no job at all. At Stone Manor, he'd been instructed that since he'd only ever been a musician, he had to become accustomed to the rhythms of a well-ordered life—and the foundation of such a life was a consistent nine-to-five job. This is what had led him to the bank: More essential than the paycheck, his work at the Alabama Street Citibank in San Francisco provided him a Sunday through Saturday routine that helped him avoid, say, wandering into a bar at two in the afternoon because he found himself with nothing better to do. It didn't matter that he needed a calculator to do even the most basic math; his manager wanted him to use a calculator to do even the most basic math.

Every morning of the workweek he took the BART from his apartment in the Outer Mission to the bank in Potrero Hill, did his job, ate lunch at his desk, then took the BART home. He'd order in dinner or microwave something, watch basketball on TV, then go to bed at ten thirty so he could be up for work the next day. On weekends, he ran errands, went to the movies, went out on the dates. And five nights a week, he went to the gym. It was a dingy chain place on the border of gentrified and ungentrified blocks in the Mission, but it had a swimming pool, and Adam could now do as much as a mile's worth of laps at a time. He knew a lot of recovering alcoholics replaced their compulsive need for booze with the compulsive need for marathons or hot yoga or baking, but he didn't think of his swimming this way. Rather, he saw swimming as an affirmation of something, a further commitment to a particular way of living. And he'd gotten to like being in the pool. The sound was pretty extraordinary: the rumbling breath from your nose, the windmill slaps of your forward palm, the muffled voices on the surface that would leap to echoing clarity when you turned your ear to inhale. You became aware of your body in a particular way in the water: the weight of your limbs, the twisting of your torso, the heat of your lungs. Swimming was a way to be alone with yourself that wasn't boring.

He was making it work in San Francisco. Anyone would agree with that. Often, when he looked around the BART, or the sidewalk in front of the bank, he saw people a lot like himself: in their thirties, on their way to work, coffee in hand, grateful to have found refuge from whatever their twenties had been about. At times, seeing those people made him feel like an impostor, as though they were the authentic version of something he could only try his best to imitate. But even if he sometimes felt like a stranger in his own life—might look up from his desk, or see a young woman in a cashmere sweater smiling at him from a table in a restaurant, and think, How the fuck did I get here?—that didn't mean that it wasn't a sufficient life, an appropriate life. And taking a clear-eyed look at who he was, what he'd done and risked and escaped and might still fall victim to— weren't sufficiency and appropriateness the essential qualities?

A cherry-red Sonata was stopped in front of the hotel; the airport shuttle pulled up behind it. It was really too bad he hadn't been able to go through with the family Thanksgiving. Next year, maybe, he'd do better.

The door of the shuttle opened with a whine and the white-haired driver got out, his face pinched, sour. He stretched his arms in the cold, shivered, and went inside the hotel, leaving the van's engine idling. Adam figured he had time to smoke a cigarette. And he put the filter between his lips, he noticed the driver in the Sonata still sat in the car, had her head bent over her smartphone. Peering through the passenger-side window, he recognized Marissa.

Adam was a superstitious person, susceptible to signs, omens, portents. He crossed the street to avoid walking under ladders, treated black cats like they carried the plague, wasn't absolutely convinced the collapse of his music career couldn't be attributed to a mirror he'd broken in a Milwaukee bathroom in 2009. He recognized this magical thinking had never served him well; what bad luck had he ever avoided? But even if this wasn't a sign, wasn't it at least an opportunity? An opportunity to get it right.

He tossed the unlit cigarette away, walked up to the car, and tapped on the window. Marissa looked up with surprise that deepened into suspicion as she recognized him. But she lowered the window. "Hi," she said.

"So I was thinking," he began. "The thing is, I returned my rental car."

"Okay."

"And you said you're going up to Vermont. That's pretty much straight up ninety-one, like I told you."

"Okay . . ."

"And my house, my parents' house, in Roxwood, could not be more on the way." She brushed a black twist of hair off the side of her face. "What I was thinking—maybe you could give me a lift? I mean, like you said, it would be a waste not to see them . . ." She was giving him the wary, vaguely irritated look he'd gotten familiar with over the years. "Only because you're going up that way. I mean, you can one hundred percent say no. It was just, I don't know, keep each other company . . ." The driver of the shuttle passed behind him, walked up the steps back onto the van. "Just an idea," he concluded.

"Okay," she said.

"Yeah? You sure?"

"Yeah, whatever, why not."

He pulled open the door, thinking how close he'd come to making the wrong choice—or, if this turned out to be the wrong one, how close he'd been to avoiding it.

II
Family

[1]
The Sonata
(Four Movements)

They didn't talk for a while. Marissa relaxed into the calm she could find while driving: the streetlamps passing one by one, the gray guardrail trailing away like a ribbon, the highway ahead narrowing toward a vanishing point it never reached, no music, no conversation, no announcements to hear or be made, just the engine thrum and the wheels and the propulsive sensation. She'd always loved driving, especially at night: the headlights of cars in the opposite lane coursing like a river, the scenery beyond the streetlamps muted, tucked in darkness—and her, unseen and unencumbered, just another gliding pair of headlights for someone else to see.

She'd hoped she might find some of this serenity flying on airplanes every day. But that hope had been disappointed. Staring out the window when she didn't have maid duties to perform, a shuttered blankness might spread across her mind, but there was no full-gas-tank, open-road freedom to it. She never entirely forgot she was in a pressurized metal tube thirty thousand feet in the air with no control over the destination.

Blasting icy wind filled the car. She looked over. Adam had lowered the window on his side. "You were falling asleep," he explained.

"No, I wasn't," she shot back.

"You can't mess around with that, though. You know what happened to the first bassist for Metallica, right?"

"No."

"You should Google it, I don't want to jinx us by talking about it." He reached his hand into the pocket of his coat. "Hey, cool if I smoke in here?"

"This isn't my car." She found the button on the driver's side and raised his window.

"Whose is it?"

She shifted her grip on the steering wheel. She didn't feel like talking. These were the last moments of the day when she wouldn't be required to be pleasant, sociable, polite. "There's this flight attendant, Alice, who's been flying for twenty-five years, so she never has to work any holidays or weekends. She leaves her car at BDL for anybody who has a layover there."

"That's cool of her. Like, we gotta have each other's backs."

This was true. The job wouldn't have been bearable unless they looked out for one another in these small ways: picking up the slack when another attendant appeared on the verge of collapsing in the aisle, buying an extra coffee for anyone else on the four A.M. shuttle, switching sections when a drunk passenger started to get handsy. Indeed, she'd thought of Alice when Adam had asked her for a ride—though she'd also been conscious of the dread she'd felt, staring at the little red pin on the map on her phone that marked her in-laws' Vermont address. Adam was a distraction from that.

They passed the big Massachusetts Welcomes You sign, with its jovial white script, as if Massachusetts had written you a personal note of greeting. "I used to drive up and down this highway every weekend when I was a kid," Adam told her. "My parents found me this piano teacher in New York, and every Saturday one of them would drive me there and back for my lesson."

"You have pretty good parents."

He made a noncommittal sound, a click of his tongue behind his teeth. "The teacher was this Russian guy, Mr. Ioffe, and he was a total fucking hard-ass. He was obsessed with posture. He had this yardstick, and before he'd let me play, he—"

Marissa's phone started ringing. She lifted it from the cup holder by her knee: Robbie. She looked at Adam. "Can you not talk for a minute?" He made a compliant zipping gesture across his lips.

She answered, held the phone against her shoulder as she drove. "Hey," she said evenly—not hostile, but not unguarded, either.

"Hey," Robbie said. "Hi."

"I'm on the way. I had trouble finding the car."

"No, it's okay." He was quiet for a moment. "I'm so over fighting with you, Izzy."

His use of the pet nickname confirmed that hostilities really had ceased. She felt her shoulders slacken. "Me, too."

"We're good?"

"Yeah, we're good." These were the words of reassurance they gave each other after every fight, gave each other more and more lately. But didn't that mean they were worth less and less? She concluded she didn't care. "I'm so fucking tired, Robbie," she told him, quietly, though there was little hope of Adam not overhearing.

"You get a chance to nap or anything?"

"Not since yesterday."

"You're a soldier, girl."

"Yeah, yeah," she said.

"In other news," he continued, "guess who turned up this morning? Laila."

"I thought she was in Germany."

"Hence the surprise."

Laila was Robbie's younger sister. Marissa had never felt strongly about her, one way or the other, but something (everything) about her bothered Robbie. Anyway, Marissa was more than happy to be his ally today. "So, what, she just flew in from Berlin?" she asked, feigning exasperation.

"Got in last night, slept at the house in Cambridge, drove up this morning to surprise us. If you'd seen my dad's face when she walked in. I seriously thought he was going to cry. Which would have been a first. Then cue a solid hour of her describing her NGO's heroic efforts on behalf of mankind. The only thing that amazes me is that Laila's been in therapy since she was eleven, and no one's ever pointed out to her that she's a narcissist?"

"Hang in there," Marissa told him. "I'll be there soon."

"Yeah, when do you think you'll get here?"

"An hour, I think. I have to drop off"—she glanced at Adam—"another flight attendant. But they live right on the way."

She heard some muffled talk on Robbie's side of the phone. "Um, Izzy?"

"Yeah?"

"My mom wants to talk to you."

Her shoulders stiffened again. "Robbie, I'm driving, I should—"

"Marissa? Marissa, it's Roz," she heard her mother-in-law say.

"Happy Thanksgiving, Roz," she said as warmly as she could manage. Fuck me, she thought.

"No—I'll be a minute, just shut—shut the door," Marissa heard Roz saying. "Marissa?"

"I'm here, Roz."

"Marissa, Robbie and I had a long talk last night." On the steering wheel, the backs of Marissa's hands were turning white with the strength of her grip. Her mother-in-law was five foot two, Jewish, a divorce attorney, one of the best known in the state; she'd married Robbie's father, six foot three, black, the son of a famous civil rights lawyer, after they met at Harvard Law School. So there were plenty of things about Roz that Marissa could admire: her achievements, her independence, her strength of character. And Marissa found she needed to remind herself of these things often whenever they spoke.

"Robbie opened up to me, son to mother." Marissa

was feeling nauseous again. "You two are having problems? Well, guess what? That's what marriage is. You thought it'd be all sunshine and rainbows? There's lean years and fat, that's life, honey."

"No, that's a good point, Roz, but I need to watch out for my exit, so—"

"You think my marriage has been a walk in the park? There was a time, and Robbie didn't know this, but I told him last night, and now I'm telling you: There was a time, right after Laila was born, when I moved out. For two weeks I slept on the couch in my office. The bottom line is, Leo and I had a decision to make. And guess what? We stuck it out. And that's what made our marriage as strong as it is today. You know how long Leo and I have been married? Do you know, Marissa?"

"Um, maybe . . ."

"Forty years in June. You don't make it forty years without getting through some times. You hear what I'm saying? Now, honey. I understand you and your mom aren't close."

"Did Robbie say that?" She worried she was pulling on the steering wheel so hard it might crack off in her hands.

"That's reality, so why hide it? But I want you to trust me, Marissa. I want you to feel you can confide in me. Can you try to do that?" Roz was too savvy to wait for Marissa's answer. "Tell me something: Does my son make you happy? Woman to woman, you know what I'm asking, in the important ways, does my son make you happy?"

"Roz . . . Roz, I . . ."

"Well, you make him happy. That'll never be the issue, I can assure you of that. You hearing me, sweetheart?"

"Uh-huh," she said, surrendering, just letting it happen, the way you had to when a passenger began screaming at you about every detail of their horrible day of travel, starting with the cab ride to the airport.

"You make my son happy," Roz was saying, "and let me tell you something, I've been around a lot of marriages. A lot of good ones, and plenty of bad ones. And you know what's true, almost without exception? If the man wants the marriage to be saved, the marriage *can* be saved. That may not be PC, and God knows I've shed more blood for feminism than most, but I'm telling you what I've experienced, firsthand. And sweetheart, Robbie wants it to work. My son would give his right arm for it to work.

"Did you know, when Robbie was born," she continued, "I took a whole year off? With Laila, there was the nanny, I was back at the firm full-time two weeks later. But with Robbie, my first, I was always there for him when he was an infant. So maybe he needs a little more attention, he's a sensitive boy, there's no point denying that, and if I'm to blame, okay. When you're a mother, you'll understand. But you never need to question how much he loves you. That's all I wanted to say. Okay, sweetheart? You understand how much my boy loves you?"

"Yes, Roz, I do."

"That's my girl. Now, could you meet him halfway on certain things? Probably. But that's not for me to say. That's the two of you, and it's not my place. But if you could meet him halfway, say, being more affectionate, remember, Jews and the African American community, we are talking about two very extroverted and physically expressive—"

Marissa was tempted to drive headlong into the guardrail. "Okay, Roz, can you put Robbie back on, my—"

"I'm done, I'm all done," Roz assured her. "One day you and I will have a glass of wine and I'll tell you some things about Leo—well, anyway, did Robbie tell you Laila surprised us? So it'll be a great day. I'll see you soon, dear."

Marissa heard shuffling with the phone. "Sorry," was the first thing Robbie said.

"Jesus fucking Christ, Robbie."

"I said I was sorry!"

"What did you tell her?" she demanded.

"I don't know, she's my mom," he mumbled.

"You're a thirty-year-old man!" She didn't care what Adam heard.

"C'mon, Izzy, I was upset, I needed to talk about it."

"What did you say about my mother?"

"She wasn't at the wedding. It's not like it's some big secret you guys don't get along."

"'Don't get along,' Robbie?" she hissed.

"I was speaking generally! Look, we're on the same side, okay?"

"Are we?"

"Jeeeeesus," he said, "you seriously want to spend this whole day fighting? Is that honestly what you want?"

She often found herself checkmated this way: forced to either swallow her anger or accept responsibility for the discord. There was a shard of rubber ahead in the road; she changed lanes to avoid it, and conceded. "No," she said. "I really don't."

"Look, you're gonna get here, we're gonna crush some turkey and sweet potatoes, we're gonna drink some beers, we're gonna watch a movie on Netflix, and we'll call it a holiday. I mean, does that sound so bad?"

It didn't; it sounded like all she wanted in the world. It sounded so great, she almost wanted to start crying again. "Let's do that," she said, and couldn't help adding, "Please, let's do that." Delia was right; Delia was always right. Marissa would get it taken care of, and he would never have to know.

"I got some good news, too," he told her.

"What?"

"Freelance gig." Robbie, when he made money, made it on freelance video editing jobs. The income was maddeningly (to her, anyway) unpredictable, but it always seemed to come just when they really needed it.

"How much, do you think?"

"Five g's."

Thank God, she thought. "That's great. That's really, really great."

"Yeah, y'know, so—like we said, we're good."

"I love you, Robbie."

"I love you, too. Drive safe." And they got off the phone.

She dropped the phone in the cup holder. Adam was leaning forward, his arms folded across his chest, his lips packed into his mouth, doing a terrible job of pretending to have nothing to say. "What?" He shook his head. "What?" she demanded.

He held up his palms, his blameless gesture. "All I want to know is, what were you doing the day they were giving out mothers-in-law? I mean, holy shit!"

She bit the inside of her cheek. "So you heard all that . . ."

"I mean, Roz! Wow. Yikes. Roz. That is one bad trip of a mother-in-law."

"I'm glad it's so hilarious to you, but if . . ." She was too tired to be indignant; anyway, she agreed with him. "You should've heard the toast she gave at my wedding. The joke was that if half the family was disappointed I wasn't black, the other half was disappointed I wasn't Jewish, so at least it gave them all something to talk about."

He laughed, maybe a little too hard. "Seriously, if Roz was my mother-in-law, I'd have fucked around on Robbie, too!"

Silence, deep enough that she could hear each rotation of the tires over the ruts in the lane. "Sorry," Adam finally said.

"I'm sick of that word."

"I wasn't the one who . . ." He was at least smart enough to shut himself up. She stared straight ahead. A few crimson leaves clung to the branches of trees climbing the embankment by the highway. Adam began humming, low and indistinct. She shot him a glance and he stopped.

Scalloped gray clouds filled the sky. In the nearer distance, streaks of blue curled around them, like ribbons. They passed bus depots, self-storage units, billboards advertising beer, fast food, Indian casinos. Every two miles an exit sign appeared, reflective white on noble green, announcing towns in pairs: Longmeadow, Hampden; Agawam, Southwick; Granville, Westfield.

After a while, Adam unbuckled his seat belt, started working his coat off his shoulders. After he'd tossed it into the back, he pulled off the sweatshirt he was wearing. "It's hot as shit in here, you might as well let me open the window and smoke," he muttered, but she ignored him. He wore a threadbare cotton T-shirt, the letters LFTR PLLR sagging in folds over his thin chest. There were tattoos on his forearms: on the right a sort of caricatured portrait of a bearded black man; on the left, thickly clustered musical notes, climbing up and down a staff. He spotted her looking, put the sweatshirt back on.

"What's your T-shirt?" she asked him.

"I dunno," he said. "A band. Maybe I was on a bill with them or something, I have about a million T-shirts."

He didn't speak for another mile, then declared, "It's not like cheating makes you some kind of evil bitch."

"Thanks." Marissa got over on the left, passing a semi. When she pulled back over on the right, she asked, "What makes you so sure, anyway?"

His legs were extended as far as possible underneath the dash, hands shoved in his jeans pockets—a pose much like the one in which she'd first seen him in the restaurant. "I don't know, you said you weren't happy about being pregnant, it doesn't take an FBI profiler or something . . ." He added under his breath, "It isn't my fault I was right."

"You ever done it?" she asked him. The car bumped in and out of a pothole she couldn't avoid, making a dull, two-part clunk.

"Fucked around? Yeah, sure. I'm not proud of it, but everybody does it, sooner or later."

"Someone ever done it to you?"

"Probably. I mean, yeah, of course."

"That girl Johanna?"

She looked at him: his face puzzled, wounded, angry. "Sorry," she said. It had been a bitter burst of temper she hadn't seen coming.

"Yeah, yeah, yeah," he said, crossing a leg over his knee, folding his arms across his chest. "Now we're even."

The stretch of highway was bordered by panels of tall wooden boards, a muted sea-green color, tree branches stretching over from the opposite side. "So why'd you do it?"

"I dunno," he answered, "different reasons." He paused. "Well, no, actually, pretty much the same reason: I was wasted. Plus, there's the whole rock 'n' roll thing, you tell yourself fucking around is part of the life, y'know? And you can get used to lying. But for the record, I never really cheated on Johanna, except when I was in a blackout." He seemed to take a moment to consider this. "I get that that's a fucked excuse. But at least I can acknowledge it, right?"

She took her eyes from the windshield long enough to give him a careful look: the dark folds around his eyes, the pitch of his cheekbones, the grooves by his mouth and up his forehead to his hairline. It was a prematurely aged face. And then it all clicked, an unexpected alignment of facts so tidy, she figured she had to have known all along: the Diet Coke, the music career that ended in shambles, the odd bursts of earnestness, the unaccustomed way he performed the simplest physical acts—sitting in a car, walking to a chair—like he was just getting used to them. He was a recovering alcoholic: sober at the moment, but working every second to remain so. It was all just as she remembered from the AA meetings she'd accompany her mother to, during the odd week every other year when Mona announced she was going to clean up—the meetings Marissa and Caitlyn would beg her on their knees to return to when those weeks were over. Marissa had a panicked instinct to pull into the breakdown lane and kick him out of the car, like she'd recognized him from a serial rapist Wanted poster. But he was trying. He deserved credit for that.

"What?" he said, noticing her look.

She turned back to the road. "I just feel bad about bringing up your ex. I was being a bitch."

"No, it was my fault, I shouldn't have brought up, y'know, how you, on your . . ."

"It's fine," she cut him off, before the apology collapsed on him.

"Anyway, me and Johanna, that was a long time ago. Troubled water under the bridge, like they say."

"Do you two still talk?"

"Nah. After we broke up, or Kiss and Kill broke up, whichever happened first officially, she moved home to Michigan, and we didn't talk again." He drummed the glass of the passenger-side window with his knuckles. "Everyone said it was a good idea that we just . . ." He made a slicing motion. "By the time we split up, she was—she was having problems. She had, um . . ."

"You don't have to—"

"She'd hear things, in faucets, or in sprinklers, like voices and shit, talking to her, singing to her. She stopped showering for like, weeks at a time. It was such a sad—I mean, Johanna was the most beautiful woman, it was pretty heartbreaking, to tell you the truth."

Marissa had a helpless, guilty feeling, having brought them to this topic. She asked hopefully, "Is she doing better now?"

"Fuck, I can't remember the last time I talked to her dad! So, she went into a . . ." He swallowed. "She was in a facility, I guess you'd say. But then she got out, and the last time I talked to her dad she was doing a lot better."

"We don't have to talk about this."

Adam shrugged. "Why not? Like I said, water under the bridge!" A moment later, he repeated, in an uneasy way, "Water under the bridge."

Marissa didn't answer, let the conversation fade away, the medians they passed covered with frozen snow—shoots of grass that looked black the only thing poking through.

The regular series of highway signs—the exits, the black-on-yellow merge arrows, the silhouetted deer cautions, the brown-and-white points of interest—was interrupted by an orange placard declaring "Road Work Ahead." Cones from the shoulder narrowed the three lanes into one—though if there was work being done on the closed-off sections of highway, Marissa couldn't tell. She came up behind a minivan with a metal Jesus fish affixed to the trunk, and as she got nearer saw the purple bumper sticker reading "Abortion Is Murder."

"Come fucking on," she muttered, slowing down behind the minivan to forty, thirty.

"So why'd you cheat on Robbie?" Adam asked cheerfully and out of nowhere. Marissa kept her gaze on the bumper sticker, like she might be able to stare it out of existence. Why couldn't she have gotten stuck behind some aging hippie's camper, adorned with harmless appeals for coexistence, the ecosystem, world peace? The real wonder was Adam's question, coming just as they'd pulled up behind that bumper sticker—as though his gift for saying the wrong thing bordered on the telepathic. "I was wasted," she told him.

He replied, "Fair enough."

The cones arced back across the lanes toward the guardrail, as if in retreat, and immediately Marissa passed the minivan, looking over to see a backseat crammed with kids staring up at seat-mounted video screens, and a middle-aged, copper-haired woman in sunglasses at the wheel, moving her lips silently, like she was singing along to something. You never knew with people, like Adam had said—whose bumper sticker would be like a long slow twist of your neck, or whose neck you might be twisting.

"I wasn't wasted," she admitted. Why not tell him the truth? Adam was a stranger; she'd never see him again. He'd never meet Robbie or Brendan or anybody she knew. "I wasn't wasted, I was . . ." Did she even know the truth, though? Had she even explained it to herself?

The highway passed under a bridge—green metal, rusted bolts. "You don't even have to explain, I get it," Adam informed her. "Being a flight attendant is probably just like being on the road—playing shows, I mean. You're constantly meeting new people, you're away from home, you've got a hotel room, and you gotta do something to unwind, so why not pick up a—"

"Would you mind just shutting up?" she asked.

"Sure, no problem," he said.

The stereotype of the life of a flight attendant being one giant spring break annoyed her to no end—as if all they did was pick up passengers and screw them in the plane bathrooms. Had the people who thought that ever been in an airplane bathroom? "Brendan was my high school boyfriend. It wasn't *Stewardesses Gone Wild* or something. We had history."

He'd shifted in his seat again. In the corner of her eye, she could see that he'd swiveled his torso to face her, his face patient, attentive. You learned to do a lot of listening in AA.

And again, why not? Delia hadn't wanted to hear any of the details—had implied she found the tawdry details offensive. Marissa didn't talk much with her little sister, she didn't talk to her mother at all. This might be her last chance to tell anyone. There was still some resistance in her, though, as if she hoped that never speaking about what she'd done might allow the events to lose their hold as memory, lose their place in reality altogether, dissolve into something like a daydream. But the proof of what'd happened was literally growing inside her by the minute. And if she were going to have an abortion (even the mental formulation of those words sent a tremble down her spine; her CCD teachers would be proud) shouldn't she, at least once, give an accounting of why she needed to? So as they drove through Springfield, and then north, roughly following the upstream course of the Connecticut River, toward Exit 19 for Roxwood, Marissa told him her whole foolish story.

"We moved around a lot when I was a kid. By the time I was sixteen, my mom had skipped out on the rent in practically every neighborhood in the greater

Boston area. And one spring we landed in a shithole one bedroom with no hot water in Needham, which is this suburb outside of the city. But it was a really nice little town, with a really good high school, and that's where I met Brendan.

"He was the best player on the baseball team, I was the best player on the lacrosse team. So in the beginning, it just made sense. It was high school. And he was also really Catholic, so he was okay with me not wanting to have sex. Some of that was me being a Catholic. But more of it was that I'd made up my mind that I was getting out of Boston. And you didn't need a sociology degree to figure out why all the girls in the neighborhoods I got dragged through growing up were stuck in those neighborhoods. Every waitress and hairdresser and manicurist from Swampscott to Mattapan had a baby or two at home. But I was going to go to college. And that meant I needed a scholarship. And they don't give lacrosse scholarships to girls who are six months pregnant.

"Brendan's family was the most normal one I'd ever been around. They were all just . . . really good people. His parents were divorced, but his dad lived around the corner, and he even got along with Brendan's stepdad. And they were all cops. Brendan's dad was a cop, his older brothers were cops. All Brendan wanted to do was be a cop, and live in Needham, and go to Red Sox games and barbecue with his brothers.

"He wasn't dumb. He knew I had reasons for never bringing him around my mom. He knew that when I said I was leaving Boston the first chance I got, I meant it. So I guess there was something temporary about the whole relationship, right from the start. But it was high school, you don't think about it. And Brendan was good to me. He was nice to me. Nobody needs to shed a tear for me, but growing up the way I did, that meant a lot. He'd take me to the movies, he'd take me fishing with his brothers. We'd make out in his stepdad's pickup, listening to Bruce Springsteen CDs. I know it's so stupid and cliché, but I swear to God there was something romantic about it. Just being normal.

"Anyway, that summer, my mom started a kitchen fire in the place in Needham, and we got evicted. We landed with all our stuff at a Days Inn up the highway. A girl from my high school worked there, it would have been humiliating if it hadn't happened to me fifty times before. My mom eventually found us a place in Waltham, somebody always owed a favor to somebody who owed her a favor—the less I knew about it the better, she said, and she was right. Waltham's an hour by bus from Needham. I guess my mom figured that fall I'd just start going to school in Waltham, if she thought about it at all. But Brendan's family invited me to live with them. My mom went apeshit, but I was eighteen by then, there was nothing she could do.

"Brendan slept upstairs, I slept in the little room off the kitchen his mother had used as a sewing room. Like I said, they were just good people. His stepdad even drove me for my recruiting trips. I think they thought I'd end up marrying Brendan, when it came down to it, no matter what I said.

"But you can guess how this story ends. I got offered a full ride to play lacrosse at Syracuse, and I took it. Brendan started going to UMass Dartmouth. We tried long distance for a while, but that never works for anybody, and it didn't help that I'd never go down to see him. In the end, we broke up. It was sad, but we weren't even twenty yet. You get over it. A few years ago, I saw on Facebook he got engaged. I think I even Liked the announcement. He Liked my wedding photos when I married Robbie. I guess that counts as—I don't know, like you said, water under the bridge. You wish someone well, even if you never plan to see them again.

"But I did see Brendan again. On a flight I was working last month. He was in his army uniform, and I'm in my VentureJet uniform. It was like we ran into each other at a costume party, or, I don't know, we caught each other pretending to be other people. Older people. He was flying to Norfolk on his way to an army base in Germany. And I had an overnight in Norfolk, so . . . We had dinner. It should have been awkward, right? It should have felt so different from when we were kids. Except it didn't. He was still so nice to me, like he thought being nice to me was important. When he got out of the army, he was going to move back to Needham, become a cop, and he and his wife were going to start a family. And I'm living in New York City and the only time I set foot in Boston is when a flight I'm working lands in Logan. 'It all worked out for you,' he said. And it'd all worked out for him, too.

"Only how can you not wonder? All the other ways it could have worked out. If I'd been that wife in Needham. Going to those barbecues, having those kids. It could've been me. Only I had to run away from my mother. I think I only wanted, for just one night— some other life, a simpler life, just to be free to be with Brendan. 'I know the real you,' he told me when he was taking my clothes off. 'I wish I did,' I remember thinking.

"And I think we were both just curious about having sex with each other, since we'd never done it when we could've. Like we deserved it, after we waited all that time. God, it's so ironic he got me pregnant, though, isn't it? Like somehow I knew it would happen, like it would happen no matter what I did. What's the word for that, when the world plays a trick like that on you?"

"Bruce Springsteen, huh?" Adam said at length, breaking the silence. She looked over at him. "'I'm on Fire?' 'Prove It All Night?' I just can't picture making out to Bruce Springsteen in high school. You didn't have Radiohead in Boston?"

The clouds overhead had thickened, sunk lower on the horizon, matched almost exactly the ash gray of the guardrail slicing beside the highway. She drew a sharp, steadying breath in and out through her nose. "That's all you have to say?" The exhaustion had sunk into her bones, even her hands on the steering wheel felt heavy. She wished she'd never told him, wondered why she had. It hadn't changed anything. Of course he couldn't help her.

"That's not *all* I have to say," he answered petulantly. "It's just something I was thinking. Look," he went on, "there's no reason to beat yourself up about it. Some things, you just chock up to a single twist of fate."

"I don't believe in fate," she answered, petulant herself.

"Are you going to tell him you're, y'know, pregnant?"

She sighed impatiently. "That would just fuck things up for good."

"No, not him, your husband. I mean Brendan."

She shook her head. "It's my fault. I told him I was on the pill. I *was* on the pill. He's married, I don't want to ruin his life, too. You don't understand. He'd want me to keep it."

"Because of the Catholic thing."

"Yes, Adam. Because of the Catholic thing."

"But you're not going to keep it."

She slammed the wheel with her palm. "Fucking hell, Adam!" she cried. "You think Robbie is going to raise some other guy's baby? What am I supposed to do? Try to convince him he got me pregnant while he was sleepwalking? And that no, he's wrong, he'd love to be a dad in about seven months? And I'll really have to talk fast when the baby comes out looking like Brendan Ryan, who's about as black as Frosty the Snowman. Either Robbie would divorce me now, or he'd divorce me later, but either way, I can't get divorced. I can't be alone, trying to afford diapers, and it's not like *flight attendant* is the perfect job with a newborn at home. What do I do when they call me to go to Dallas the next morning? Pack the baby in my rollaboard?" She noticed he appeared a little terrified. She looked at the speedometer—the needle was trembling above ninety-five. "Sorry," she said, pressing the brake. She was sweating; she pulled her coat open, fumbling with the belt, then fumbled at the armrest, lowered the driver's-side window. "No, I am not going to keep it," she said over the roar of air through the window, the compacted coming-and-going moans of cars in the opposite lanes. She shut the window. "I'm not that stupid."

When he spoke, his voice was calm, reassuring. "Hey, you gotta do what you gotta do. It's not like you'd be the first person. Johanna got an abortion, when we got pregnant."

She knew better than to get him talking about Johanna again, but she couldn't help herself. When would she get the chance to talk about this, either? "What happened?"

"It wasn't very complicated. We were fucking without condoms, and eventually, she got pregnant!" He laughed weakly. "It was shitty, I guess. But what else were we going to do?"

She felt cold now. She pulled her coat closed over her chest. "You still think about it, though?"

"Sometimes," he answered with a shrug. "But everybody said it was the right decision. And I don't think it would have changed anything." When she glanced over, for once he sat very still beside her, his hands resting on his thighs. "No, I don't think it would have changed anything," he repeated, a kind of surprise in his voice, as though he'd never thought about it. Then he tossed his hands up. "But look, like I said, you shouldn't be too hard on yourself. As far as Brendan goes, I get it. We all have that one that got away, that itch we never scratched in high school. Who can resist the chance to actually scratch it? Plus, y'know, the guy's in the army, shipping out the next morning."

"He was going to a base in Germany, not to Afghanistan."

"Like there's never been a war in Germany!" She smiled a little. "You can tell Roz you were being patriotic!" She smiled more fully, and Adam came out with an uncannily close impression of her mother-in-law's nasally alto: "Do you know how many soldiers I slept with after I got married? Do you know, hon? All of them."

She laughed, and Adam did, too, really laughed, widening his smile, his eyes. It was pretty pointless laughter, considering what came next: carefully avoiding conflict with Robbie; coping with her in-laws; working another overnight; and later, but not too much later, stealing an afternoon and getting an abortion, and then somehow preserving, rebuilding her marriage.

It seemed like more than she could handle—but she'd never been a quitter: Her story had reminded her of this, if it accomplished nothing else. You kept going, you didn't wait for applause or congratulations, you kept on going, forward.

Silence returned to the car. The signs floated by—places, ads, merges, turnoffs.

You kept going forward, since where else was there to go? Once again, she put her stupid hand on her damn stomach, without meaning to or knowing why.

[2]
Walmart and the Gas Station

Adam found it harder and harder to sit still once the name Roxwood started appearing on the signs: 18 miles away, then 13, 5, 2, like a jittery countdown. By the time Marissa pulled off 91, his legs were bouncing at the knees, the fingers of both hands playing tremolos in the air of the dashboard vents.

Driving along a two-lane street, Route 8, they came up to a complex of big-box stores that'd sprouted like mushrooms since the last time he'd driven this way. "Hey," he told Marissa, "I have an idea."

She eyed him sidelong, not slowing down. "I really need to get up to Vermont, Adam."

"No, I know, but I was thinking . . . It'd be better if I showed up with a coffee maker."

"A coffee maker?"

"Before I left, I broke the coffeepot. Did I mention that? So if I have a new one when I come back . . ."

"It's Thanksgiving morning. Nothing'll be open."

He sped up his tremolos. "Maybe not, but, I dunno, maybe," he said with a hopeful shrug.

They came to the intersection with the right turn to the stores; for once that day, Adam thought, he caught a piece of luck, as the light changed from yellow to red just as they approached. "Two minutes," Adam promised. Her hands on the wheel didn't move. "What if we drive around the parking lot, and if everything's closed, we get back on the road? The house is only, like, five minutes from here." The thought of walking back into the house without the coffee maker was like imagining walking in naked.

She slapped the turn signal with a sigh. "Only because I need to find a place to pee."

This was going to work great, he told himself. He could get the new coffee maker gift wrapped. Maybe he could buy the paper and tape and do it himself.

But he saw immediately that Marissa had been right. The stores had the graveyard silence of places of commerce closed for business: barred gates pulled in front of glass doors, long rows of nested shopping carts chained in place. All that was missing were tumbleweeds, he observed bleakly. He was about to give up and to tell Marissa to forget it when they drove by the Walmart, where a line of tents stretched to one side from the entrance. The tents were blue and red and army green, some shoulder-width narrow, others appearing large enough to accommodate eight or ten. At the end of the row stood a longer line of people, mostly men, in heavy winter coats, gloves, beanies. "Looks like they're about to open!" Adam said.

"Or it looks like they'll be standing here for hours," Marissa answered. "That's why half of them are in tents."

"Lemme jump out and ask."

She rubbed an eye with her fingertips. "Why do you need a coffee maker again?"

"A peace offering!"

"Can't you just apologize?"

She made it sound so easy, as if it was just a matter of saying the words. "I'll be two seconds," he promised. Her phone pinged from the cupholder; she stopped the car with a jerk.

"Two seconds," she said, picking up the phone. "I'm already late." She looked at the screen and frowned.

"What is it?" he asked.

"Nothing. My sister's texting me my mom's address."

"Why?"

"Because she hopes I'll temporarily lose my mind and—" She cut herself off. "Are you going or not?"

Getting out into the cold felt like dropping face-first into freezing water. He slammed the car door behind him and half jogged to the entrance. But even fifty feet away, he could see that the interior of the store was dark, deserted. He balled his hands into fists, blew on them as he looked over the doors, searching for some posting about when the store might open.

"Fuck," he muttered. He took out a cigarette and lit it. Behind him, he heard a car honk; he raised his hand in acknowledgment, not needing to turn to check who it was, and walked over to the line of tents. The third was one of the larger ones; a heavily bundled man sat in the portal in a lawn chair, a space heater between his legs, an iPad playing a football movie in his lap. He glanced up as Adam approached. "Can I get one of those, man?" he asked, pointing a gloved finger at Adam's cigarette.

"Yeah, sure," Adam said, offering him the pack. He pulled off the thick yellow work glove he wore, took out a cigarette, put it to his lips, and lit it with Adam's lighter. Adam heard Marissa honk twice, but he ignored it.

"Appreciate it," the man said. "My brother was supposed to come by with a resupply this morning, but no sign of him yet." He was late middle-aged, with patches of grayish stubble on the tops of his cheeks, and wore sunglasses on a neoprene band and a camouflage canvas hat with earflaps. He reached into his canvas jacket, produced a silver flask, and offered it to Adam. "Would be grateful to repay the debt."

Adam shook his head. "Nah, I'm allergic."

"You get hives or something?"

"No, I turn into a giant, self-destructive asshole."

The man frowned, then shrugged. "Ten-four," he said, took a sip himself.

"So are they opening soon, or what?" Adam asked.

The man shook his head as he returned the flask to his coat. "Another three hours or so."

"Shit. How long've you been out here?"

"Eighteen days."

Adam whistled as he blew the smoke from his mouth. "I wouldn't sit out here for eighteen days if they reanimated Elvis and he did a one-night-only show in there."

The man chuckled. "If you only knew, brother. Tent's got a generator, Wi-Fi, a bunk with a minus-thirty sleepsack, a grill, and a hot plate. It's as good as being at home. Quieter, actually." He winked. "My brother comes by every other night to relieve me. Hot shower, see the kids. He did the oh-eight-hundred to eighteen hundred, Monday through Friday, last two weeks so I could go in to work. This is our fifth year out here. We've got the whole thing down to a science." He leaned forward and took a black, three-ring binder from under his chair, handed it to Adam. There was a piece of masking tape on the front, on which was written in Sharpie, "WALMART DOOR BUSTERS 2016." Adam opened the binder. Inside were torn-out pages from a Walmart circular in plastic sleeves, items on each page circled in red marker: cell phones, laptops, video games, HDTVs, a snowblower. "That's the kill list," the man told Adam with satisfaction.

"So you'll, like, run around trying to grab this shit?" asked Adam, flipping through the binder.

The man chuckled again, ashed on the sidewalk. "Negative on that. After the employee got trampled in Long Island a few years ago, they have a whole system. In a couple hours they'll give out numbers to everyone in line, and then let us in in groups. You get tickets for the bigger items. Like I said, it's a whole system."

"Huh," Adam said. He had stopped on a page with a red arrow pointing to a little kid's bicycle—pink with a cartoon princess's face on the seat. "And then you'll give this stuff as Christmas gifts?"

"A couple things," the man replied, leaning over to put the cigarette out on the concrete. "Most of it I'll put up on eBay. I'll probably clear a few hundred bucks in the end, but if you crunch the numbers, you don't even make minimum wage. It's not about the money. It's about the experience."

Adam watched the trail of smoke rising from the tip of his cigarette, wafting skyward and disappearing in the air. As someone who had spent years of grueling hours in front of a keyboard for far less than minimum wage, and often in environments far less hospitable than this man's tent, he concluded he was in no position to judge. In fact, he felt like he understood: the man's shared effort with his brother, the myopic and thus liberating focus on a particular goal, however obscure to the larger world. Fuck, this guy was practically a kindred spirit. "What's your name?" Adam asked.

"Reginald."

"I'm Adam. Good to meet you, Reggie."

"Reginald." They shook hands. He heard Marissa honk three times: staccato, staccato, marcaaaato.

"Look, Reginald, would it be cool if I stayed in your tent until they opened? I gotta pick up a coffee maker."

"Can't do it, Adam," he said gravely. "That'd be cutting."

"Right . . ." His eyes fell again on the iPad. "Hey, do you have a charger for an iPhone in there?"

"iPhone, Android, whatever somebody might need out here."

Adam took his phone from his pocket. "Would you mind? It's been dead all day."

"That one I can do for you."

As Reginald went inside the tent to plug in the phone, Adam jogged back to the Sonata. He passed a man leaning against the back of a silver Crown Vic, sipping from a thermos, dressed in a Red Sox hat and a heavy red-and-black checked coat. The man gave Adam a peculiarly antagonistic sneer—curling his lips behind the rim of the thermos, narrowing his eyes accusatorily. Panic briefly tightened Adam's chest, as if he'd been caught. But caught doing what? He hadn't done anything, he reminded himself, returning a what-the-fuck glare. This guy was just an asshole.

Marissa was flipping through Facebook on her phone when Adam got to the car. He tapped on the driver's side window; she lowered it, dubious. "Why aren't you getting in?"

"This guy has an iPhone charger," he told her. "He just plugged mine in."

"You really are incredible."

"I know, so lucky, right?" Then he realized he'd misunderstood. "It'll just be, like . . ."

"Two seconds?" she said curtly.

"Sorry," he said.

She tossed her phone into the passenger seat. "You see that gas station up there?" Over the roof of the car, he could see the gas station at the top of the parking lot: six pumps and a shop under a green-striped roof on pillars. "I'm going to fill up the tank and pee, and if you're not there when I'm done, I am sorry, I am going to have to drive to Vermont. Okay?"

"I'll be there," he promised.

"I'm not kidding, Adam," she said, then raised the window and drove across the lot to the station.

He knew she wasn't kidding—she really would leave him there. And he wouldn't blame her, either. She was too smart, too practical, to put up with much more of his shit. This was something you became attuned to when you were an alcoholic: whose kindness you could take advantage of, and exactly how far. It was a heartless way to go through life, sure, but when your priority was getting your load on, day after day, you needed other people to help attend to details like where you slept, whether you ate.

As he walked back toward Reginald's tent, he glanced over to the space where the dick in the Sox hat had parked, but he'd vanished. Those spasms of guilt were pretty common since he'd stopped drinking—like he was an escaped convict, a murderer on the run or something, trying to escape the cost of all the heartlessness and fucking-up by acting normal. All he could do was start to do better, he told himself. He needed to be more like Marissa: practical, self-sufficient.

He handed Reginald another couple cigarettes in return for charging his phone. The battery was still in the red, but at least the screen could light up now. Whatever relief this gave was immediately displaced, though, by a sickened feeling when the messages waiting for him appeared: four new voicemails, six new texts. He decided there was no point reading or listening to any of them. Instead, he walked to the edge of the sidewalk and called Kristen.

It didn't even ring before she answered. "Adam?" There was a pained, cautious note in her voice: She didn't know what she'd hear.

"Hey, Kristen," he said, as calmly—soberly—as he could. A long pause. He could guess what was happening in that pause: her relief, her anger. "I'm an asshole." She didn't answer. "Kristen?"

"I'm here," she said. "I'm here at the house, with our family. Where are you?"

"Y'know that Walmart they opened on Route 8 . . ." Another pause; he could hear her breathing, long and slow, like a yogic calming technique.

"What the hell, Adam," she finally said. "What the hell."

"I'm trying to find a new coffeepot!"

"Do you know what you did to Mom and Dad?"

"I texted Jack—"

"Are you coming over today or not?" she interrupted.

"Yes," he said firmly—and he couldn't help adding defensively, "Why do you think I even flew out here . . ."

"Then I'm coming to get you."

"Are you serious?" he shot back. "You think this whole time I've been—"

"I don't know, Adam, and to tell the truth, I don't give a shit. But if you think I'm going to let you just disappear on everyone for another three hours—"

"Okay, okay, okay. Just chill out, all right? Y'know that gas station, the BP? I'll be waiting there."

"Okay, I'll chill out, Adam," she said, with brutal sarcasm. "You just keep your ass at that gas station." She hung up.

Reginald was watching him, a knowing smirk beneath his camo hat. "And people say I'm crazy being out here three weeks every winter."

Adam smoked another cigarette as he walked across the parking lot. The lines on the blacktop marking the spaces looked to him like staffs of some arcane musical language, waiting for notes. His anger at Kristen vied with his resolve of a few minutes before to get better at all this shit. They didn't trust him; they'd never trust him, and why should they? He wanted to run away again, all the way back to San Francisco. But it was too late, he told himself, and he had to face what he'd done: what he'd done this morning, and what he'd done before that, the long compounding chain of Things He'd Done that stretched back farther than he could or cared to remember.

Marissa's red Sonata was parked in front of the gas station shop, but he didn't see her. He wasn't going to leave without saying goodbye, though; if Kristen showed up, she'd have to wait. He stood by the back of the Sonata, lit another cigarette with the one he'd been smoking. Almost simultaneously, Kristen's BMW minivan shot into the station and stopped with a tire screech across two spots. She'd hurried.

Kristen shoved the door open and got out, staring at him with a look that tangled relief and hatred so thoroughly, it would have taken Adam all day to pull them apart. "God, you're skinny," she said. Her hair was very short now—cut to the middle of her neck, a smooth wave across her forehead. She had on a black quilted coat, zipped to her neck, black leather boots, silver bulb earrings. He flicked the cigarette in the direction of the gas pumps. Unfortunately, nothing exploded. There really would be no escaping.

"I need to wait for my friend," he told her.

She folded her arms over her chest, took some long, winded breaths, as if she'd been running. "Your friend. Of course."

He leaned back on the Sonata, tried not to meet her gaze. It was like being near her turned him back into a little brother: young and petulant and a little in awe.

"Nice minivan," he said.

And she was an inch from his face. "Oh, fuck you, Adam," she shouted. "Just fuck you. You want to explain to me what you're trying to do to us? Why you're punishing us? And for what? For what? Because I didn't want my kids to see their uncle passed out on the lawn?"

He'd turned his face to the side, stared down at the lightning crack in a frozen puddle on the ground. "I'm not punishing anyone," he told her, with a distant, eerie calm, like he was only listening to himself speak, too.

"Bullshit!" she shouted. "Bullshit! Then why do you keep acting this way? Why do you keep torturing us, every chance you get?"

"Yeah, yeah, yeah," he said, trying to focus on the crack—trying to cope. Rely on your coping strategies, his one-on-one therapist at Stone Manor would always tell him. Use your coping strategies. Only he couldn't remember what they were.

"And you know what the sad part is? I was the one who convinced everyone to invite you! I paid for your goddamn ticket, Adam!" They hadn't told him that; he'd thought it was his parents. "Because you told me how *great* you were doing!" she was shouting. "And how do you think it makes me feel, when Mom spends the whole morning sobbing at the kitchen table? Did you ever think, for a second, how it makes me feel to have to explain to my children—"

"Really fucking bad!" he said, swinging around to face her. "I bet it made you feel really, really fucking bad, that your brother is such a goddamn loser who keeps ruining shit for you, over and over and over. I can't imagine how ashamed you are to—"

"Oh, just shut up. Will you just shut up for once?"

"And let me go down on the ground and kiss your boots for *convincing* everyone, doing me this big favor, *paying*, when obviously nobody wants me there, I mean, what a wonderful person, what a wonderful sister you are."

She had her eyes closed, shaking her head. "I am your only friend in this family. I am your last friend."

"I don't even recognize you anymore, with this persona you have now, of this like, like, rich soccer mom, this Burberry Nazi or whatever you're supposed to be."

Her face was momentarily wounded, then tightened again with wrath. "Sorry I didn't want to get high and go to shows for the rest of my life. Sorry I grew up and became an adult. Sorry if my little brother nearly drinking himself to death ruined the scene for me."

"Yeah, well, as long as we're blaming people, are you sorry for giving me sips of Zima in the backyard when I was eleven? Have you ever thought maybe it's your fault that I—"

Her neck and shoulders jutted toward him, and for a moment he thought she was going to hit him, and he recoiled. But then her whole body went slack, like some cord inside her had snapped, and she sank to the ground, sat on the curb and started to cry. "You're so mean," she was saying. "You were never mean. When did you get so mean?"

Adam was shaking. All he could think to do was to walk into the gas station, walk to the cold cases, take out a case of Budweiser, rip it open, and just stand there and drink beer after beer—drink beer after beer after beer. He could almost hear the crackle and fizz of the can opening, could almost feel the cold ring pressed into his lower lip. He went so far as to turn his head to look through the shop's window. Marissa was standing in the doorway, a cup of coffee in her hand, a stunned, deer-frightened look on her face.

The unmistakable fear in her eyes wrenched him back into himself, to the reality of it all: This was happening. This was real. And it was all too late. He could never undo any of it. He couldn't look at Kristen, instead he looked back at the crack in the ice, how it zigged, how it zagged.

Eventually, her sobbing got quieter, petered to silence. Her coat rustled as she stood. "I don't think we were ready for this," she announced. "Not you, not me, not any of us." He knew there were so many things he had to say, but he didn't think he could summon his voice—like any words were buried and compacted deep and silent in his chest. "I'll make up something. How does that sound to you? I'll make up something. I'll tell them it was your decision. I'll tell them . . ." Her voice wavered. "How great you're doing."

He heard her open the car door, he heard the door shut, he heard the minivan pull out onto the street. He sat down beside where she'd been sitting. He tried to explain to himself why he'd done what he'd just done. But it was all so ugly and violently stupid and cruel, crueler than ever, what explanation could there be?

Revoltingly, a series of digital kicks were popping in his head, looping: "Oops! . . . I Did It Again" by Britney Spears. Oops, I did it again.

"You need to go to a meeting." Marissa was standing beside him. She put the plastic bag down on the blacktop, sat next to him on the curb. "I can take you to a meeting." He discovered he was too ashamed to look at her, either. "My mom, sometimes, would decide to go to meetings. She wouldn't want—your sister wouldn't want—"

"You don't know shit about it."

She was silent for a moment. "I guess not," she said. "I guess not." She put her hand on his shoulder. It occurred to him he'd like to cry, but it would be so unfair of him to cry, he wouldn't allow it: not that, not self-pity, too.

"You'll be okay," Marissa said. With some terrified animal instinct, he pushed his face in her shoulder. And then he couldn't stop it. Worthy or not, the sobs started bursting from his chest: "Aguh, aguh, aguh," he heard himself sobbing.

"Don't give up," Marissa told him. A while later she repeated, "Don't give up."

[3]
The Russells'

She couldn't just leave him. "I couldn't just leave him," she rehearsed telling Robbie in her mind—telling Robbie, Roz, Laila, Leo. She shouldn't have said the thing about Adam being a flight attendant because she'd need to maintain that lie, and the list of deceptions was already long enough. But what choice did she have? He didn't get up after he stopped crying, just sat there twisted on the curb, like a crack had opened in his body—the right side stiff, supported on one arm on the concrete, the left drooping over itself toward the ground. Maybe it was all his fault: All he'd needed to do was say sorry, or say nothing at all, just stand there and take it. But she knew by now that he was not the sort of person who knew when to keep his mouth shut. And even if it was his fault, did it make any difference?

He looked so ruined, so shattered, slumped there on the curb outside the gas station. She had few pretentions about the kind of person she was, maybe fewer than ever, given what she'd done to Robbie. But Marissa couldn't leave him like that.

And so she helped him up by his two hands, like he'd gotten knocked on his ass on the lacrosse field. He didn't object, he didn't resist; the barren look on his face didn't change. She led him to the car, opened the door for him, went so far as to reach across him and buckle his seat belt. And then she got back on the highway, back on 91 North, heading toward Vermont and her husband and her in-laws.

The highway ran straighter here, the ribbon of asphalt pulled taut under charcoal clouds. There were hardly any other cars, as if they were the last ones still to get where they needed to be that day. Adam didn't speak. He sat with his face turned toward the passenger-side window; all Marissa could see of him were half a rounded ear and clumped stalks of black hair above his collar. Eventually, she turned on the radio, listened with half attention to a call-in show about pets: an incontinent cat, a pug with a yeah-probably-fatal tumor. The trees along the highway thickened as Marissa and Adam traveled farther north, the spider-arm branches reaching out above the road to form a sort of tunnel.

It was as the pet show went to commercial after a discussion of ferret law reform that Adam at last sighed loudly, turned off the radio, lowered the window an inch, took out and lit a cigarette. She was relieved he was no longer catatonic, but still, "Could you not? Please?"

"It's sort of essential right now."

"I told you, this isn't my car."

"So buy some air freshener or something."

"Will you just put it out?"

"What do you do when people smoke in the bathroom on the airplane?" he asked, with oddly blithe curiosity.

"Open the emergency door and throw them out. What do you think we do, Adam? Would you put it out?"

"Fucking junior high in here," he mumbled, and flicked the cigarette out the window. Then, more sharply, he added, "Your friend better have lung cancer or something, I mean, Jesus fucking Christ . . ." He'd closed his fist around his pack of cigarettes; she watched as he opened it and stared at the crushed box, a few of the cigarettes split and seeping curlicues of tobacco. "Here's the thing," he said toward his hand. "She's not usually like that. Kristen, I mean. My sister."

"Sure," Marissa answered, uncertain where this was going.

"Like, you probably think she's some rabid crazy bitch right now. But the truth is, she's a really great person. I shouldn't have said what I said. She was right, I was being a total asshole. I don't know why. And what she said about bailing today, putting my parents through that—she was right about that, too. I'm really sorry about all of it."

His tone was strangely detached—not insincere, exactly, but it was like he was reading from a script someone else had written. "Maybe you should call her and tell her that."

Adam grunted bitterly. "Yeah, like she ever wants to talk to me again." He pushed the broken cigarettes through the gap in the window, and closed it. "There's something else," he announced. "I shouldn't have talked to you about Johanna. I don't want you to get the wrong idea about her, either. What I told you about her being in the institution—you should just forget I said that. It's not anybody's business, okay? And with the cheating—that was really only at the end, after things were already all fucked up. We were really in love. Okay?"

It sounded close to a demand. "Yeah, okay," she said.

"You can't put these things into words but we just

got each other. When we were together, or we were writing music, we just knew what the other one was thinking. It was motherfucking magical. Do you understand what I'm saying?"

All at once she remembered the first days of her and Robbie—how they'd lie naked and packed together like sardines on the narrow dorm room bed, just talking and talking for hours, like they'd never been permitted to talk to anyone before, sharing every memory, every secret, like she'd been holding onto them just so she could tell him.

"Yeah, Adam, I understand."

"And if she cheated . . . It wasn't because she was a bad person. She just didn't quite understand what people wanted from her, but she wanted to give it to them, so bad. You've gotta understand how beautiful she was, and how gifted, I mean, Johanna found melody in the clear blue sky. Someone like that, people are drawn to them, and the weird part is, it can make you sort of lonely . . ." He hesitated, like he'd gotten a little confused in his own thoughts. "But we had each other. Y'know?"

The question was urgent now; when she looked over at him, his eyes were wide, pleading. There was some affirmation he was looking for, but Marissa didn't know how to give it to him. Maybe she should have just let him smoke the fucking cigarette. "She sounds really special," she said. "I'm sorry it didn't work out."

He stared at her for another moment and then it was like the light of need was switched off in his face. He went back to sulking, went so far as to pull his knees up and hug them to his chest. She gave a worried glance to his sneakers on the fabric of the seat, but didn't bother giving him shit about it. He'd taken enough shit, warranted or not. She missed Robbie—not the Robbie she'd get when they arrived at the house but the Robbie she'd call from bed while he was in the kitchen making her huevos rancheros on a Sunday morning. The Robbie she never had to explain herself to, the Robbie whose growing up could not have been more different from hers but who understood, too, what it was like to long to flee from your family. She'd forgotten that about him—how earnestly he used to talk about feeling like a stranger among his parents and sister.

Adam reached over and turned on the radio, scanned among the stations, paused momentarily on some song and before she could come close to identifying it, muttered, "Oh, fuck no," and turned the radio off. "If you want to get depressed, listen to the radio," he said grimly. Everything shadowed and sunken and creased in his face appeared to have become more so. "Suicide music . . ."

"Look, Adam," she began. "It's sort of important that things go well today."

"Uh-huh," he said, without interest.

"I'm not exactly my in-laws' favorite person to begin with. And things with Robbie are . . . complicated."

"That's one word for it," he said under his breath. Before her anger could take hold, he swung his hand nonchalantly. "Don't sweat it. I'm great with parents."

"Yeah, I'm sure," she replied, skeptical. "But I told them you were a flight attendant, okay? So you have to, like, say that to them, too. Tell them we worked the flight from Seattle together. And if anyone asks you—"

"Flight attendant. I got it."

"Adam," she said, getting frustrated. "I'm counting on you. You can't—"

"Can't what? Fall off the wagon, drink all their bourbon, tell them you're pregnant, and steal the coffee-pot?" She couldn't tell if this was a joke, but she wasn't within a mile of laughter. In fact, she was considering whether she would be punished for her compassion, and if the smarter thing would be to leave him on the next curb she could find. Whatever ruin he'd made of his life, she couldn't allow him to make one of hers, too. But when she looked at him, his expression was so remorseful it was almost tender. "I know the last thing I deserve is to be in this car," he told her, his voice quiet, strained. "You picked my ass up a couple times today when you didn't have to. I know that I'm a dick but I'm not a dick like that. So I am a flight attendant with nowhere else to be today, and I am so thankful to be with them in their home, and by the way, I love doing dishes."

"Okay . . . ," she said. "Fine." A little needle of worry was still boring into her chest, but her instinct was he'd at least do his best. "Don't worry about the dishes," she muttered as they pulled off the highway at the Brattleboro exit. "It's not that kind of Thanksgiving."

The Russells' country cottage (so-called) was a couple miles outside of Brattleboro, in the town (village) of Wantastiquet, on a winding, wooded road, edged by a leafless thicket half-buried in snow. The driveway of number 51 was steep and narrow, with two switchbacks; Marissa took a measure of pride in being able to mount it even when it was covered with snow (Robbie had trouble), but on this late morning the blacktop was clear and freshly salted. She pulled in behind a Range Rover that she identified from the Harvard decal as Laila's. The house's façade featured a trio of great, sanded tree trunks, extending from the ground to the upward slanting roof. Two levels of floor-to-ceiling windows glowed yellow in the cold overcast midday. Adam studied the house for a moment after he got out of the car. "So your in-laws . . . ," he said. "They're, like, rich."

"Pretty much," Marissa answered.

He paused another moment; then, as he started up the slate steps twisting around the side of the house, he added, "Atta girl."

She didn't move, a fuck you poised on her lips, but he had already disappeared around the house. There hadn't been anything malicious in his tone. It was more like a congratulations. She weighed his words another second, but by now he would already be at the front door, and she didn't doubt he might ring the bell and just start talking to whoever opened it.

She hurried up the steps, taking care not to slip on their ice-gleaming surface, and came around the house to the garlanded front door just in time to see it open. A total stranger stood in the doorway: a trim young Asian man in a white button-down shirt. "Robbie," Adam said, with a sort of gravitas. "It's good to finally meet you." He stuck out his hand. The stranger blinked a couple times, shook.

"Happy Thanksgiving," the stranger said uncertainly. "Can I take your coat?"

"Yeah, thanks, man," Adam answered, walking in.

"And if you wouldn't mind taking off your shoes," he requested; he spoke with a faint but detectable accent. "There is mud."

"No, there isn't, but sure, you got it," Adam replied, pulling off his sneakers. "So did you and Marissa meet when you were, like, a foreign exchange student?"

"Jesus Christ," Marissa said, interrupting this as she walked in. "That isn't Robbie."

"I'm Fred," the young man said helpfully.

"So you're a friend of Robbie's, or . . . ?" Adam asked.

Fred shook his head. "I came from Craigslist."

"Craigslist?" Adam responded, as if more confused than ever.

"He means they hired him off Craigslist to help out today," Marissa said, the needle of worry expanding into something more like a drill.

But in the next moment, Adam was all smiles, and Fred was all smiles, too. He had a certain charm, she reassured herself; it didn't last long, but maybe they'd be out the door this afternoon before it wore off. She lifted her hair behind her head as she took off her trench coat, she straightened her blouse, she told herself she'd seen them a thousand times and either they were accepting of her poor-white-Boston ass by now or they weren't. Her heart thumping its way out of her chest wouldn't change anything. But she couldn't help remembering again (it was one of those memories that only got more embarrassing with time) the first time Robbie told her his parents wanted to meet her, had invited her to join them at a ramen restaurant—and ramen to her was twenty-five-cent slabs sold at Stop & Shop. So she'd been confused and pissy until Robbie had explained (without condescension, to his credit) that ramen restaurants were "a thing." This set a precedent of discomfort that had never really been broken.

By now, Adam and Fred had started chatting away about Chinese basketball players or something. Marissa had the sudden flash of hope that meeting him today had been lucky after all—that she'd stumbled on the perfect person to bring to a potentially awkward Thanksgiving. He'd smoothed things over with the waitress—maybe he could smooth over any conflict he wasn't responsible for. "To be honest, I don't even think about great players, I only think about great teams. It's not tennis, y'know?" Adam told Fred as he kicked off his shoes.

They walked up the stairway—sanded half-log steps, latticed cedar railing—toward what was called the great room. "Let me do the explaining," she said to Adam under her breath. She could hear a woman's voice—rapid, assured, a touch husky: Laila. As her head rose above the level of the floor, the first thing she saw was Mash, the Russell family dog, leaping from Laila's arms. Marissa was not a fearful person, but dogs fucking terrified her, even this floppy-eared spaniel, which was yapping and growling at her as she edged up the stairs, her back against the wall.

"Marissa!" Laila cried. She hurried across the room, lifted up the animal. "He only does that because he knows it scares you."

"Right . . . ," Marissa said, watching Laila's grip on the dog mistrustfully. Laila walked up and threw a free arm around Marissa in a hug. Marissa tried to lean her torso away from where she knew Mash's mouth would be, but Laila was strong, willowy—ran marathons, did hot yoga. She took a step back, gave Marissa a wide-eyed, smiling examination, Mash still growling at Marissa behind his sharp little teeth. She reached up, ran her fingers through Marissa's hair. "You don't know how lucky you are to have follicles that obey the fundamental laws of physics."

"Right," Marissa said, not sure how to respond. "You look great, too."

"Liar," Laila shrugged. Her skin was the same light brown shade as Robbie's, but where his face was square, his chin firm, her face was a long oval, crowned with a nimbus of coiled black hair, splashed on the right with blonde. She wore square, black-framed glasses, Harvard sweatpants, a faded Boyz II Men T-shirt. "I flew international yesterday, I'm not even pretending to try."

"At last," Roz said from behind Laila. She was seated on the leather couch by the fireplace, wearing a (frankly gorgeous) blue-and-silver knit jacket over her stout frame, had a copy of the *New Yorker* in her lap, a thin, watchful smile on her lips. She got up and crossed the room; in lieu of a hug she squeezed Marissa's biceps. "We were about to call the state police," she said, eyeing Marissa, her look more subtle but no less probing than her daughter's. A full foot shorter than Laila, there was no question that she was the more intimidating of the pair. "You're still in your uniform? You came right from the plane or what?"

"She makes it work, though," Laila said. With fastest-gun-in-the-west quickness, she had her phone out, was taking Marissa's picture before Marissa had time to smile or object—then was typing with her thumbs while keeping Mash in a headlock with one elbow.

"You feeling okay, honey?" Roz asked, peering at Marissa's face. "You look exhausted."

"I flew an overnight, so . . ."

"On Insty, check it," Laila said, holding the phone

up in front of Marissa's eyes. Marissa saw a washed-out image of herself, looking stunned and, yes, exhausted, with the caption

Sis-in-law gourg in her uniform, per always
#workingclasshero #hairenvy #familytime

"Oh, cool," she said to Laila. "Where's Robbie?"

At this point, Adam appeared behind her on the stairs. "Hey-o," he began with a dopey wave. "Didn't want to interrupt."

"Who's this?" Roz asked.

"Adam, he—" Marissa started.

"I'm Adam," Adam interrupted. "I'm a flight attendant. Marissa and I flew in together from Seattle. Roz, Laila, it is a super privilege to meet you. Okay, so, you know how you clearly have a warm and loving and accepting family? My family, not so much. Long story short, I'm gay, my family is not down with that, and honestly, they do not treat me very well. And because Marissa is the greatest woman on the planet, like seriously someone I admire, she was like, 'Well, come over to my family's.' And I was like, 'You can't be serious.'"

"Not serious?" Laila said, her face awash with pleased indignation. "Of course you're eating here."

"Are you sure?" Adam asked. "Because I can get an Uber or something, I—"

"First of all," Laila declared, "Uber has not penetrated the Wantastiquet market. And second, we are not turning our back on you. Due respect, but this is the year of our Lord two thousand and fifteen: Fuck your family's retrograde notions."

"Honestly?" Adam said. "Honestly, that is wonderful to hear."

"Are you crying, sweetie?" Roz asked Marissa, because she was squeezing the bridge of her nose with her eyes closed.

"I'm allergic to dogs," Marissa said, which she had mentioned at every Russell family gathering she'd attended for the last decade.

"We'll throw him in the closet," Laila told her. Then she let out a bouncing, boisterous laugh. "'In the closet!' Right, Adam?"

"Ha!" he laughed.

"Roz, he's totally eating with us, right?" Laila said to her mother.

Roz looked Adam over. And then she shrugged. "You want to eat with us, you'll eat."

"Awesome," Adam said. "Tremendous. Fantastic." He let out a laugh, as exuberant as Laila's. "To feel welcome!"

Robbie had appeared in the doorway at the back of the room; he stood leaning against the jamb with his hands shoved into the front pockets of a billowing black sweatshirt. He was several inches shorter than his sister, and was slouching, to boot, the fine features of his face locked in a look of irony and scorn. Marissa could imagine her husband skulking in doorways like this his whole childhood, almost basking in his resentment at being forgotten in the presence of his younger, taller, more outgoing sister. He grinned a little as Marissa's eyes met his, and gave a sidelong glance at Laila—and Marissa felt the recurrence of that tiny miracle that any marriage depends on for survival: She knew exactly what he was thinking. She passed between mother-in-law, sister-in-law, guard dog, crossed the room, and kissed him on the mouth.

"Hi, Izzy," he said, his hand on her hip.

"Robbie!" Adam called. "It's really great to finally meet you."

"Um, hi," Robbie answered. "Who're you?"

"Marissa's flight attendant friend," Laila announced. "His family has a problem with his sexuality, ergo, he's going to eat with us."

Robbie shot Marissa another sidelong glance at this, said, "Got it. Well, glad you're here, dude."

His hand was still on her hip; she covered it with her

own. "This fucking day, Robbie," she whispered under her breath.

"Now who is this little mutt?" Adam asked, taking the dog from Laila. Mash began licking his face with frantic affection.

"Mutt?" Roz answered. "Take a look at his papers, then see if you want to call him a mutt."

"That's Mash," Laila explained. "It was a nickname for Art Blakey, my dad's favorite musician. He was a sick drummer."

"He must be a real jazz aficionado to have heard of Art Blakey," replied Adam, half-playful, half-sarcastic.

"Can we go downstairs for a couple minutes?" Marissa whispered to Robbie.

They left Adam tussling playfully with the dog, and walked down the window-lined corridor to the back stairway. "So who is that dude?" Robbie asked her.

"Just somebody with nowhere else to be today," she answered, glad she'd found a way not to lie. Maybe later there'd be a chance to tell him the whole truth. "Where's your dad?"

"Where do you think?" Robbie answered, with a note of bitterness. "His office."

Marissa could never fully identify with the simmering antagonism between Robbie and his dad: Whatever one of them did, the other seemed to regard it as a betrayal of some distinctly masculine obligation. But then, she'd never met her own father. The most Mona would say about him was that he was a bastard and a "full Italian," as if this ought to be enough for Marissa to triangulate her own identity in terms of paternity. She liked to imagine him a million miles from Boston, not doing anything particularly noble or otherwise, just living a conventional life and not contacting her because Mona had never told him of Marissa's existence. It was as good a theory as any other. In any event, if Marissa couldn't understand precisely why Robbie found his father so vexing, the larger pattern was familiar enough: your parent as your nemesis. "That sucks," she told him.

"Something's up, I don't know," Robbie continued. "Some agency probably wants another ten grand in appropriations or whatever."

"Yeah," said Marissa, having lost interest in the subject. They turned down a hall at the bottom of the stairs, went into the bedroom the Russells called "the minaret room," for the black-and-white photographs of minarets on the walls, taken by Roz's father. Marissa didn't know what a minaret was until she walked into that room. An antique wood dresser stood against one wall, twin painted lamps stood on the bedside tables, a beaten quilt lay across the king-size bed: rustic, seemed to be the idea. Robbie's Nike gym bag was open at the foot of the bed, overflowing with clothes he'd wedged inside. She resisted the instinct to fold them, instead let herself fall sideways on the mammoth bed, curled her legs to her chest, and closed her eyes. She heard the door close, felt the mattress dip with Robbie's weight as he sat down next to her, put his hand on her calf. "You all right?" he asked.

"Did she have to say I look exhausted?"

"It's my mom being my mom."

"I was up all night. How am I supposed to look?"

"She's not a happy person," he said, flopping back on the bed. "We were playing Boggle this morning, and Laila was talking about, I don't know, how she doesn't think she'll have kids because of the water table or something, and I just mentioned how kids aren't really our priority right now, either, and the next thing I know my mom knocked the fucking board over and walked out of the room. Loco, right?"

This story had started what felt like a brushfire in her chest, but she ignored it, and instead pulled her legs up higher, curling deeper around herself. "Can you believe I have to fly again tonight?" she asked, indulging the self-pity.

"Fuck it," he said. "Just stay here."

"And just get fired," she replied; attendants without decades of seniority who blew off night flights got axed, pronto.

"I told you about that freelance gig . . ."

She didn't respond. She could sense the fight that was two remarks away waiting to pounce on them, like a mugger; he had to sense it, too. "Hey," he said. He'd brought his face up to hers. "Open your eyes." She did. She was close enough to see each individual coil of black hair in the straight line across his forehead, to see the mingling shades in his brown irises. She edged nearer to him, lifted her leg over his thighs, put her head against his chest. She spent her first two semesters at Syracuse frightened as a kitten, going nowhere but dorm, classes, library, lacrosse. She should be back in Boston, engaged to Brendan, waitressing at Legal Seafood, standing up for Caitlyn: She'd thought it every day. And then she met Robbie, who grew up with kids who were all at Harvard or Yale, who felt like the black kids didn't get him and the white kids didn't feel comfortable around him. But fuck if he and Marissa didn't feel comfortable around each other. By the end of sophomore year, they were living together, and had never lived apart since. She closed her leg over his thighs. You had to know what you could live with and what you couldn't live without. And she was sure she couldn't live without these wordless moments of belonging.

She felt Robbie slide his hand beneath the waist of her skirt, under the elastic of her stockings and panties, rest his hand against her tuft of pubic hair. This wasn't him initiating, she didn't think, it was just how he liked to sleep—with his hand there, for some reason. Men were such a collection of secret needs, secret fears. How many could you indulge? Maybe knowing that was the key to a successful marriage.

She probably would have drifted off to sleep then, but now he was initiating, closing his fist and gently tugging the hairs, the way she liked him to sometimes. But rather than get turned on, she started a mental catalogue of all the ways she didn't look good, feel good: her hair greasy, the fabric of her blouse stiff under her armpits, clamminess around her feet and the backs of her knees. "I should take a shower."

"You want company?"

"Sure, okay."

They got up from the bed and went into the bathroom. Robbie locked the door behind them—another habit of his, expressing some other category of nebulous fear. They got undressed without really looking at each other, like people comfortable with each other's nudity, or like people sharing a locker room bench, their nudity not really the point of what they were doing—she couldn't say which. But taking off her uniform felt wonderful, as if her work day ended only just then. She'd been acting something like Adam's flight attendant, too, it occurred to her: at his service, all morning long.

She paused as she looked at the shower, as if it shone bright against her fatigue: a glass-walled cube in the corner of the room, tiled with black stone, a shower-head the size of a pizza fixed parallel to the floor below it. Atta girl, she heard in Adam's voice, as if he was perched on her shoulder like the little devil in a cartoon. She was suddenly so sick of him. And she recognized that for all her lamenting of her fate and her fortune, she just might be the luckiest girl to have ever got out of the Shittier Boston Area. And all she had to do to preserve that good luck, or all her hard work, whatever you wanted to call it, was have an abortion and keep her mouth shut. Surely, better women had done worse.

Marissa stepped into the shower first, turned the nozzle, stuck her foot under the waterfall cascading from overhead. A rain shower, they called it. Satisfied with its warmth, she stepped into the stream, stood with her face inclined downward, letting the water soak into her hair, feeling its tendrils get heavier and heavier on her back, shooting jetties of water down her buttocks and thighs. Her eyes closed again, she heard the door open, Robbie step in. Instinctively, she wrapped her arms around his neck, like they were dancing. She was sorry, so sorry, so sorry—only she couldn't say it. He put his hands above her hips, by her stomach, and she had to tamp down a burst of panic: There was nothing for him to notice. It couldn't be bigger than a grain of salt, could it?

She heard the squirt of a bottle and he began to rub the shampoo into her hair. "I love you, Robbie," she told him.

"I love you, too, Izzy," he answered, working the shampoo from her scalp down the length of her hair. It was all so tender and fragile she began to cry. He wouldn't notice that either, with the noise and the water.

"Why's it been so bad between us?" she asked, like a plea.

"I dunno. Why talk about it?"

Fair enough. She opened her eyes, her head still bent down toward his chest. She could see her nipples pressed into the copper of his pectorals. God, how they used to fuck: gleeful, shameless, a pair of recent virgins indulging every touch and taboo they could imagine, like it was their own secret kingdom, no rules against anything. Where had that gone, that revelry in each other? It was nobody's fault. Time passed, you got older. It happened to everyone, familiarity settling in like a fog until you stopped seeing each other.

Why permit that, though? Didn't you need to fight for things? Wasn't that all she'd ever done?

She lifted her head and pushed open the shower door with her knuckles, pulled a towel folded over a metal rod and brought it into the shower with them. As she dropped it to the tiled floor, Robbie asked her, "What're you doing?"

"Sucking your dick," she answered, which sounded dumb, but she was determined. She arranged the already sopping towel underneath her knees and knelt just about exactly eye level with his erection. When she was in college there were all kinds of outlandish porno-inspired things she might have done or said at this moment to enhance the event, but none of them seemed necessary, and so she tucked her lips over her teeth and did start to suck his dick. Nostalgia blow job, she heard in her head. Apology blow job. Last hope blow job.

Atta girl.

Twenty minutes later, she was wrapped in a towel and standing at the sink, brushing her teeth at the sink furiously for the second time that day. Robbie was naked and loving it—dancing like a bee showing the others where the honey was, his cock flapping back and forth.

Men were so simple, she thought, spitting water and toothpaste into the sink and starting to brush again. It took so little to make them happy; only, it didn't last.

As she brushed, he came up behind her, kissed her on the neck. "I needed that," he said. "We needed that."

"Yeah, yeah," she said dryly, working the toothbrush in her mouth.

"Want me to get you back?"

"I need to see your parents in a minute." And it took her considerably longer than a minute to get off, and then she'd have to shower again . . .

"After, then. I'll give you something to think about when you're on that flight," he added in a joking whisper.

She guessed they'd both be so stuffed later all they'd do would be pass out on the bed—which sounded just fine to her—but she told him, "It's a date."

He kissed her neck again and danced over to the toilet, kicked up the lid with his foot, started to piss, humming. She felt sick. She dropped the toothbrush in the sink, grabbed its sides, squeezed her eyes closed. "You all right?" he asked over the thrum of his urine.

She felt like her stomach was trying to climb up toward her throat.

"Just . . . light-headed," she managed, swallowing down bile.

"You gotta get more sleep, Izzy," he told her. Then, a moment later, "Didn't you puke the other morning?"

"Delia had a stomach bug, I think I caught it from her." The nausea passed. The lie had come so quickly, so naturally. She opened her eyes—she hadn't wiped the condensation off the mirror, could only make out the contours of her face, globs and splotches in the dripping gray sheen on the glass. After she had the abortion, she'd never tell him another lie, she promised herself. Or was that a lie, too? It didn't matter. You swallowed as much bile as you had to. She repeated Delia's words to herself: He never has to know. She picked up the toothbrush and started brushing again.

"Did I tell you I finished the latest draft of the screenplay?" he said, shaking the last drops of piss from his dick.

"Yeah?" she said, doing her best to sound impressed.

"Yeah, Tuesday night."

"So now what?" she asked, looking at him over her shoulder. He lifted one foot in the air, flushed the toilet with his toes.

"On Monday I'll go over to the copy place, have new bound copies made, then give it to Zach and those guys to read. Get their notes, see where I'm at. It might need one more rev. I'm still waiting for that agent guy to call me back." She nodded, smiled around the toothbrush, returned to the sink, and spat. "What?" he said.

"What?" she answered.

"That's what I'm asking you."

They were back at the edge of the chasm, staring down into all they knew the other one was thinking. "Nothing," she said. "That's great news, Robbie."

There was a pause. "Okay, then," he finally answered. And then he walked out of the bathroom.

And there you had it: Just like that, all the goodwill of the day—the smile at seeing each other, holding one another on the bed, the blow job in the shower—it had all evaporated. They didn't even need to have the fight anymore. Just knowing the fight was there to be had was enough. She could walk out of the bathroom and they would have the same argument they always had—about money: the problem that encompassed all their other problems or was merely the canary in the coal mine of a marriage that was all out of goodwill.

She'd come out of the bathroom, he would have his jeans on, begin with something like, "Is it wrong for me to expect you to be happy when I accomplish something?"

She'd sit down on the bed in her towel, wearily—trying to show him, in the way she sat down, just how weary she was. "I *am* happy for you."

Sharp and accusatory, "Is that true?"

And then, running out of patience—from the flights, the day, from all the times she'd been forced to give the same reassurances—she'd reply with, "I'm sorry, Robbie, but how many drafts of that screenplay have you written this year?"

He'd answer through flat lips, chin pushed out, his eyebrows forming a spastic V between his eyes, showing her the effort it took him not to lose his temper: "I've *explained* this to you. It is a *process*."

"Okay. That's fine. But all I want to know is—"

"You make me say this a million and fucking one times—"

"—when the process ends!"

"Jesus Christ . . ." Dismissive, like she was an idiot.

"What about your short?" Because he'd made her mad now.

"Honestly, Marissa, just don't."

"You were working on that short for *months*. You spent *months* on your laptop editing it."

"What do you want me to say!" Defensive, indignant, swinging his hurt feelings like a cudgel. "It was a shit project! Sometimes you find that out the hard way!"

"You didn't even submit it to the festivals!"

"Yes, because it was shit. You think it's a good strategy to send around bad work? That wouldn't be very *smart*, would it, Marissa?"

You shared your insecurities with people you loved— why? For reassurance, for protection. Because you believed you could trust them never to turn those insecurities against you. And while he had her stunned, "You knew what I wanted to do with my life. I told you that a long time ago."

"A long time ago I was twenty. Now I'm thirty-one! I want to have a family, Robbie, I want to have the freedom to—"

"Jesus, here we go again. You had expectations, Marissa, when we got married? Is that what you're trying to say?"

And here, annoyed by the absurdity of the accusation, of what he was implying (or maybe feeling somewhere that what he was implying was not quite as absurd as she wished to think), here all the Russell and Syracuse and Needham in her would vanish, and only Cavano would be left. Which is to say, she would lose her temper. As loud as she could: "My expectation was that my husband would get a fucking paycheck at least once in his life! I'm such a dumb bitch, right, Robbie, because I care about paying the rent?"

"Like we'd ever had a problem paying the rent. You are being hysterical."

"I don't want to take money from your parents!"

"Right, you want to be independent."

"I do want to be independent!" Screaming now.

He'd be pressing his fists into his temples, like he was trying to squeeze his contempt or disgust or whatever it was out of his eyeballs; he'd make threats that ended without the hook of consequence. "You know what, Marissa? You know what, Marissa? Sometimes I really think . . ." Or maybe he'd drop to the floor like a toddler, let out long, slow, deep groans. "All I ever wanted, all I ever wanted—"

If the latter, and if self-restraint was still recoverable, she might hurriedly say, "I'm sorry, Robbie. I know you're doing your best, you—"

But it was usually too late. He'd bury his face behind his hands, sob into them, wail, "I feel so alone. I feel so alone."

She did, too. And how awful that was, because if their relationship had ever been anything, it was a promise that neither of them would ever feel that way again.

Had they just been too young when they got married? Sometimes she thought so. If he'd believed she'd always be content waitressing while he got the odd freelance job and worked on his screenplays, it was probably because for many years, she had been. What had changed? Something biological—her body screaming at her to have a kid? No, she suspected that in the end, the problem was all the things that hadn't changed, and could never change: the differences between them, the way they'd been raised, what they thought about money, what they thought about themselves. Marissa had never changed.

"Fuck," Robbie said.

Startled, she turned from the mirror, almost slipped on the damp floor. He was still naked, staring at her from the doorway. "You look like you saw a fucking ghost."

She nodded. "I really am happy. About your screenplay." It might do them no more good than throwing a penny in a fountain, but you had to try.

Something tightened briefly in his face, then softened. "Thanks, Izzy. I know you are." Izzy: She wanted to cry again. Instead, she rubbed her hand all over the skin of her face, like she was trying to rub out the fight they hadn't had.

"Will you get my bag from the car? The keys are in my coat."

"You got it." She watched through the bathroom door as he pulled on a pair of boxers and jeans, took a T-shirt from his bag, pulled it over his head.

"Robbie," she said as he was sticking his left arm through the T-shirt's sleeve. He turned around. "You know how you say sometimes you don't know how to make me happy?" He nodded a little. "You shouldn't say that. You do make me happy. We're good."

He smiled a little. "I know we are. You're tired," he added, sympathetic, consoling. "We gotta find some time for you to get some sleep." He winked at her. "We're so good."

She managed a smile; he went out into the hall, closing the bedroom door behind him. She left the bathroom and dropped down on the bed again, not bothering to lift the towel as it fell open at her back. She felt a sort of carousel in her forehead of all the things she might feel, think, but found she was too tired to take hold of any particular one—fear and hope, sadness and guilt, resistance and surrender, rising up and down, repeating, repeating. Her eyes fell on Robbie's laptop, sitting on the bedside table. She sat up, the towel falling to her thighs, opened it, typed in his password—a vestige of trust that seemed to do them little good. She stared at the screen for a moment, then remembered and typed "kiss and kill" into the search field.

The page popped full of links: reviews, interviews, articles. Adam was right, this did look like success to her. She picked an article at random and scrolled to the middle, not sure what she was looking for. "War-shaw's notoriously virtuoso if too often Byzantine synths make a strikingly PB-and-J-right pairing with

Mayfield's bell-clear vocals. You feel they'd both be better off doing something else, but for as long as they're together, there's plenty to enjoy." Marissa didn't find this terribly enlightening. She went back to the search results, clicked on a video. A much younger version of Adam appeared on the screen—singing, playing a keyboard, a brightness in his eyes she would have noticed even if it hadn't been so entirely absent in the person she'd met that day. And onstage beside him was a young woman playing guitar—slender, her hair dyed silver, with striking, elfin features, and great round eyes. She really was beautiful. The sound was muted, and Marissa didn't bother turning it on. She just watched this happier, healthier, in all ways more alive Adam, watched the ethereal woman next to him— watched as they played and sang and bopped around onstage at some outdoor festival, the crowd swaying and dancing and smiling. She thought of all the things that had once and maybe still bound her and Robbie together—trivial, essential: the sense of not belonging in their own families; a willingness to listen; an instinct to comfort; sex, in-jokes, Mexican food, Harry Potter movies . . .

On the screen, Adam and Johanna played and sang silently. It was like an act of bravery encased in amber.

Laila gave Adam a tour of the house: the media room in the basement with the leather recliners and the projector and the popcorn machine; the chef's kitchen with the wood-block island and eight-foot refrigerators and Fred heating dishes in three ovens; the dining room with the salvaged Brazilian rosewood dining table, already set with the crystal and the china and a centerpiece overflowing with orange roses and chrysanthemums. Roz had gone into the master bedroom, Robbie and Marissa were in one guest bedroom, Leo was in his office, so Laila elected to skip most of the ground floor. She led Adam up the stairway at the back of the house into a lofted room with exposed beams, floor-to-ceiling windows overlooking wooded hills rolling down to a frozen lake. Instruments adorned one wall of the room: a Gibson J-200, a lovely humpbacked mandolin with ivory inlays, a cream-colored alto sax, a battered mbira. Opposite these were custom oak shelves, filled end to end with records in sleeves. A pair of leather recliners sat on a Turkish rug in the middle of the room; a turntable on a black pillar stood nearby, beside a cabinet of speaker equipment.

"This is the conservatory," Laila told him.

"Where Colonel Mustard killed Miss Scarlet with the lead pipe?" Adam answered.

Laila laughed. "I know, it's so Roz and Leo."

Somehow, he managed to notice the most compelling thing in the room last, a gorgeous six-foot Steinway grand in a corner by the window, fallboard up, lid up, brass pedals polished, the black maple of the cabinet shining like onyx: ready for business. Adam hesitated, then couldn't resist. He walked over and with his index finger pressed down middle C. Sound filled the instrument like light fills a lamp—a half-step flat. Adam scowled. With the same finger, he pressed A above middle C. He could taste the sourness of the vibrations at the back of his throat. "Christ," he said. "When was the last time this was tuned?"

"Nobody really plays it," Laila answered. "Leo made Robbie and me take lessons when we were kids, but we both sucked. It's essentially ornamental. Do you play?"

"Used to."

"Go on, then," she teased.

He pushed down the sostenuto pedal with his sneaker, feeling a sort of mournful sympathy for the piano. All this craftsmanship and beauty and the instrument was as good as pickled in formaldehyde; or worse, actually—rotting neglected on a shelf. Maybe he should sit down and play, show her what this thing had been built to do. Even years out of tune, it was a better instrument than many he'd played on. He could just work C major, walking bass line, like he used to do for hours and hours at the last bars he worked in, when he was so blotto he could barely sit up, or pull an arpeggio-laden "Round Midnight" out his ass or a forty-minute "Rhapsody in Blue." She wouldn't know if he faked his way through half of it. He imagined striking the keys so ferociously the piano would break apart before he was done: the strings snapping and popping like gunfire, the top board slipping from the prop and cracking in half, the legs buckling on the casters, the ivory chipping and splitting, the keys pounded at last into dust. He imagined playing the piano to death, pretty much. He knew he was angry, only he wasn't sure at who. Kristen? All of them? At Stone Manor, they'd have insisted he was mad primarily at himself, and they were usually right about these things. He wiped the dust off the keys with his sleeve, gently lowered the fallboard over them. This wasn't a day to be crossing the lines he'd drawn for himself. "All I remember is 'Michael Row Your Boat to Shore.'" The skin around his eyes felt warm with fatigue, but he could keep bullshitting like this all day if he had to. It was a skill he'd honed with practice. At Stone Manor, they encouraged positivity.

"Laila," a low, disembodied voice said out of nowhere.

Adam looked around, confused. "The fuck?"

Laila lifted her toe (her feet at the bottom of her sweatpants were bare, the nails painted a lavender shade) toward the wall behind Adam: a little round intercom was set at the top of the stairs. "It's so you can find people in the house without looking for them. I call it the 'voice of God' system."

"Laila," the voice repeated.

"You going to answer?"

She rolled her eyes. "I don't play that surveillance state shit."

"Me, neither," Adam agreed, though not really clear what she meant. It was pretty obvious she was smarter than him. He also hadn't failed to notice that from her blond-stained afro down to her ten painted toes, Laila was a good-looking girl: cute face, cute body, if a little on the broad-shouldered side. But he figured if he restricted himself to flirting, he wouldn't be breaking his vow to Marissa to keep things cool. Anyway, where could the flirting go, since he was pretending to be gay, too?

He walked over to the shelves, began inspecting the record collection. Each shelf had a little brass label screwed beneath it: "Classical A–L," "Pop/Rock A–L," and so on.

"Leo keeps the really expensive ones in a fireproof safe in Boston," Laila told him.

"They probably can't hurt anybody there." She laughed again. "And to think I used to keep my records in egg crates."

"Yeah, my dad gets pretty anal about his *things*. It's one of the ironies of the modern American liberal, how progressivism and consumerism aren't seen as mutually exclusive."

"Totally." His eyes moved quickly over the Pop/ Rock K's, then shifted to the spines of the other albums. It was like anybody's dad's collection: the titles conventional, predictable, uninspired. You had your *Pet Sounds* and your complete Beatles, your Hendrix and your Joni Mitchell and your Creedence. So there was a first pressing of *Exile on Main Street*—whoop-de-doo. Some of the stuff in the Soul/R & B section was more enticing. He slid one off the shelf he decided he wouldn't mind hearing.

"So, that still might cost two thousand dollars," Laila warned him.

"You can trust me," he told her. And yes, Adam might shatter the family coffeepot on Thanksgiving morning—fuck, he might shatter the Holy Grail if it turned out to be made of glass and his mind was elsewhere when Jesus passed it to him. But he wouldn't shatter a record, not by carelessness. He pulled the cardboard sleeve out of its plastic covering, slid out the disc and freed it from its paper sheath—felt the disc's weight as he pressed its edges between his two palms, turned its ebony face in the light, inspecting the concentric ripples on the surface. Not a scratch. Good for Leo. Adam hadn't even managed to sell his records—just left them in the last apartment he'd shared with Johanna. He brought the record to the stereo, placed it on the turntable, wiped its face with the synthetic cloth tucked on top of the receiver.

"It's all sort of pathetic, though," Laila announced, flopping down in one of the recliners. "When my dad was my age, he wanted to be a musician—a jazz drummer. He gave it up when he went to law school. This room is, like, eighty thousand dollars' worth of overcompensation."

"I know a lot of drummers who'd trade places," Adam answered, pushing buttons on the stereo.

"Still, though. It's like a museum of broken dreams."

Adam looked up from the stereo. Her legs dangled over one arm of the chair, her head was propped on the other as she stared into the ceiling, a contemplative look on her face. The comment had surprised him, like when a band he'd given up on came out with a chord progression that was actually sort of interesting. "Can I ask you something?" he said.

"Sure," she answered, turning her face to him, cheek on the chair's arm.

"Like, what's your deal?"

She brightened. "I started an NGO in Berlin that helps dissidents living under nondemocratic regimes access the Internet without risk of government surveillance. We facilitate anonymous VPNs in China, Iran, Cuba. Places like that. It's an extension of my master's thesis."

"Oh," said Adam. "You speak German?"

"*Ja, aber,* you don't really need it."

"Right . . ." Okay, definitely smarter than him, and she was not just a book-smart nitwit, either, like a lot of college girls. From what he understood of her work, there was even something a little punk rock about her. She was really kind of a badass, Adam concluded.

"You like being a flight attendant?" she asked him.

"What? Oh yeah, it's great. You fly all over the place." The lying was problematic, from a Stone Manor perspective, but at least it was for a good cause. He returned to the stereo, pressed the protruding PLAY button on the turntable. He turned up the volume and watched the mechanical arm lift its head, glide an inch to the left, lower itself to the spinning record. And next he heard what he considered the most beautiful sound in all of recorded music: the staticky, pregnant murmur as the needle approached the grooves of the first track. Beyond this liminal hush, anything could follow. It was what the universe sounded like before the Big Bang, Johanna used to say. He sat down in the recliner next to Laila's as the first bars filled the room—slouched down in the chair, his legs extended.

"What's this?" Laila asked.

"Al Green."

Whatever did end up playing was always a disappointment, one way or another, but the voice was as great a consolation as one could hope for. And there was no denying the sound quality was fantastic: big and warm and intimate—money well spent, he'd remember to tell Leo.

"Is Al Green the one who got shot?" asked Laila.

"Nah, Al Green's still alive. You're thinking of Marvin Gaye, he got shot by his dad." Adam paused. "Or maybe you're thinking of Sam Cooke. He got shot by, like, a night manager of a hotel or something." Another pause. "Or maybe you mean Otis Redding. But he died in a plane crash."

"Fuck, that's a depressing list."

"Kind of. But I think about that a lot—maybe it's

better if these guys just disappear one day, instead of turning into sad, old parodies of themselves."

"'Runners whom renown outran, and the name died before the man,'" she commented.

"Laila, are you dressed for pictures?" the deep, disembodied voice asked. This time, they both ignored it.

"I met Al Green once, y'know," Adam said.

"Al Green? For real? What was he like?"

"I don't know, he was a pretty weird dude . . . But soulful, too, y'know?"

"How'd you meet him?"

Adam didn't answer—didn't feel like explaining what he'd been doing at the Montreux Jazz Festival in 2008. And Laila didn't repeat the question; she seemed to share his instinct to make way for the grace and tenderness of what they were hearing. If Adam closed his eyes, he could see the voice, like curling liquid tendrils, flowing free across a void. Making music was incessant failure and frustration—but God in heaven, he still loved hearing it.

In the gap before the next track, Laila asked plaintively, "So am I wrong to hate myself for never listening to this record?"

"You shouldn't hate yourself for anything. No one can listen to all the great music in the world, it's just impossible."

"So would you say Al Green is your favorite singer?" she asked him, oddly formal now.

"I don't really think of it that way. What's the point of ranking these things? Does it actually mean anything if you put Al Green above, like, Leonard Cohen, or Freddy Mercury, on some imaginary totem pole of All Singers Ever?"

"All hierarchies are inherently reductive, I agree with that."

"I dropped out of college," he confessed.

"Oh yeah?" she replied admiringly. "I wanted to a few times, but I never had the balls." Is that what it had taken to drop out of college? Balls? Sort of the opposite, he'd always thought.

"I'm just saying the more you talk about these things," he continued, "the further you get from them. You want to know how good Al Green is? Listen to his music. And if you don't know after that, reading an article that shoves him between Lou Reed and fucking Emmylou Harris isn't going to help you."

"So it sounds like you're saying," she responded carefully, "consider the music qua music, without attention to relative aesthetic—"

"I'm saying don't trust rock critics. In fact, don't trust anybody who says 'I'm going to explain this,'" he pointed into the air, in which Al Green's voice floated, "using *words*. Do you know how many books people have written, trying to *explain* the Beatles? I mean, throw on *Rubber Soul*, it's pretty obvious what's going on there. But no, they gotta dissect it, break it down: Is this song thirty percent Paul and seventy percent John? Or fourteen percent Ringo? Or they act like the whole band was an experiment to determine which of them was 'the best Beatle.' Like it makes you some kind of courageous idealist if you argue that George was the secret genius behind the whole thing. Hey, newsflash, George Harrison's just the best guitarist in the ashram without the other three. But he was *in the fucking Beatles*. I'm pretty sure that's his high watermark as an artist. I mean, do these people even understand what a band *is*? Do they understand why anybody plays music at all?" He waved his hand with frustration. "Everyone's stuck inside their own heads, everyone's stuck in their own lives. Only sometimes, when you play music with other people, or for other people, and no, not only then, but sometimes, I don't know, in a band, in a *good* band, you feel like for once . . ." He struggled to find the right words, felt the familiar gasping futility of it. "You're in it together," he finally said. "You're in it together. And no, it doesn't happen all the time, and when it does, it never lasts, but just for that song or those five bars or those fifteen seconds or whatever it is, you're in it together. What's the point of slicing and dicing that moment, since it's a miracle it happens at all? You can play two hundred shows a year, you might get there five times."

He'd strayed so far from his original point, he'd lost track of what he was talking about. Laila was pushing herself up in the chair to stare at him, her T-shirt bunched up above her belly button. "You used to be in a band, didn't you?"

He felt embarrassed, felt like he was guilty of everything he'd been accusing everyone else of. What did he care about rock critics? Or George Harrison? "Yeah, a few of them, whatever."

"I think you're pretty soulful, too, Adam."

"Well . . . Thanks, I appreciate that."

"Do you want to go to my room to get high?"

He opened his mouth to say no, but before he could, he asked, "On what?"

"Weed, man, chill out!" she laughed. "This isn't Burning Man!"

Pot had never been a problem for him, but he knew better than to fuck around on the slippery slope. "I'm okay. But I'll watch you smoke, if you want."

"Okay, great. Let's do that. Let's go do that right now."

As Adam got up, he heard footsteps on the stairs:

heavy, unhurried, like a cop knocking on the window of your car. A moment later a large man appeared at the top of the stairs, his skin several shades darker than Laila's, but unmistakably her father: tall like her, with the same high, flat forehead, the same ovular face, even the same tussock of incongruous hair, his a fraying rectangle of white in his beard. He wore wire-frame glasses and a maroon cardigan over his broad shoulders, and took in the scene before him with a dour expression that, despite the music, seemed to effect a sort of vacuum of disapproving silence around his person. "You two have made yourselves comfortable," he observed.

Poor Robbie, was Adam's first thought: to have a guy like this for a father—plainly the sort who'd unironically deploy phrases like "Not while you live under my roof" and "You have your homework to think about"; who'd hold himself gruff and remote until he insisted on conversations about how shitty your life was turning out; who'd generally carry himself as if because he'd gotten his rocks off at the right time of the month, he'd been vested with some form of implacable authority over a personal fiefdom: his family. Adam's own father was nothing like that. His dad was the type who cried during movies and gave hugs (though, to be fair, the tears and the hugs had in recent years become as unbearable to Adam as any assertion of paternal privilege). Still, Adam saw in Laila's father the dad of every girl he'd dated in high school, every aggro bouncer and backstage heavy and boots-and-braces meth dealer he'd ever crossed paths with.

But he'd made a promise. He stood up, held out his hand. "Hello, mister—er, hello." He'd intended to say Sir, couldn't quite get there. "I'm Adam, I'm a friend of Marissa's."

"Senator Russell," Laila's father answered, his voice a predictable *basso profundo.*

"Jesus, Daddy." Laila said to Adam, "You can call him Leo."

"That's a strong grip, Leo." This seemed to be the point of the way Leo was shaking Adam's hand.

"You're a friend of Marissa's?" Leo asked, not releasing his grip.

"I think I said that already? We work together. We're flight attendants. Hmm, ho. So do you use one of those hand exerciser things when you're watching CBS, or are you a rock climber?" Adam was smiling, but marshaled every other part of his face to contradict the upward bend in his lips.

"Okay, then," Leo said, finally releasing Adam's hand. "What did you say your name was?"

"Adam."

Leo regarded him with poker-faced stillness.

"Adam Warshaw."

"Okay, then." Leo moved his gaze over to Laila, her ankles crossed on the arm of the chair, her arms behind her head, her shirt pulled up above her lower ribs. She returned a look of blasé disgust she'd probably been honing since puberty. "You could find a more seemly way to sit in that chair, I think," he said to her.

She yanked her T-shirt down over her navel. "As it happens, Roz and I invited Adam to stay for dinner. I assume it'd be more *seemly* to make our guest feel welcome?"

He ignored this. "You didn't hear me over the intercom?"

"I think I've made my feelings about the intercom abundantly clear."

"It's time to get dressed. The photographer will be here in twenty minutes."

"Speaking of things about which I've made my feelings clear . . ."

"Hey, if you guys want, I can take the picture with my iPhone," Adam offered.

Father and daughter were momentarily united in giving Adam a bemused, pitying look. "It's not that kind of picture," Laila explained. "Come on," she said to him, standing, giving her T-shirt another perfunctory yank. "You can help me pick out what to wear."

"Sound system is amazing, Leo," Adam said as he walked by him.

Leo responded with a stiff nod, remaining at the top of the stairs and looking into the conservatory as Adam and Laila descended. And Adam had an impulse to turn, and apologize for the sarcasm and the shit-eating grin with which he'd spoken, and assure Leo he meant it: The sound system was amazing. He'd been hit with an unexpected stab of shame, like he owed Leo better than this—leaving him alone with the Al Green, in a room Leo had erected to something both he and Adam had tried and failed at.

"He's not always such an asshole," Laila said on the stairs, once Leo was (probably) out of earshot. "Something's going on in Boston, he's been in his office all day. And believe it or not, he really values his family time. Real talk, though"—and here she lowered her voice—"I don't think he likes white people."

"Um, didn't he marry a white person?"

Laila laughed. "Roz is probably the white person he likes least!"

At the bottom of the steps, she opened a door in the hallway—he was about to follow her into the bedroom when his phone rang. He'd forgotten it was charged. He yanked it out of his jeans pocket: Jack was calling. Inchoate death metal screaming rang in Adam's head. He hit the IGNORE button—big, red, round, exactly like an emergency exit button ought to look—then texted Jack.

Headed back to SF. Have a great day!

He hit SEND, turned off the phone, went into the room after Laila.

A neatly made-up king-sized bed occupied most of the square room. The blinds were pulled down over a pair of picture windows, black-and-white photographs of Greek statuary lined the walls. On a shelf opposite the foot of the bed sat a cluster of colored glass sculptures, small and globular. "They call it the sculpture room, because of the . . ." Laila motioned toward the photos, didn't bother to finish. As Adam walked in, she reached behind him, pulled the door closed. "So be honest. Is every family totally fucked, or is it just mine?"

Adam thought about it for a moment. "I'd say if you leave me out, my family is doing pretty well."

She patted him on the chest. "You're right, they're wrong. Never forget that." She frowned in an impressed way, patted him on the chest again. "You do Pilates?"

"Swim."

"Your boyfriend's a lucky man."

He gave her a puzzled smirk before he remembered.

"Oh, right. No, I don't have a boyfriend. We broke up because . . . He kept fucking other dudes. He was super dishonest."

"Sucks," she told him. "Been there. He was good-looking, right? You can't trust good-looking guys."

She turned and crouched at a purple hard-shell suitcase on the floor beside the bed. "I wasn't kidding about Leo and my mom," she told him as she opened the suitcase. "When we sit down to eat, count how many times they talk to each other. Their marriage is such a sham," she declared, fishing around inside the case with her hand. "Which is why it pisses me off about the photographer. Just the hypocrisy of it. We send these pictures to half of Massachusetts and—" She looked over at him. "Do me a solid and don't touch those?" He'd drifted to the shelf of glass sculptures, had lifted a green one shaped roughly like an apple, and was peering through its opaque surface. "They're probably the most expensive piece of artwork in the house." He replaced it on the shelf. She pulled out a palm-sized chrome vaporizer, and switched the device on. A little curving infinity symbol lit up in red on its face. "Look, I don't begrudge them their misery. If they want to live a lie, so be it. But this parading of ourselves as a symbol of twenty-first-century postracial harmony . . ." She took a long, contemplative hit from the vaporizer, exhaled out the corner of her mouth, and sat down on the bed, folding her legs underneath her. "I accept that we have to make sacrifices for my dad's career. But spending every holiday in a fucking Potemkin village, it just gets depressing." She took another hit, let the smoke drift between her lips. "It's complicated, though," she allowed, blowing the rest of the smoke from her mouth. She tossed the vaporizer on the comforter, stood, and went to a closet in the corner. "Leo isn't well-known nationally, but walk through certain neighborhoods in Boston, he's like DeNiro in *Godfather II*. Everyone has a story of this time he saved their gas station, the time he got the landlord to fix their pipes, the time he got a street plowed after a blizzard. The fact is, my father is a hero to a lot of people. And I respect that." She was surveying a quartet of dresses dangling from hangers in the closet. "But doesn't his happiness and my mom's happiness count for anything at all? Or mine and Robbie's, when we were growing up?" She was quiet for a moment, as if pondering this, then took a green dress from the closet, held it in front of Adam. "Nice, right?"

It looked a lot like every other green dress he'd ever seen, but sometimes the answers were easy. "Yes, very."

"Tracy Reese. It's one of the two shades in the visual spectrum that's actually flattering with my skin tone." She laid the dress on the bed, smoothed it with the back of her hand. Then she turned again to face Adam, who leaned with his back against the door. "Sorry, I'm high. What was I talking about?"

"Uh . . . Your dad's a hero, but your parents aren't happy?"

"Right. Exactly. And that's the thing: family, integrity, personal responsibility in the black community. That's pretty much my dad's entire political brand. Divorcing his wife after forty years of marriage doesn't quite align with that, know what I mean?" She crossed her hands at the wrists, grabbed the hem of her T-shirt, pulled it over her head, and dropped it on the floor. She wasn't wearing a bra, and Adam wasn't sure what to do with his eyes. They darted over her narrow hips, fitness-magazine abs, breasts curving over her highest ribs, tiny, nearly black nipples before he got them to settle on a point just above her eyebrows. Laila picked up the vaporizer, took a hit, and sat down beside the dress. "Roz sometimes says they stay together for *us*. Which is bullshit. I mean, Robbie and I are adults. I came within an inch of getting arrested at the Turkish border. I think I can handle my parents consciously uncoupling." She shook her head, her breasts shaking a little, too, like they agreed. "Real talk, though . . . Sometimes I think they're right. Well, not that they're *right*," she corrected herself. "But . . . They're trying to set an example. Sacrificing their personal happiness for the greater good. Does that sound corny?"

"Um," Adam said, trying without success to force his gaze up to the smear of color in her hair.

She shrugged and her breasts shrugged, too. "It's okay. I know it sounds corny. But I think about it. So does Robbie. You're willing to back burner your own needs, your own freedom, because . . . well, 'cause it's the right thing to do!" She rolled her eyes at herself. "Trust me, it's not easy being the child of State Senator Leonard Russell Jr. The granddaughter of the Reverend Leonard Russell. My dad says there are places in Alabama where they still wouldn't let black folks vote if it weren't for my granddad. I did the research, it's actually kind of true. And then I think about what I'm doing . . . I know it's important. I think it's important. But the reality is, my work consists mainly of going to conferences and smiling at fund-raisers. That's not exactly marching into a cordon of baton-wielding cops. And then with the whole mixed thing. It can all feel a little . . ." She bounced the vaporizer in her palm, seemed to consider another hit, decided against it. "Bitches made comments in college about my white mom. *Believe* me. And then Robbie with Marissa. Whom I *adore*, by the way. But do I feel an obligation sometimes to end up with a black guy? Yeah, I do. But it's like, is my body really the latest frontier in the fight for racial justice? Aren't there obligations I owe to my *self*? Whatever the fuck that is. Or is it all just a waste of time? I'm chasing my own tail of self-acceptance, and no matter what I do, I'll never be black enough, or Jewish enough, or anybody enough . . ." She looked Adam in the eyes, her expression earnest, stoned. "You get it. You're gay in a family that privileges hetero norms."

"My family's pretty cool, for the most part," he told her guiltily, because whatever complaints he might have about his parents and siblings, they were nothing if not tolerant. When they hassled him about voting, it was always for Democrats.

"But don't you ever feel like you're just gonna drown in everyone's expectations for you?"

He was relieved he could be truthful. "All the fucking time."

"Can I ask you something?"

"Sure."

"You ever been with a woman?" She laughed at herself, an easy, charming, THC-floating laugh. "Sorry to drop the rhetorical level down to an episode of *Gossip Girl*. Seriously, though. Have you?"

"Been with a chick? Uh, yeah." He cleared his throat. "Actually, kinda often."

She nodded gravely. "So you're mixed, too, right?

Gay, straight, bi . . . Mixed is the new black. Mixed is the new everything! Sexuality is a matter of degrees on a spectrum. The gay-straight dichotomy didn't even exist before the Victorians. It certainly didn't exist the eight weeks I was getting my pussy eaten out by Elissa Finkelstein. My poor subconscious! Doing whatever she could to obey my mother's implied directive to seek out a nice Jewish doctor!"

It was getting harder for Adam to follow this, what with the jargon and the breasts and the pot. But as far as the sexuality spectrum, or whatever, went—given a few ecstasy-fueled nights he'd wound up in bed with the Deployers' bassist, he could be truthful again, saying, "That's a good point."

"I mean, who's black? Is Barack black? Is Beyoncé black? Her mom is part Irish, for Christ's sake! Her weave is *blond*. And bitches talk shit about the struggle and my white mom?" She lay back on the bed, and tucked her hands loosely into the waistband of her sweatpants. "Black and white, gay and straight. They're just labels, they're just boxes, and soon we'll be free of them altogether. In one more generation, birth won't obligate us to anyone or to anything: family, race, nationality, religion. Friendship will become the only authentic form of human connection, because it's the one connection you *choose*. Did I mention I had my eggs frozen?"

"I don't think so."

"It's one less thing to worry about. Got my eggs frozen and an IUD put in. What about you? You're pretty careful, right? I swear I'm not asking because you're gay."

"You mean, careful like with condoms? Uh yeah, totally, no doubt, uh, no question . . ."

"Well, then, either you're gonna fuck me, or I'm going to need some time alone." Her hands disappeared beneath her waistband.

This wasn't the first time a woman had thrown herself at Adam. You wouldn't get rich playing music, and you wouldn't get famous—but if fucking total strangers appealed to you, it just might be the profession for you. When Kiss and Kill was at its peak, he couldn't make it from the stage to whatever passed for a green room without some woman or other groping him, propositioning him, making death-eyes behind Johanna's back and winking at him. But a woman demanding sex and starting to masturbate in her parents' house on Thanksgiving—this was something new, even for him. He understood she was probably just bored, and mad at her dad, and horny and stoned out of her gourd. But did he really care why this was happening? his cock seemed to ask by way of chafing against his jeans. Nope, he decided, he did not.

"Say more bullshit to me," he said as he unbuttoned his pants.

"Be more specific," she exhaled, her wrists flexing and unflexing above her waistband.

"Just say a bunch of words."

"Oh, ah, objectivist, epistemology . . . normative, dichotomy . . ." She seemed to be getting off on this, too, pausing to gasp for breath between terms. "Semiotic . . . appropriation . . . hegemonic . . . ontological," she gasped, "despair . . . masculinity . . . teleological collapse, osnos. . . ."

"I'm not gay," he told her as he yanked her sweatpants to her knees, saw her fingers working frantically on her clitoris, like a DJ scratching out the same two-note drop again and again and again. "I'm not a flight attendant."

"I'm not mixed," she cried. "I'm neither. I'm a fat nobody. Somebody's *daughter.* I'm a pure nihilistic bitch."

He pulled her by the ankles to the end of the bed. "I'm a stupid alcoholic loser." He pushed her hands away, and she brought them to her face, shoved half her fingers in her mouth, bit down. She lifted her head when she noticed he'd paused. "'S th'onny way ih cah cum," she explained. Then she bit down again.

It was at that moment—far too late, like always—

that it occurred to Adam that this was not a good idea: that beyond whatever passing pleasure they'd get out of the next couple minutes, fucking Laila would not do her any good, and it would not do him any good. At least when you fucked a stranger, you could imagine it to be whatever you wanted. But he knew Laila just well enough to recognize the solitude they wouldn't be fighting here, but affirming. They'd fuck and they'd never have anything to say to each other again. And what about the promise he'd made to Marissa? Wouldn't fucking her sister-in-law be on the short list of things she would explicitly instruct him *not* to do? Unfortunately, though, by now his erection was only a quarter inch away from Laila's pussy. So what choice did he have? He glanced for a moment at the shelf with the little glass sculptures—red, milky, blue. Then he looked back at Laila, diligently crushing her fingers between her teeth. "I had one friend left," he said as he began to fuck her.

"Ih nu-uh ehh uh ove oo!" I've never said I love you? I know one thing that's true? It was like trying to decipher screamed metal lyrics. Then, "Ihh, ihh, ehhhh," loudly, as she came. She lay still for a bit, and he could hear the light squeak of the bedsprings as he went on. Then she patted him on the thigh. "You should finish up. I need to shower."

[4]
Thanksgiving Dinner

The photographer had a storklike appearance: a long, pliable neck, slender legs extending from a round torso. She wore black pants and a black sweatshirt, had pale, unblinking eyes, reminiscent to Marissa of quarters, and took photographs like she had five other jobs that afternoon. Fred had been pressed into her service, was holding up the silver light-reflector disc wherever she told him. As Marissa came into the dining room, Laila was posed with her mother at the far end of the table. The dog clutched to Laila's chest only added to the peculiar formality of the scene: Laila dressed in a knee-length green dress with cap sleeves, her fixed smile broad enough to expose the slender gap between her front teeth, her neck and shoulders stiff as she held one hand on her mother's lower back, the other hand clutching Mash, crammed for the occasion into a Red Sox sweater. Roz, meanwhile, grinned thinly, her forehead coming up no higher than her daughter's shoulder. The table before them was set with such polished and scrupulous splendor—china, silver, crystal, linen—Marissa was afraid to get within five feet of it. She had never felt less a part of this family in her life.

When Laila noticed Marissa lingering in the doorway, she raised her chin to grin over the photographer's shoulder, lifting her eyebrows in an oddly conspiratorial way. "Eyes on me," the photographer ordered. The camera or the lens or something made a hissing sound after every picture: *click-flash-hiss, click-flash-hiss.* The photographer inspected the shots in the digital viewer. "Nice frames. Okay, Mom, let's move you to the other side of Daughter."

"I'm going to stay on this side," Roz answered. "But they'll want some without the dog. Marissa, honey, hold Mash for a minute?"

"I'm allergic," Marissa reminded her.

"Oh, I knew that, sweetheart!" Roz turned to Fred. "Ted, can you, and hold up the thing?"

"Yes, no problem," Fred answered, by all appearances perfectly content to have another opportunity to be of service. He extended an arm, took Mash in the bend of his elbow, and held up the reflector with his free hand while making kissing faces at the dog.

"Daughter, an inch closer to Mom. A little more life in the smiles. Mom, loosen up the right hand, you're not made of stone. Good." *Click-flash-hiss.* "Nice frame."

Adam appeared beside Marissa at the door. "Hi," he said, not looking at her. Above his stubble his cheeks were flushed, somehow his hair had gotten matted on both sides now, giving him a crude asymmetrical faux-hawk. He put one fingernail between his lips after another, like he couldn't decide which one to bite.

"You okay?" she asked him.

He dropped his hand. "Why wouldn't I be okay?" he said sharply. He glanced at her, made a grunting sound under his breath, and turned back to the scene at the head of the table. "You clean up nice."

She returned an annoyed glance, but in truth, she was grateful at least someone had noticed that she'd showered, paid down twenty minutes of sleep debt, changed into clean clothes: a red cashmere sweater, black pants, a silver pendant necklace Robbie had given her. Adam, however, smelled like a cheap motel room or something; she was about to ask him about this when Laila suggested, "Hey, what if we do some with all the girls?"

"Let's get everything on the list first," Roz answered. "Robbie, finally," she added as her son entered the dining room. He'd put on a V-neck sweater over a white button-down, scowled as he looked at his mother and sister arranged at the table.

"We're doing this for Dad, is he going to bother to show up?" he asked.

"Do I look like your father's secretary?" Roz snapped. "You have something to ask him, go down to his office and ask him."

Robbie stood by Marissa, rested his hand on her shoulder, then on her back, then dropped it to his side. "You were asleep when I got back," he said to her.

"Yeah, I passed out. What were you doing?"

"Playing *Gears of War.*"

"Daughter, turn your head a quarter inch to the right. Nope, to the right. Good." *Click-flash-hiss.*

"Why can't we do some with the ladies of the family?" Laila pressed. "It'll take ten seconds, Mom."

"Your father forwarded me the list from the press office," Roz replied. "I'm trying to get us through the list. But if you want to waste some time, sure, come on in, honey." She gestured to Marissa.

Marissa really, really hated having her picture taken. Even in her wedding photos, she displayed the same stunned, fugitive-in-the-searchlight look. She shoved a handful of hair back behind her shoulders, took position beside Laila. "Who's this?" the photographer asked.

Laila began, "This is—"

"This is my son's wife," Roz interrupted.

"Son's Wife. Okay. These are just for composition." *Click-flash-hiss, click-flash-hiss.*

"You got some rest, hallelujah," Roz declared, surveying Marissa. "You looked like the walking dead when you got here. Honestly, sweetheart, it isn't healthy."

"Cute necklace," Laila commented. "Guess who picked it out?" Her eyebrows bounced up and down again. Marissa did wonder sometimes about Laila's eagerness to prove her affection.

"Okay, Son's Wife, let's get you on the other side of Mom." Marissa moved around behind Laila and Roz, stood by Roz's shoulder. "Okay, Son's Wife, let's turn those shoulders into Mom. These are *family* photos. And see if you can do something about your hair, we're a little helter-skelter on the right." Marissa was pulling at her curls with a kind of panic when the photographer abruptly lowered the camera. "Right, so, Daughter has a nipple situation. Can we get the heat turned up maybe?"

"Are you not wearing a bra?" Roz said. "Thanksgiving dinner, and you're not wearing a bra?"

"Wow, we are *so* not having this conversation," Laila answered with a high-pitched laugh.

"No one wishes it was still 1969 more than me, but as I have been telling you since your bat mitzvah—"

"You mean the time I hadn't hit puberty and you wanted me to wear—"

"You know what?" the photographer said. "Forget it. I can Photoshop out the nipples. Let's go back to smiles. Son's Wife, stop thinking about your hair." *Click-flash-hiss.*

So far, Adam and Robbie had been standing beside each other in silence, which Marissa managed to be grateful for even amid the photography trauma, but now she saw a big, out-of-nowhere grin break out on Adam's face, like he'd just remembered what a terrific mood he was in. He went so far as to clap Robbie on the back. "It's good to meet you, man," Adam announced.

Robbie gave him a puzzled but amiable-enough nod. "Yeah, same."

"Marissa says you make movies! So, like, what are they about?" Though Robbie only turned his face as though to scratch his chin, Marissa could feel his inner groan as if it were her own. He got so uncomfortable telling people about his work—even when Laila wasn't around. "I watch a ton of movies, you'd be surprised, I bet I've heard of a lot of the people who influenced you," Adam was saying. Can you please for fucking once shut up? she mentally begged him.

"Back to Earth, Son's Wife. Eyes here." *Click-flash-hiss.* "Need to do better with these, people. Go to your happy places."

Gazing at the black eye in the center of the lens, her mouth pulled apart with a toothy grin she knew would never fool anyone as to her proximity to her happy place, Marissa heard Robbie answer, "The film I'm writing now is like a meta-, um, deconstructed indie horror." He did his best to sound nonchalant, but Marissa wondered if anyone could miss the little ripples of self-consciousness and standoffishness and resentment shaking over the surface of his voice. "Not blood and guts horror, but more psychological, sociological commentary. It's sort of a twist on, okay, think vampirism, but as an allegory for crack and gang warfare in South Central in the mid-nineties. Like subverted blaxploitation horror."

"Subverted blaxploitation horror?" Laila said from the head of the table. "Bro, we have got to work on your elevator pitch."

"I've read the script," Marissa chimed in. "It's really, really good."

"So if I catch you talking, it's a wasted frame," the photographer announced.

"It sounds pretty cool to me," Adam said to Robbie over the *click-flash-hiss*. "What're you thinking for the soundtrack? N.W.A., obviously. Ice-T. Tupac—who was actually born in New York. You ever heard of Schoolly D?"

"Yeah, so," Robbie responded, clearing his throat, "a central conceit of the film is how the black community was corrupted by these interwoven forces of addiction and fetishistic consumerism and nihilistic violence. Basically American culture itself, y'know? So I definitely plan to tell that story musically, like, how we got from 'The Message' to Suge Knight."

Laila asked, "Are you going to be able to afford the rights to any of those songs, though?"

"Have you noticed no one's even talking to you, Laila?" answered Robbie.

"I'm only trying to help!" she cried.

"Smi-i-i-i-iles," the photographer said.

Under his breath, but loud enough, Robbie murmured, "If I ever need help spreading Russian bukkake videos all over the planet, you'll be the first person I call."

"What did you say?" Laila snapped. "What did you say? That was a cruel thing to say."

"Mom, help me out here," the photographer pleaded.

"What do you want me to do?" Roz sighed. "Their

whole lives they've been at each other's throats. And who suffers? I suffer."

"The Guardian Group is agnostic with regard to how people use their freedom of expression," intoned Laila.

"And I'm sure the girls in the bukkake videos really appreciate that," answered Robbie, taking out his phone, swiping his fingers across its screen.

"You know what, Robbie? You know what? This has nothing to do with me. This is about your own insecurities, because the Group has a seven-figure budget and was named one of the most innovative nonprofits in the world by *Fast Company*, and the only people who'll put money into your movies are Roz and Leo."

Marissa stared at Laila over Roz's head, indulged fantasies of reaching over and wrapping her fingers around Laila's throat. Her allegiance to Robbie was always sharpest when she felt him under attack. But she wished Robbie could come up with a better retort than momentarily lifting his hand from the phone to give Laila the finger. The photographer by now had the camera at her shoulder, was firing shots up toward the ceiling. "Big waste of time here, people."

"Personally, I see both sides," Adam offered brightly. "I never made a dime when I was playing music. On the other hand, I love bukkake videos! Ha ha ha!" Roz and Laila adopted nearly identical looks of dismay, like they'd managed to forget Adam was there, and weren't so happy to be reminded.

Roz said, "Somebody want to explain to me what a bukkake video is? Or maybe I don't want to know."

"Mrs. Russell?" Fred said to her.

"Ms. Lichtenstein," she corrected him.

"I should put the food back in the ovens, if you aren't going to eat . . ."

"No, no, no, that's a good idea," Roz said, shaking her head wearily. "Let's bring out the food and do the candids. Give us all a break. Go ahead and bring the food up, please, Ted."

Fred balanced the light reflector against the wall, set the dog on its feet on the floor. Laila intercepted Mash as he raced menacingly toward Marissa, teeth bared. Dog in hand, Laila pulled out a chair, sat down, held Mash before her face. "What's that, honey? Yes, I do think Robbie has deep-seated inadequacy issues because his younger sister is three inches taller than him."

"Gotcha, I have issues, but you started therapy when you were nine," said Robbie.

"I suffer from *depression*, asshole. It is a *disease*."

"I'll never understand why you two treat each other the way you do," Roz commented. "I bet at my funeral, you'll make peace, is that the idea?"

"What are we even doing right now?" Laila complained. "It's not like we can shoot the candids without Daddy." She pulled out her phone. "Fuck it, I'm texting him."

Marissa walked the length of the table to Adam. "Bukkake videos?" she whispered hotly.

Adam raised his palms to her. "I was trying to break the tension!"

"Don't. Don't break the tension. Don't do anything. Just stand there. Okay?"

"Ooookay," he mouthed, rolling his eyes toward the ceiling, like he were indulging her craziness. Then he added under his breath, "I'm just trying to fit in around here." Something twitched in or pulled at his face, like a hidden regret, a suppressed smile. Abruptly, she realized what he smelled like. She swung her head to Laila, now tossing the dog in the air and catching him before her face; Marissa swung her head back to Adam, the regret having spread into a sort of guilty terror.

"Are you fucking kidding me?" she whispered, her lips barely moving.

"Her idea," he mouthed.

She could hear the breath coming in and out of her nose, like she'd transformed into a snorting bull; the fearful way he leaned back made her aware of her hands, balled into fists at her sides. A cascade of foul-mouthed loathing, encompassing every one of his fuckups and outrages over the entire day, was right there on the tip of her tongue—and she wanted as badly to let it loose as she'd previously wanted to go to sleep. She wasn't sure she could control it another instant when Leo walked in, his tread shaking the flatware on the table lightly. His eyes settled first on Adam and Marissa, standing an inch apart by the door, as though he'd caught them at something (which he had, though Marissa doubted he could guess at what). Next, he turned his flat, impassive gaze to Laila and Mash at the table; to Robbie, staring down into his phone; to Roz, looking over the pictures on the camera with the photographer. His disappointment with what he saw appeared total, but he dropped it all on his son, as he often did. "Something in there more important than what's going on out here?" he said to Robbie.

"You're the one who's been in his office all day," Robbie answered, putting his phone in his pocket.

"There's a difference there I shouldn't need to explain to you," Leo responded dully. "What's next?" he asked the photographer.

"Let's get set for the candids," Roz ordered the photographer.

"Okay, then," Leo said to the photographer.

Fred was just then carrying in the first two platters of food on oven-mitted palms: wilted Brussels sprouts, sweet potatoes topped with a layer of deflated marsh-mallows. As he set the food down, Roz assigned every-one their places: Leo at the head of the table, then Laila at his right, Marissa across from Laila, and Robbie to Marissa's left. Seating herself at the head of the table opposite Leo, she asked Adam to wait until the candids were finished before sitting down. "We don't want to confuse people," she explained to him.

"Yeah, sure, I get it," Adam said with a complicated blend of gratitude and indignation. He leaned back against the wall, hands stuffed in the pockets of his jeans, like a human asterisk to the whole affair.

"Are we doing the carve-the-turkey shots?" the pho-tographer asked as Fred set down two silver trays of cranberry stuffing.

"No one's carved a turkey in this family since Grandpa died," Laila said. "The only one here who knows how to cook at all is Marissa."

Marissa didn't, in fact, and wondered why Laila believed she did. She was about to correct the record when Adam, breaking out another abrupt, oversized smile, chimed in: "If microwaving burritos counts, I'm Julia Child."

But the family appeared to have reached a collective decision to ignore him. Roz ordered Fred to take the dog down to the kitchen, and now, all in its place, she suggested, "How about some grace shots? My husband can say grace."

Leo pondered his wife, his eyes behind his glasses calmly surprised, calmly resentful. Then he pushed the glasses up his nose an inch and said, "Certainly." He reached out and took his daughter's hand, Marissa's hand; they all joined hands. *Click-flash-hiss, click-flash-hiss.* To Marissa's relief, Robbie gave her fingers an affectionate squeeze; it was easy to lose track of their current terms of engagement.

Leo, his hand big, heavy, inert, around Marissa's palm, lowered his head. She watched Laila lower her eyes with piety so childlike Marissa suspected it was ironic. She looked down at her own plate, ringed with a painted chain of interlocking petals. "Bless us O Lord for these Thy gifts," began in her head, like a reflex.

"Friends, family . . . welcome strangers." Leo paused. "My father used to say that every family is its own Eden. I always took those words for comfort, but as I get older, I wonder if he didn't intend something more than comfort. A gentle warning. Because Eden didn't last. Maybe a family is just as fragile." He paused again. "Well, today is a day in honor of a feast when bread was broken by red man and white man, immigrant and native, exile and host. We know that's all a myth, and like every American myth, the truth is considerably bloodier. But we cling to the myth, for no better reason than because we need it. We failed in the past. We fail in the present. But maybe someday, we'll find ourselves worthy of Eden. And all we lack will be restored. Amen." He dropped Marissa's hand.

"Jesus, Daddy," Laila said, raising her eyes.

"Were you not supposed to be taking pictures?" Roz demanded, turning to the photographer. And then, seeing she was crying, said, "Oh, for the love of . . ."

"That was really fucking beautiful, dude," said Adam from the wall. It looked like he might cry, too.

"Sorry, sorry, sorry," the photographer was saying, wiping her eyes. "My mom was a quarter Wampanoag. This is a complicated day for us. Can we set up again—would you all, just, like you were before . . ."

"No, that was seriously beautiful," Adam repeated.

"They heard you," Marissa told him.

"Okay, everyone, heads down, let's go," Roz ordered.

Laila said, "Oh, *Jeez*-us, Roz . . . "

"Is it my fault she can't do her job?" Roz answered. "Is it my fault? Come on, let's go, heads down . . ." *Click-flash-hiss, click-flash-hiss,* as they all looked down at their plates, though this time Leo didn't take Marissa's hand.

"So are we eating or what?" Robbie asked after they'd been posed in this manner for a full minute.

"Okay, the rule for eating is that you don't do any eating," the photographer answered, all business again. "Pass some dishes back and forth, though. Smiles wouldn't kill you." *Click-flash-hiss,* as they half-heartedly pantomimed a Thanksgiving meal.

At length, Laila let out a plastic chuckle. "I'm sorry, why are our holidays like bad Ibsen?" She looked at Adam. "Tell the truth. This is the worst Thanksgiving you've ever been to, isn't it?"

"Nah, I've had worse than this," Adam answered.

"Oh yeah?" Robbie said, curious. "What happened?"

"I don't remember," Adam replied casually, folding his arms across his chest. He laughed. "I don't remember. The thing is, I—"

"This food looks great," Marissa interrupted. "Is the caterer from around here, Roz?"

"Oh, he's a big boy, dear," answered Roz. "He wants to tell his story, let him tell his story."

"Thanks, Roz, I really appreciate that," Adam said, lifting a shoeless foot to the wall behind him—settling in for story time, Marissa concluded with dread. "It was a year my family was doing Thanksgiving at my brother's house in Framingham. My parents were there, both my siblings, all their kids. The whole gang." His tone was forthright, matter-of-fact—confessional, as earlier, in the car. "And—you all have heard of mulled wine, right? It's like red wine, you put oranges and cloves and shit in it, and you heat it on the stove. Y'know, New England in winter, big pot of hot wine. It's festive."

"I've had it a time or two," Leo said mildly. "Festive. Like you said."

"Well, anyway, you'd think—how drunk could you get off mulled wine? I guess I tried to find out!" He laughed again, one of his laughs without a floor of happiness, just an empty, throat-shaking sound. "I mean, I probably showed up drunk to begin with. Like I said, I don't remember. But it's a good bet I had a few on the drive over. I used to keep an eighth of peppermint schnapps in my glove compartment, because cops think it's mouthwash or whatever if they smell it on your breath. Anywho. I was at my brother's, drinking the mulled wine, and I guess to cut me off they hid all the mugs. So after I tore around all the cabinets for a while, I just, uh, dunked my head in the pot. I probably thought it was a joke, y'know, for the kids. But the thing was, the burner was still on. So everybody panicked, they thought I burned my face off, they started dunking my head in ice water. I've still got this one little scar, down here . . ." He tapped the stubble on his face beside his left ear. "Anyway, spending Thanksgiving afternoon in the burn unit, that sort of tops all the constant bickering you guys got going on, y'know what I mean?" As he'd talked, his voice had gotten progressively heavier, like he was drifting, word by word, into the shame he'd been too drunk to remember incurring. He ended with a painful grin—a last, broken-winged attempt to conjure some humor.

Marissa's worst Thanksgiving had been spent sitting across from Caitlyn in a McDonald's: a little girl babysitting her younger sister while their mother "took care of some business." They sat there for five hours before the guy pushing the mop by for the hundredth time gave up and called the cops. When Mona finally showed up at the police station, she said their aunt was supposed to be watching them. They didn't have an aunt, Marissa wanted to scream—but her mother had taught them never, ever to talk to cops.

Adam was looking at her. He smiled weakly, apologetically. But her anger at him had evaporated. Some other feeling had replaced it, too dense, too intricate for her to parse. She wondered if her mother remembered leaving her and Caitlyn like that; she wondered if her mother felt the same shame over it that had sunk into Adam's features. She hoped so.

In any event, Adam's story had struck the Russells

dumb. They stared ahead mutely, hopelessly, Laila baring her teeth behind a square of lips, thinking God knows what—though if Marissa had to guess, it was probably something along the lines of, I can't believe I fucked this guy.

"Did I mention I'm sober now?" Adam finally announced. "Nine months and four days!"

"We'll leave the wine downstairs," Roz said. "We don't need to make anybody's life harder."

"Don't worry about it, I'm around it a lot." Adam looked at Marissa. "On the airplanes!" he added abruptly.

"Here's a radical notion," said Robbie. "How about we start eating?"

And in this way, the awkward silence was broken. Adam took a seat between Roz and Laila, angling his chair to face away from the latter. The photographer went downstairs to the kitchen to eat with Fred. And everyone at the table piled their plates with food.

As they began to eat, Laila described a talk she was giving at a UN summit on free speech in Switzerland the following month. "They have me on a panel with this queer Turkish blogger and Ed Snowden's lawyer in Europe," she explained, pushing a dollop of creamed spinach on her plate away from the mashed potatoes.

"It conflicts with this other panel in Stockholm I'm supposed to do, but there's nobody else at the Group I trust to do that one, either. I'm spread so insanely thin, I feel like I spend my whole life in airports."

"You should be grateful you found an endeavor worthy of your best effort," Leo told her.

"What matters is that you're getting people's attention," said Roz. "That they're *listening*." Robbie sawed viciously into a slice of turkey. Marissa reached under the table to put her hand on his knee, but he moved it away.

This was the family back on its bearings, though, after the jolt Adam had given them. Listening to Laila talk was something all the Russells knew how to do: the reactions and resentments all clicked into place, like it was a song, and they each had their parts.

And as Marissa finished off her first scoop of stuffing, she realized she'd been starving. Maybe it was remembering that Thanksgiving in McDonald's: God, she'd been hungry that day; it was as if she could still smell the greasy odors of the place, jeering at her empty stomach. As Laila continued on about German surveillance laws, Marissa ate indulgently: turkey smeared with gravy and cranberry sauce, sweet potatoes swirled up with their marshmallow topping, glazed Brussels sprouts bursting between her teeth. She didn't care that the food was lukewarm, had an overcooked dullness: There was more on the table than she could eat.

Buttering her third dinner roll, she checked her watch: a little before one thirty, still another five hours before she needed to be back at the hotel in Connecticut. For the first time that day, she had plenty of time. Laila was wrong, this wasn't a terrible Thanksgiving, she concluded. In most of the ways that mattered, it was the opposite. Whatever else they were, they were a family. The tensions, the gripes and grudges coursing beneath every word didn't only pull the Russells apart; they bound them together. If there was unhappiness here, it had the virtue of intimacy, familiarity.

Adam had begun tapping his crystal wineglass with his fingernail, watching the twisting path of the bubbles in the seltzer Fred had poured him as they floated up to the surface. He flicked the glass too hard, nearly toppled it over, caught it over his plate just in time. What would become of him? Marissa wondered. Would he ever find the place where he belonged? What quality did she possess that allowed her to keep at least a toehold among the Russells, while he couldn't even make it to the table with his family?

A shrill ringing startled her enough that she dropped her fork on her plate. Leo took his phone from the pocket of his cardigan. "Weren't you just giving Rob- bie shit about this, Daddy?" Laila said.

Leo didn't answer. He rose from the table with a token "Excuse me," and walked from the room, the dishes shaking a little as he departed. The adrenal fear of the startle lingered with Marissa, and she would think later there was some sense of foreboding in this. Her mother had always told her that the Cavanos had "the sight"—a dubious gift, as old as the rocks of Sicily, not to forestall disaster, but rather to feel in its wake like you saw it coming the whole time.

"These screens are so toxic, though," Laila was say- ing. "It's a real threat to public life when we can't pay attention to one another for five minutes."

"You are fucking obsessed with Instagram likes," Robbie pointed out.

She shrugged. "I'm not saying I'm immune. Any- way, most of what I do on Instagram is about building awareness for the Group."

"You post your breakfast every morning."

"You're the one who checks it."

"You know what I think's depressing?" Adam joined in. "How you go to a show and people don't even watch the band. They just hold up their phones. I mean, you don't have to watch this on video. It's *happening* to you."

"Even ISIS is addicted to social media," Laila resumed before Adam could elaborate further. "Think about that. Motherfuckers want to live in the sixth century, but the one thing they want to bring with them is Twitter." She pushed a scrap of turkey into a mound of mashed potato. "None of it matters, though. Thirty, forty years tops, the ice caps will be melted, and this whole shitshow will be underwater."

Roz was watching Laila with a sharp little smile. "You won't get off that easy, princess."

"May I speak with you in my office, Marissa?" Leo was standing in the doorway.

Marissa looked at him: His face was as expressionless as a sheer cliff; she felt her cheeks burning. "*Entschuldigen?*" she heard Laila saying. "Speak with her in your office?"

"What do you want to talk to her about?" Robbie asked.

"If you don't mind, Marissa," Leo answered.

She looked at Robbie, and he shrugged. She knew that if her husband was ever going to stand up to his father, it would've happened a long time ago. She got to her feet, conscious of the risk of knocking her chair backward.

"What are you guys going to talk about?" asked

Adam, suspiciously, eyes moving back and forth from Leo to Marissa.

Leo only turned and walked from the door. Robbie gave Marissa a bemused half frown. She didn't know what else to do besides follow after Leo. "Why all the drama?" she heard Laila say as she went out.

"If you think he tells me anything, you're out of your mind," Roz replied.

Marissa followed Leo's back—broad, slightly stooped, draped in the maroon cardigan—down the stairway to the end of the hall, into his office. He closed the door behind her as she walked in. It struck her how open and airy the rest of the house was compared to this close-walled room: dark-paneled, a perfect square, the only windows a triptych of rectangles at the top of one wall, letting in three patches of light that fell with a kind of uselessness on the red ikat rug. Leo's desk, stained a color like merlot, stood low and imposing before ceiling-high bookshelves, stacked and stuffed with books: leather-bound tomes, scar-spined paperbacks, fat dictionaries, rows of numbered volumes. You could call the room cozy, or you could call it claustrophobic, but in the grip of her deepening dread, it struck Marissa as something vital, and sinister, like she'd joined Leo inside the organ of some animal. The photographs on the walls were a little reassuring, at least, in that they featured people: portraits of Robbie and Laila as teenagers; black-and-white images of Muhammad Ali, Malcolm X, a few other black men she didn't recognize. The largest photo was of the bearded man she knew to be Robbie's grandfather, marching at the head of a crowd beside Martin Luther King Jr.

"Have a seat, please, Marissa," Leo said, motioning to the leather upholstered chair opposite the desk. She sat, crossed her legs, arranged her hands on her knee, felt stupid, and put her hands on the arms of the chair. She was reminded again of the time Robbie had first invited her to dinner with Roz and Leo at the ramen restaurant. She'd been so nervous that afternoon she went to a Barnes & Noble, stood in the aisle and read three chapters of an etiquette book. But there was no silverware on the table at the restaurant to choose from, and Robbie had laughed at her when she mentioned writing a thank-you note.

Leo regarded her with his usual impassiveness, his eyes, the precise shade of brown of Robbie's, at once still and stinging, like an ice cube melting on the back of your hand. The desk was bare except for an ink blotter, a lamp with a triangular paper shade, a stack of books in one corner (*A People's History of the United States, The Wretched of the Earth, Oil!*). It occurred to her this was the first time she'd ever been alone with her father-in-law.

Leo announced, "I've decided to run for governor."

Marissa pressed her lips together uncertainly: This was why he wanted to talk with her? "Robbie didn't tell me that."

"No, I haven't told the children."

"Well, that's . . . That's great news."

"I'm too long in the tooth, no voter outside of Boston has ever heard of me, and I've been in office so long I've made enemies of half the statehouse. Still. There's a school of thought I'll win."

It was almost as if he were asking her opinion—though this had to be impossible. "Um, congratulations," was all she could think to say.

He pulled at the white tuft in his beard, as though irritated she wasn't taking his point, or maybe with his own difficulty making it. Evidently taking a different tack, he told her, "I've always tried to make you feel welcome in this family."

"Thank you," she said, though if this was true, she hadn't noticed.

"I can appreciate that it's no simple thing," he went on, "becoming part of a family. Does Robbie ever talk about his grandparents on his mother's side?" Marissa shook her head. "I wasn't welcome in their home while her father was living. It's not that I was black, mind you, though I doubt that helped. It's that I wasn't Jewish. And these people were communists, mind you. But somewhere the communism ended, and the Jewish stayed put. They were probably as surprised as Roz."

Marissa felt more lost in the conversation than ever. "No, yeah, he never told me that."

"Robbie may not know. We told him, but he may not have listened. Both Roz's parents were dead by the time the children were born. All in all, it was pain that benefited no one. Everyone wants to do better than their parents," he continued. "It's the solemn promise you make yourself when you see your child for the first time. I expect you know what I mean?"

Panic spread from her stomach to her fingertips— but no, she told herself, he didn't know. He was talking about Mona. "Yeah," she said. "I do know what you mean."

"My father," Leo continued, "was a great man, but a very hard father. A very fearful father, you might say. His father was an Alabama sharecropper, and from what I've been given to understand, my father was very gentle, compared with him. Did your mother ever put her hands on you?"

She had an inexplicable instinct to defend her mother. "She would never do something like that." And now she was angry, hearing herself sticking up for Mona, the greasy fast food odor as if still fresh in her nostrils. "But yeah, there were a lot of things she did to me and my sister I'd never do to my kid."

Momentarily, his expression softened, something nearly sorrowful appearing briefly in his eyes. "I admire you, Marissa. You never let your origins hinder your rise. And that's what America is supposed to be, isn't it? We're judged by the content of our character." Abruptly, he grinned, a long, crooked, unsettling smile. "I've been wondering a great deal lately about the content of your character." He placed his palms flat on the ink blotter. "Okay then," he said, and he wasn't smiling anymore. With his right hand, he slid open a drawer, took out a manila envelope, and placed it in front of her. "No one else has seen this."

The envelope was unmarked, bulging, sealed with a little gold clasp: bland, ominous, immutable. After staring at it for a moment, she realized she had stopped breathing. She looked back at the photographs hanging on the wall. One featured a man wearing a sort of conical fedora, a cigarette dangling from his lips, the keys of a piano reflected in the lenses of his sunglasses. "Who is that?" she asked.

Leo turned his head slightly, looked back at her, took his time answering, as though he suspected this might be some sort of trick. "Thelonious Monk," he said at last. "A great American jazz pianist."

When he said the name, she remembered where she'd seen the face: It was tattooed on Adam's arm. And it seemed to her again such an awful fucking waste—Leo loved music; Adam loved music. So why shouldn't they be upstairs in the conservatory, listening to records, arguing about musicians and bands no one else in the house had heard of, maybe eventually playing together—becoming, against all odds, and despite every expectation, something like friends? No point wishing for a better world now, she reminded herself.

"Let's get this over with," she said.

"You need to open that, Marissa."

But she didn't. She knew perfectly well what it contained, and would not stoop to the indignity of opening it and reading through its contents while he sat behind his desk and watched. Her fury made it very easy for her to compose her face, but she worried if she undid that clasp, pulled out the first damning piece of evidence, the airplane-falling, stomach-plunging sensation she was enduring might get the better of her. It was all very simple: She had been caught.

"It's necessary to be practical," Leo said. He added, "We had to be sure." Then: "A man wants to be governor." She looked at him, astonished, because it sounded like an apology, and an apology would be a greater cruelty than even he ought to be capable of. "It is not a matter of trust. I hope you understand that. It is a matter of being thorough, as thorough as our opposition will be. Every unknown requires looking into, and by us first. We hoped there wouldn't be anything to find . . ." And it was like the envelope burst open to fill the silence that followed, and she imagined everything she assumed was inside swirling around her in the air: photographs of her and Brendan, sworn testimony from their waitress, a swatch of the sheet on which they'd fucked . . . He was still talking; she realized she'd stopped listening. ". . . admiration for you. But I can't allow my family to be embarrassed." For the first time he sounded angry. "This adulterous behavior cannot continue, Marissa."

She managed to get offended. "I made one mistake, I'm not a . . ." But then she realized what he'd assumed. "No, Adam isn't—"

"I don't care what he is," Leo interrupted. "But that man is no flight attendant."

There was no point explaining—the truth wouldn't help her. Adam was a stranger she'd met in a hotel lobby who she'd brought to their Thanksgiving dinner under false pretenses. And yes, she did it for good reasons, but those reasons wouldn't help her, either. And now Marissa laughed, laughed like she'd never heard herself laugh before, the way Adam sometimes did: a miserable, air-wringing sound. Saint Marissa—when what she'd needed to do was leave his ass at the gas station; when what she'd needed to do was be more like her mother.

"I don't expect you to have a perfect marriage," Leo went on. "Robbie is a particularly . . ." He seemed uncomfortable finishing this thought. "I don't expect you to have a perfect marriage. But my position aside, what father would abide what you've done? You cheated on my son. You brought this other man into my home. It is what it is, Marissa. I have my obligations to Robbie to consider. Therefore . . ." Like his son, he didn't wield the sharp end of his threats; but unlike Robbie, he made his meaning unmistakable.

"Therefore, if I don't tell him, you will," Marissa finished for him.

"It is what it is." He folded his hands over the ink blotter. "We hoped there wouldn't be anything to find."

"Who is 'we,' anyway?" she asked, her indignation gaining traction again. "Who did you have watching me?"

"Frankly, I don't know. I never met anyone face-to-face. These are people, professionals. From experience,

I'd assume it was a middle-aged white man. The type that's invisible in public spaces."

He'd paid strangers to follow her, men he'd never bothered to meet in person. She lifted her hands to her head, closed her fists around her hair, pulled until she knew she wouldn't start screaming at him the next time she opened her mouth. He was right, she had to be practical. "Please," Marissa said. "Please don't do this to us."

"I don't feel I have a choice. You were the one who had a choice."

Tears sprang to her eyes; she closed them until she had herself under control again. "This will kill our marriage."

He joined his fingers on the ink blotter, to signal that he and Marissa were finally getting down to business. "I don't see that that has to be the case. I don't see that that has to be the case at all. The survival of a marriage is a matter of evolution. A marriage can take many forms. I'm prepared to pay for a couples counselor I know in New York. I think you'll find you both can live with more than you'd think."

Something in the comment repulsed her. All of it repulsed her: the room, the envelope, the men watching her, and most of all him—ripping her and Robbie's relationship up by the roots and holding it before her eyes, without even altering his inflection much. He really would be governor.

"As I said, I admire you, Marissa. I take no joy in this." She glared at him, wondering whether this was true. He pulled at the tuft in his beard contemplatively. "My father often said there were men in the movement who spent their whole lives climbing the mountain, and when they reached the top, they became the mountain themselves. But so be it. I intend to be a good governor. I intend to help people in this state. The people who are growing up in the same circumstances you did. I hope you'll take that into account." Whether this was bullshit, whether it was sincere, she had nothing else to say to him. He'd found a way to live with himself. She would have to do that, too.

She picked up the envelope, pulled open the door and walked out, slamming the door behind her. She'd like to think the photographs fell from the walls and shattered, but she knew that was more justice than she could expect.

The hallway was dazzlingly bright. The light hit her with a wave of vertigo and she had to hold herself up with a hand on the wall. Eyes on the buffed floorboards, she made her way to the bedroom—the minaret room. (Who the fuck were these people?)

She'd already repacked her rollaboard, her purse stood neatly on top. (Then again, who the fuck was she?) She needed to lie down, but equally she needed to flee, but before she could do either she heard Robbie's voice. "Izzy? Where are you?" He was speaking to her over the house's intercom. No, she had to flee: It was a necessity, as bone-deep-urgent as any need she'd ever known. She grabbed her purse, shoved the envelope inside, pulled her bag down the hall. The sound of its wheels rolling over the wood floor was so loud she assumed the whole house would come running. So she went faster. She knew she needed to talk to Robbie; but even fighting for her marriage seemed shameful now. The worst of her had turned out to be true: She was nothing but a skank Boston gold digger who'd fucked up the one good thing in her life because she couldn't keep her pants on. She could hear her mother saying it, the staccato and dropped R's and viciousness.

She yanked her coat from the hanger in the closet, stuffed her feet back in her heels, and hurried outside. Either there was ice on the first stone step or she forgot about the steps altogether—her feet came from underneath her, she reached out desperately but her hands found nothing but air. The next thing she felt was her lower back smacking stone as she tumbled down the steps until she skid face-first into the ice-slick snow of the lawn. Her purse had spilled open around her. Before the pain set in, she clawed after the quarters and lipstick and tampons, as if getting them back in her purse might fend it off.

By the time she'd shoved everything back inside, her ribs and back and left hand were screaming, the pain as if sharpened by the freezing air. But then—"Oh no, oh no, oh, please God, no—" She leapt up, her back clenching so fiercely she gasped. But there were no sharp, shooting pains in her abdomen—was that what it felt like? Frantically, she unbuttoned her pants, stuck her hand down the front of her underwear, pulled it out, and stared at her fingertips: no blood. She closed her eyes, forced herself to count to one hundred. She heard the retreating sound of car wheels on a gravel road. A breeze across the lawn played savagely at her stomach where her coat and sweater had gotten pulled up. She tugged them down. She checked again. Still nothing. Maybe she was okay.

"Izzy?" she heard Robbie say from the top step. "Are you bleeding?"

She couldn't look at him, so she sat down gingerly on one of the steps. The lawn descended away from the house, overlooked an arc of spruce trees, boughs weighted with snow. A mottled gray sky rose behind them. "What the fuck? Are you all right?" He'd walked down the steps to stand beside her.

"I cheated, Robbie. I'm pregnant."

The wind blew through the trees, shaking off clouds and clumps of snow. His voice very calm, he said, "This isn't happening. This . . . this isn't happening." She lifted her hands to her face and began to sob into them.

"You're a fucking bitch, you know that? You're a fucking, fucking bitch." He didn't sound very convincing. But it didn't matter; she believed it. Her hands were soaked with tears and snot, but it was like the sobbing would never stop, like it poured out of her from some inexhaustible well at the bottom of her, at the bottom of everything she'd done. "Who was it?" he asked, his voice squeaky and breaking, like he was going through puberty. "You don't get to cry!"

She pulled in lungfuls of air over gasping breaths, and wiped her face again and again on the sleeve of her coat. Finally, she got the sobbing to stop, though she could feel tears still leaking down her cheeks. "He was nobody. An ex I saw again. Nobody. It doesn't matter."

"Who?" he demanded.

"Brendan. From high school. We ran into each other . . ."

"And you're fucking pregnant? You are such—you

are such a stupid little bitch." The anger was sincere now, raw, like she'd never heard in his voice before. She curled over, waiting for him to grab her by the hair, drag her down the steps, around the corner of the house to the driveway—pummel her; run her over with the car. But Robbie would never, because Robbie was a good person. And she was so much worse than stupid.

"I'm sorry—" And she started sobbing into her hands again.

"Stop crying!" he screamed, his frantic, furious voice echoing across the lawn.

By the time she finished this time, she felt as empty as if she'd been scraped out with an ice-cream scoop. The damp on her face clung like it was frozen across her cheeks and chin and nose; her teeth started chattering. He sat down next to her. "Why?" he asked. She looked at him for the first time. It was as if each part of his face had been pulled off and then shoved back in place, he looked so shattered and astonished.

All she could do was try to explain. "I was lonely. I was angry at you. I don't know, I don't know. But Robbie—" She grabbed his shoulders, grabbed fistfuls of his sweater. "I will do anything. Anything, anything, anything." The full force of her will condensed to this single vow: If he told her to walk on water, if he told her to punch her way through a brick wall, she would find a way.

But as she stared at him, she could see him retreating, she could see him drawing away from her as plainly as if he'd stood up and walked across the lawn. "But see, what I'm thinking right now is that I hate you." He nodded to himself. "Yeah, I think that's how I feel about you, Marissa."

"I will do—"

"Shut up," he said, brusque, disinterested. He sighed, a small puff in the air. "The fact is I've been lying to you, too. I haven't had a freelance job in two years. My mom's been writing me checks. And the thing is, there's nothing wrong with that. Only you make me feel like such a . . . And now this, it's . . . it's like fuck you, y'know?" He said it almost casually. Then he brought his lips to her ear, and whispered, intimately, "Fuck you." He stood up and brushed off his sweater, though there was nothing to brush off. "You can go now. You can get the fuck out of here." And he walked up the steps, went inside, and closed the door.

She was shaking with cold by now; her face and fingertips had gone numb—all she could feel, really, was the pain from her fall, and the regret was so vast she didn't know where to begin to feel that, either. She groaned, and the sound of the groan surprised her—like it was a noise she never heard herself make.

She pictured in her mind the inside of the car: locked doors, heat pouring from the vents. This image propelled her to her feet. She lifted her purse to her shoulder, picked up her suitcase where it had landed on the lawn, and started gingerly down the steps, ignoring as best she could the various splintering sensations. And as she came around to the driveway, there was Adam, sitting on the hood of the car, smoking a cigarette.

She must have looked worse than she'd even imagined, because the cigarette tumbled from his lips. "Oh, shit, what did they—" She held up a finger, cutting him off as she dragged the suitcase to the car. She pulled the car key from out of her pocket, but her hands were shaking so badly she couldn't get it in the door to unlock it. "Hey," he said, his voice gentle, respectful. "Why don't you just chill for a minute?" It was the way you talked to a drunk.

She handed him the key and he unlocked the door, leaned in, and pressing down the brake with his hand, turned on the engine. She watched him crank the heat all the way up, and then moved aside so that she could sit down. She got her ass in the seat, but her back suggested lifting her legs in was going to be a problem, so she remained with her feet on the driveway, half in, half out, her fingers pressed against the vent by the steering wheel.

When the feeling returned to them, she said, "Can I have a cigarette?"

He put two in his mouth, lit both, and handed her one. She inhaled through chattering teeth, and held the warm, tobacco-rich smoke in her lungs for a long second before exhaling. "Can I ask you one question?" he said. She nodded. "He hit you?" She shook her head. "Because I heard some shouting, and if anybody hit you, I mean, fuck, I'm a peaceful person, but—"

"Stop it, Adam." She'd had her fill of unconvincing machismo.

"Okay," he agreed.

She smoked the cigarette, her first since she was twenty and Robbie made her quit, down to the filter, then asked for another one. As Adam handed it to her, he said, "You've got a cut above your eye there." She reached up. "Right eye." She touched a space above her eyebrow and winced. "It's not like you'll need stitches or anything." He added, "I'm really sorry about Laila, I . . ." She glared at him and he shut up again.

She took another long drag on the cigarette. Then she slid her purse off her shoulder, and tugged out the envelope. It took her a minute to get her fingernail under the arms of the envelope's clasp, then finally she pulled out a sheaf of papers. The first was a copy of a handwritten letter of complaint some passenger had written about her. ("She was EXTREMELY rude to me and did NOT say she's sorry!!") Next was a copy of her credit report—admittedly, enough to make any father-in-law wary. Then she got to what must have been their crown jewel, a page with an eight-by-ten photograph stapled to it: her, at a table at the Chili's in the Norfolk airport, seated across from Brendan, in his fatigues. He was holding her hand over the table. She looked happy.

"I'm fucked, Adam," she said.

"I'm really sorry," he answered.

The photograph made her want to start sobbing again, so she opened the stack to the middle, and came upon a streaked printout of a mug shot: a defiant, black-eyed woman, sneering at the camera—tough, pretty, her hair fighting its way free from a ponytail.

"Who's that?" Adam asked.

"That's my mother." Marissa could make out the date on the placard Mona held at her chest, 6–8–82, four years before Marissa was born. On the back of the page were scrawled a few notes:

colorful character
bookmaker? Italians? Bulger?

DUIs, fencing

No convics

"She looks like you," Adam told her.

Marissa agreed. Years younger and a hundred pounds lighter than she'd ever seen Mona, the resemblance was unmistakable: the almond-shaped eyes, the thick dimple in her chin, the outward curved nose.

Adam said, "So I need to tell you something." She looked up at him, and he was holding a pale blue glass ball in his palm.

"What the fuck is that?"

"Art. Expensive art. Your in-laws' art." He went on, "I don't know, they're not even bad people, I just felt like . . ." He shrugged. "I don't know."

"What the fuck is wrong with you, Adam?" she asked, exhausted. "What the fuck is wrong with you?"

He shrugged more definitively, wedged his cigarette in the corner of his mouth, and walked with the ball to Laila's Range Rover. He balanced it carefully on the door handle. "She'll find it there," he announced as he walked back to Marissa. The coat seemed to have gained a size over the course of the day, his eyes to have sunk still deeper into his skull. He looked like a refugee who'd wandered out of the woods: a vagrant, a stray.

He produced a crumpled tissue from somewhere, offered it to her. She didn't know whether it was meant for the cut, for her nose . . .

"Are you still in love with Johanna?" she asked him.

As she might've guessed, this set off a spasm of unhappy fidgeting, from his fingers to his feet. "Yeah, I'd say so," he finally answered.

"And you think she'd be happy to see you again?"

And all at once he was perfectly still. "Yeah," he said somberly. "Yeah, I think she would be."

"Let's go, then."

"Where?"

"The bus station. You're going back to her."

He swallowed. "What about you?"

"I'm going to spend Thanksgiving with my mom."

III

Once More, with Feeling

[1]

The Johanna Impromptu on the Way to the Brattleboro Bus Station

When Adam dreamed of Johanna, there was never any music. He didn't dream of listening to her play, or of playing with her, or of writing songs with her, the tugs and tussles and wrong turns and eurekas of composition. And he didn't dream of speaking with her again, or sleeping with her again, as he sometimes did with other exes, nor did he any longer have the dream he had right after it ended: running into her again in the most mundane places, a pharmacy, a food court, and ta-da, there she was.

No, Adam's recurring dream about Johanna was always set in the moments before they played. They'd just walked onstage, in the days when the Kiss and Kill crowds were swelling like destiny—dozens, then a hundred, then more. All around him was the swirl of swooping spotlights, the cheers and screaming, a mass of expectant strangers, eyes and noses and open mouths drifting from the edge of the stage, and the eighty-eight keys under his ten fingers, tasked with making sense of it all. In the dream, he didn't know what city they were in, he couldn't remember what they were supposed to play, if it was a set opener or an encore, he couldn't remember how a keyboard worked at all, as had sometimes been the case when he was a little boy, in a jacket and throat-strangling tie, and he was expected to come out with Brahms' Rhapsody in B Minor from memory. And then he'd look up, and on the other side of the stage would be Johanna, guitar in her hands, her blue eyes luminous, still, waiting for him. She'd mouth the name of the song—"Any Given Sunday," "Still Life," "Naomi"—her chin would nod in time, and he'd know with perfect calm what to do. And then he'd wake up.

In the passenger seat of the Sonata, Adam pressed his handprint into the plush, sand-colored fabric of the seat near his thigh. Marissa hadn't known how to get to the bus station, so she'd searched on her phone, then propped it against the stick so she could watch the scrolling digital map as she drove. They'd turned off the Russells' winding lane onto a sharp, unbending street, wooded hills on either side. They were eleven minutes away, according to the phone's display. "We'll be there soon!" Adam announced, his voice loud and a few steps flat of enthusiasm. Marissa nodded stiffly, making it clear there wasn't going to be any talking. Occasionally, she glanced at herself in the rearview— pulling a scrap of leaf from her hair, licking her thumb to wipe at the inkblot-test makeup stains under her eyes. But other than that, her jaw was set, her eyes were on the windshield: She was taking him to the bus station; he was going back to Johanna.

But there were some things he needed to explain to Marissa—only he didn't know how to begin. Explanations were not his strong suit, and he'd found in the process of getting sober, in the day-to-day of sobriety, demands for explanation were constant: Why'd you start drinking? Why'd you stop? Why'd you quit playing? Why'd you move to San Francisco? And what about Johanna? All his explanations seemed to lack something though; there was a blank he could never fill, and that blank actually represented the greater part of what he was trying to say.

If he wanted to explain to Marissa about Johanna— what could he tell her? Even the simple question she'd asked left more out than it let in. Was he still in love with her? Sure, of course. But what did "in love" mean? The words had gotten so tired and overplayed, you couldn't even hear them anymore, like Frank Sinatra's voice, like the first bars of Beethoven's Fifth. If he said yes, did Marissa know what it was like, from those first searing vivid moments, when she sat down next to him on the piano bench? Lifted her hands behind her head to tie her long hair in a loose knot, the frilled straps of her sundress slipping inches closer to her neck, took two of the three guitar picks pressed between her lips and set them carefully on the bench beside her knee, tips together, in an hourglass shape, and drew the third pick down the open strings of the acoustic in her lap, a quick, full, jaunty check or demonstration that she was in tune, and, so—let's go.

Adam had heard of her but never met her. She was someone they talked about in the low-end Brooklyn indie-punk scene: Johanna, with the big blue headlight eyes, who sang like Joanna Newsom and played guitar like Annie Clark. And he almost hadn't come out that night. It was the dead February of a brutal winter. From the window of his apartment in Williamsburg, he could watch ice floes sliding solemnly down the East River. He was creeping up to thirty; the Deployers had broken up; and he felt sort of in between things or maybe past the best things—sitting in for a show with this band, playing keys for a studio session with that, dipping his toe in half-assed groups that formed over beers and broke up the next week when the drummer's girlfriend kicked him out of her apartment, and he had to sell his kit and move back to wherever. He was playing music all the time, listening to music all the time, hanging out almost exclusively with people who did the same—and in this way, living a life very close to the one he'd dreamed of. But what seemed most urgent was the music he wasn't making; the recognition his talent wasn't getting; the inescapable fact that it wasn't happening for him.

So when Parker (whatever happened to Parker?) texted him about a party in Bushwick, he thought maybe he'd rather just stay in and smoke weed and listen to *Lateralus* for the millionth time. But, as fate would have it, Adam changed his mind. And after doing a few laps of the packed and sweat-smelling apartment, and finding the usual crowd of acquaintances and randos, musicians and hangers-on, trust fund DBs and the graying guys with the ridiculous nicknames (Dr. Funkenstein, Pheromone Ben, Montclair Matty) you always did at these parties, he sat down with over-it-all defiance at a battered upright against the wall in the living room, and started playing. And after a while, Johanna sat down next to him.

She was twenty-two then. Long, ropy limbs, blond hair dyed with streaks of blue, fine cheekbones, eyes presented in Technicolor. She tied her hair in a loose knot, she drew her third pick down open strings, and they began to play. Without looking at each other, without saying a word, they took, gave, begged, surrendered, fought, kissed, killed. God, she was great, she was so, so great, he thought. She was the real thing.

The pedantic robovoice of Marissa's phone demanded, "In a quarter mile, turn right onto Middle Street." Looking up to the windshield, Adam saw they were passing through a residential neighborhood: ranch homes, shoveled walks, slumped two-ball snowmen, a diamond Children at Play sign—the suburbs. Every lawn had a tree, the black, leafless branches forking like cracks in the low gray clouds. They were eight minutes away.

Because here's the thing, Adam could tell Marissa— playing music with someone isn't like sitting next to them in a fucking cubicle. When he was a kid, he played alone, and the music he played had been written by men who'd been dead for hundreds of years, and the highest aesthetic achievement he could attain was to play the music *correctly*, and if he felt any other presence with him at the piano, it was of the dead composer glaring at his fingering, a man who a century or two before had written something so refined the world was compelled to keep listening to it forever. He didn't deny that Chopin was perfect. But the dusty folk-rock legends on Kristen's mixtape were *alive*. And even a drummer who couldn't keep time and a guitarist who couldn't play more than a dozen chords were alive, too. It was no great revelation, but it had been a revelation to Adam: Music was something you could do with other people. The intimacy of it didn't have to be terrifying or oppressive. It could be liberating. And most times, no, you didn't attain some transcendent communion of souls. But sometimes you did. You could play music with a woman you'd never met and twenty minutes later know her better than people you'd spent your whole life with. Was there a word for that? Holy, maybe.

After they played together like that, it was no surprise they had the mundane "shit in common," things to talk about when they weren't playing, or writing, or fucking like they believed if they came hard enough, often enough, they could reverse the rotation of the Earth. She'd been branded a prodigy at a young age, too—her gifts making her as unaccountable to her actuary father and stay-at-home mother as Adam was to his family. The afternoon he met her parents, he watched a color-bleached VHS of Johanna, age five, her hair preposterous with curls and ribbons, singing "Amazing Grace" onstage at some megachurch, every syllable a corkscrew of vibrato. So they'd both from early on become accustomed to other people thinking of them as a little strange. But they got each other. So no one else in the world mattered.

"Would you stop that?" Marissa said.

"What?" He noticed he was flicking the metal lock on the glove compartment latch.

"Turn left onto Hamill Road!" the voice instructed. Marissa signaled, turned. The Sonata rolled onto a covered bridge, the darkness abrupt and droning with the sound of the car echoing against the walls. "Da, da, da," he sang, harmonizing with the sound.

"What?" Marissa said.

"Forget it."

He could tell Marissa he and Johanna made each other happy. They were good together. There was a perfect frankness to her gestures of love toward him: She baked him a cake on his birthday (misshapen and hours in the making and borderline inedible, the sugar and cinnamon quantities mixed up—but she baked him a cake!); she bought him coats and hats and gloves at thrift stores all winter, boxes full, more than he could ever wear; she reassured him when he woke from the anxiety dream that plagued him, the one where all his fingers fell off, promised him that even if that did happen, she'd love him anyway. It might sound like the unremarkable stuff of any relationship. But Johanna understood from minute one what it took them weeks of group and individual sessions at Stone Manor to put together: that Adam could never be told often enough, plainly enough, that he belonged; that he was normal; that he was loved. And he did the same for her, offered her that same unaltering affection—tried to, at least. Because she needed that, too.

That North Star love only became more important as everything else started to accelerate around them—as the music they made got better and better, and more and more people noticed it, wanted it, wanted to *pay* them for it. She was into New Wave, would listen to Howard Jones songs again and again and again. Adam could find his way into that. They arrived at a sound that was elaborate without being dense, pop—inviting and symphonic. Their sound was "exciting," the A&Rs told them. Before they knew it, their lives were ten shows a week, magazine parties and playing on TV, Kafkaesque meetings with label executives, reviews, interviews—but they were in it together. She never let him forget it, he never let her forget it. Or anyway, he did his best.

Because if he were honest, he'd have to admit that Johanna was a difficult person to know how to satisfy at times. Maybe if he were honest, he'd have to admit that Johanna was a difficult person to know—even for him.

She understood that, better than anyone. She found her differences from other people more alarming, more isolating, than Adam did. Part of the problem was that she was just very fucking beautiful: at eleven, lanky, gangly, teased for looking like she'd popped out of a UFO; at twelve, stared at by grown men, approached on the street by model scouts. Assumptions accrued to her face: that she must be mysterious, or wise, or flighty, or angelic. And this fostered a kind of paranoia in her. She was never convinced which affection and what scorn she deserved, and which belonged to the accidents of her big eyes and symmetrical features. When Adam could tolerate hearing about her exes, Johanna complained of an emotional sleight of hand her former boyfriends and girlfriends performed: fucking, dating, falling in love with some idea of her, and leaving her in a solitude that grew the longer the relationship lasted and the clearer that gap became.

Johanna's greatest preoccupation, her fear, was that she was weird—not charming, manic pixie weird, but weird in a way that separated her, permanently, from a body she didn't belong in, from people who surrounded her without being able to comprehend her.

Sometimes, in the middle of shows, she'd stop playing and singing, and just stand there, stare out at the crowd—and the crowd would cheer louder and louder,

imploring, demanding, impatient, smitten, until finally
she'd lift her guitar and resume the song. At first, Adam
figured this was a trick to get the show going, or maybe
the same stage fright that afflicted him. But eventually
she admitted she needed that pause to convince herself
that they were cheering for her, and not some chimerical
Johanna Mayfield that they could see, but she couldn't.

Johanna didn't trust the people she met. She'd get
quiet, mean. Or she'd overcompensate, and throw herself at them, take from them whatever physical or emotional affirmation she could get. She cheated on Adam
in all kinds of ways. He'd lied to Marissa, it began right
from the start. Why wasn't Adam enough for her? He
tried to be: singing her to sleep at night when her mind
raced with fearful insomnia, playing to her from his
classical repertoire, Bach, Schubert, all the shit he'd
promised himself he never, never, never had to play
again—and never would've except sometimes she'd sit
there contented at the end of the piano like Lucy in
Peanuts. He forgave her her cheating, her days-long
silences, her inexplicable furies or spasms of laughter;
he swore to her that he understood all of it, that even
if there were parts of her he couldn't peer into—that
she couldn't peer into—he at least knew they were
there, and it didn't change his love any more than hers
would've changed for him if he woke up fingerless.

They were good together, he could tell Marissa. They made each other happy. But he started drinking more. And she got sick.

Four minutes from the bus station now.

He'd have to make Marissa understand that Johanna wasn't to blame for his drinking, any more than she was to blame for her sickness. After all, it wasn't like he'd only started drinking when he met Johanna Mayfield! Adam had always loved drinking—since junior high, when it felt like capital-A anarchist rebellion, when it felt like you were really doing something for once. And then later, in college, and even among the Deployers, he was always the one who wanted to keep going: another shot, another bar. He didn't get depressed when he drank, he got bigger, brighter—happier, for fuck's sake. What was wrong with feeling happier? And if he drank more and more in the face of the gathering unhappiness—it wasn't Johanna's fault. As they taught at Stone Manor, some people can recognize and take action when their life begins to fall apart. And other people run screaming for whatever makes them feel better fastest. Adam did a lot of the latter.

When they'd played songs off the first album so many times it just felt like work, and then they'd get offstage and find themselves tense and quiet around one another; when the same thing started to happen with the way they fucked; when she'd seem distracted and withdrawn, making him annoyed and suspicious, which made him clingy and resentful, which made her withdraw further; when they'd try to write new songs and got nowhere and so they'd avoid trying again later; when he returned to their apartment to find her sitting on the end of the bed, pages and pages of scrawl-covered paper scattered at her feet, and she finally looked up to tell him she was transcribing the bangs and hisses of the radiator; when they missed meetings with the label; when she let all three guys in another band fuck her one night; when she'd spend hours in the tub, filling, draining, filling, draining; when he tripped down the steps of a fire escape, splitting his face open and breaking his wrist, and couldn't play for a month; when the label sent them down to Miami to the mansion of some producer who could "jump-start" the second album, and ten minutes after they walked in the door Johanna disappeared, and Adam finally found her outside on the lawn, face down in the grass and ear pressed to a gurgling garden hose—Adam's response to all these moments, and the thousand others like them, was always the same: He'd have another drink. When the record company finally canceled their contract, it was like a mercy.

Spend enough time in bars, you realize that endings

are always less remarkable than people think. It was nobody's fault. Every band breaks up; every relationship either explodes or cools like a dying star. And if it seems extraordinary, that's probably because it happened to you.

The red brick façade of the Brattleboro bus station rose in the windshield.

He tried to help her. Even after they'd broken up, he tried. He tried talking to her, he tried talking to her parents, to her friends, to doctors, to psychiatrists. But Johanna didn't want help, then. And his drinking blunted all his efforts. He needed help he didn't want then, too. "Alcohol dependence is a clinical disorder," his individual therapist at Stone Manor, Wendy, would tell him, day after day. "Just like schizophrenia." Adam didn't argue with her, but she'd inevitably repeat the words again the next time, like she thought he hadn't been listening.

Marissa turned off the engine, left him in the car, went into the bus station to buy him a ticket to Ann Arbor, where he'd told her Johanna's parents lived (which was true). She'd taken the keys with her, which he had to admit was pretty shrewd. He probably wouldn't have stolen the Sonata to escape from this, but it was possible.

The last time he saw Johanna—autumn, years ago

already. He'd come up for air, so to speak: six weeks sober following his first go-round in rehab, just detox and two weeks of groups at a city hospital. His family had staged an intervention. They hadn't even needed to say anything: finding himself ambushed in his apartment by his parents, Kristen, Jack, and a dead-faced, skeletal stranger, he couldn't say yes fast enough—anything to keep them from reading the handwritten letters they had clutched in their hands. (He'd squandered so much goodwill and forgiveness. How much more could he expect?) Johanna by then was living in an inpatient facility on Lake Huron. Nobody thought it was a good idea for him to visit, but he went anyway. He'd imagined, as he made the drive from Austin, a whole song cycle that he could write about the trip. But he quit playing before he got around to writing it.

He parked in the visitors lot of Great Lakes Psychiatric Care, a campus of brick buildings with wide wings and modest landscaping on top of a hill overlooking Lake Huron. He'd never been to the Great Lakes; he remembered as he walked from the car being stunned he couldn't see to the opposite shore, like it had to be an optical illusion. They met in an empty cafeteria: mopped orange floors, an odor of lemon-scented disinfectant and steamed vegetables. The windows were barred, but there was no big-chested male nurse keeping an eye on them, as Adam had imagined there'd be. Johanna walked in unaccompanied, her hair cut to just below her chin, her face vague, swollen, dark folds crowding her eyes. She wore baggy jeans and a Michigan State hoodie—an outfit so humdrum-suburban he thought she must be wearing it as a joke. "Hi, Adam," she said as she sat down, her voice quiet, throaty, like she needed tea. She gave him a subdued, vaguely suspicious look, then turned her head toward the window.

Silence piled on top of silence. He felt like he was chasing what to say down a long corridor, falling farther and farther behind. Her body looked so small in the sweatshirt; he imagined if she raised the hood, she'd just disappear among its folds. At intervals, something like a mocking half smile would start to spread on one side of her mouth, then sag to nothing; otherwise, she didn't appear to have any reaction to his presence at all.

He remembered touching every part of the table where they sat—legs, gum-caked underside, metal torsion bars, like his hands might finally land on the words he needed. Anyone who believed there was anything romantic about madness, or drinking, or recovery, or love just snapping in two, should've been made to endure that silence. As he sat in the car waiting for Marissa, he wondered if he'd ever escaped it.

Finally, desperately, he got to the ostensible reason

he'd given himself for visiting. He pulled a small digital recorder from his pocket, played Johanna some songs he'd been working on: just him singing, accompanying himself on the piano in a Y gymnasium. Midway through the second song, she picked up the device, pressed stop. "What are you doing, Adam?"

He felt she'd wounded him in a way she never had before—because even at their worst, she always listened to his music. "I thought, I don't know, when you got out of here, we could start working on some new stuff."

"I can barely read a magazine," she said bitterly. "You think I'm going to write songs again?" She scratched a small zit tucked behind her nostril. "I'm sick, Adam," she told him, with a brief smirk. "I have to adjust to a new normal. Anyway, you shouldn't blame yourself."

He frowned. "For what?"

"I know you did your best. You just fell in love with the wrong person."

"What the fuck does that mean?"

"And I'm sorry I cheated on you all those times. I just got lonely." She smirked again.

"*You* got lonely?" He was shouting now.

The corner of her mouth edged up toward her cheek. She noticed him notice, and rubbed her face in annoyance. "It's the meds. It won't stop."

His anger seeped away, and with it the last of his

hopes; it wouldn't have made a difference if he'd never come at all. "It's okay," he reassured her. "You look good, Johanna."

She sighed, like the little burst of conversation had worn her out. "I gotta go take a nap. I get so tired. It's because they make me take so many pills."

She stood up, started toward a set of double doors beneath a Residents Only sign. She stopped, turned, and her smile bloomed out of nowhere, and all that time and injury collapsed into nothing, they were right back on the piano bench. "Do you remember that one show we played?"

"Which show?" he asked desperately.

"The really good show. You know."

"When—you mean, in Seattle when we—or no, at Fire and Water, in Northampton?"

"The really good one." She was getting impatient. "You remember."

All his weight was on his hands pressing the edge of the table, like he might leap over it and grab her. He sat back. "Yeah, I remember."

"We were really good that night. We really connected. That's what it's all about, right?"

He'd have a drink as soon as he got out of there. He promised himself. "Sure. That's what it's all about."

She nodded a little, and turned back to the doors, his

mental jukebox cruelly playing every Genesis ballad at once. There was no sense to it, there was no soundtrack for this. Every note that'd ever been played was no match for the double doors swinging shut and his last glimpse of her back. And five months later, she was dead.

Marissa got into the car, handed him an envelope with a bus ticket. "Lotta stops," she warned him. "Gimme your cell phone." She took it, and he watched her save their respective numbers on the two phones by calling her phone with his. "By the time you get there, I'll be on the ground in Seattle. Give me a call once you talk to her, okay?"

"Yup, you got it," he said brightly, taking back his phone.

She eyed him. "I paid eighty bucks for that ticket, Adam. You're going to go to Ann Arbor and call her, aren't you?"

"That's the plan!" he answered. "Where are you headed?"

She reached up toward the dark gash above her eyebrow, thought better of it.

"My mom lives in Athol now."

"Wow. Good luck," he said.

She leaned across the stick and wrapped one arm around his neck, letting go before he could hug her back. "I'll talk to you tomorrow. Right?"

"Absolutely!" He got out of the car and pushed the door closed.

Could it have been different? What if he'd said something more—something better? Wendy said no, everyone in the group sessions said no. Marissa probably would say no, too: No, of course not, you can't think that way. Johanna had a clinical disorder, and in the end, she didn't get better. That was the inevitability; that was the explanation.

But even so.

How could he not wonder if it might've turned out another way—if he'd said the right thing, or simply "I love you," pitched at just the right tone, or if the songs on the recorder had been a little better. Might it have been enough to deliver her from the nightmare of all her fears come true, an inmate in an insane asylum, enough to deliver them both to some other, circumscribed life? Him measuring out her pills, her driving him to AA meetings, television, taco night—not what they'd ever expected, but in it together.

Marissa waved through the window, and he gave a broad, happy wave back. She put the car in gear and drove to the end of the block. The car paused at the intersection, signaled, turned, was out of sight. The wind twisted around him on the sidewalk; big, scattered snowflakes drifted in the air, like ash.

So that was the explanation—the best he could do. And if there were gaps, evasions, mistakes obvious to anyone, well, that was him: Adam being Adam. And if the whole story sounded like a lie, hey, if you had to know, that's why he stopped playing, too. Because the chords started to sound like lies—like laughter.

Anyway, whatever happened, you had to find a way to cope, like Wendy said.

He followed a couple other people through the revolving door into the station.

[2]
The Lotus Field
Apartment Homes

Marissa waited at the last stoplight before her mother's apartment complex as a man spoke on the radio in a calming, indoor voice about drowned refugees. She didn't usually listen to the news, but it was the first station she'd found, and it'd gotten very quiet in the car.

The light changed, she crossed the intersection and continued down the street. Momentarily, she glanced into the mirror on the driver's side—and as she did, the face of the driver in the car behind slid into view, framed perfectly in the rectangular mirror: a white man with a square auburn goatee, a shadow slashing his forehead. Her mouth went dry, she considered slamming the brakes, but then he made a turn, the face slid away. There was no one following her anymore, she told herself: They'd already gotten what they wanted. And right now, she had better reasons for feeling tense.

The street ascended gradually, passing converted duplexes and squat apartment buildings set close to the empty sidewalk. It was a nice little neighborhood, all in all, the signs of wear nothing a crew of painters and an upswing in the economy couldn't fix. It was certainly nicer than most of the places she'd lived growing up.

"You have arrived at your destination," her phone announced. A brown wooden sign etched with yellow letters stood in an oval of cleared snow:

THE LOTUS FIELD APARTMENT HOMES
APARTMENT LIVING
A/C & CABLE

She turned off the street onto the drive to the apartments, stopped beside the sign, put the car in park, turned off the engine. Ahead, the strip of blacktop ended in a square of parking lot, bounded by three identical buildings: two-story, horseshoe-shaped, beige siding with white trim, long and flat like shipping containers. Marissa leaned her head back on the headrest. God in Heaven, what the fuck was she doing here?

It had to be almost five years since she'd seen or spoken to her mother. Hadn't she been better off? Even going this far had stirred the old familiar bitterness that sat at the bottom of any thoughts of Mona—because what the fuck was her mother doing here? What was the point of all the T rides from one far-flung, end-of-the-line corner of Boston to the other, their worldly possessions reduced to what could be stuffed into shopping bags, if her mother one day would just up and move to Athol? Marissa would've liked to have spent her childhood in the Lotus Field apartments—safe, stolid, so profoundly ordinary it was its own form of grace. Why the seediest nooks and crannies of Dorchester or Hyde Park while she was growing up, and now, when it didn't matter anymore, a place with *cable*? It was like Mona did it all on purpose, just to—

The cut above her eye throbbed, like it was reminding her she knew better. To assume Mona had lived in Boston for decades then left for Athol to spite Marissa was to assume Mona did anything for any discernible reason at all. *Why* was a question you had to let go of when dealing with Mona Cavano: She was impervious to *why*. And Marissa realized, too, the anger throbbing in her temples to make the cut ache and now her back and ribs start up again, as well (it had all been feeling better after the gas station ibuprofen), had less to do with Mona than it did with Leo, with herself, with the whole fucking ruin she'd made of her life today. Maybe

that, then, was what she was doing here. After everything, this was the only place she belonged: with her
mother. More concretely, the thought of spending the
next three hours sitting in a hotel room at the Sheraton,
staring at the ceiling or at the television or at the dark
behind her eyes, hoping Robbie would call while certain he wouldn't, struck her as simply unbearable. So,
here she was.

Already, the cold was working its way into the
car, diluting the leftover warmth. She turned on the
engine, drove up to the parking lot, and pulled in
beside a battered Crown Vic, its backseat piled past the
windows with cardboard boxes, trash bags, bundles of
newspapers. She tucked her purse under the seat, then
changed her mind and brought it with her as she got
out of the car. She locked the Sonata, double-checked
the address Caitlyn had texted ("bldg C, apt 2") she
double-checked her face in the driver's-side mirror.
She'd washed off everything in the gas station bathroom: dirt, snot, blood, makeup. For that sliver of an
instant before she could filter her own mental portrait,
she looked worse than a mess in the mirror: She looked
old. But at least the Band-Aid over her eye looked clean.
It was a day to count your blessings.

She edged sideways through a gap someone'd hacked
out of a waist-high bank of snow and followed the as-

phalt path to the door of Building C, limping she liked to think only slightly. Her heels snapped on the asphalt, the wind swirling fine gusts of snow across her path, like smoke. The door of the building was painted metal, the wire-reinforced glass affixed with a smattering of Protected by Armitron Security stickers and the business cards of twenty-four-hour locksmiths. On the strip of buzzers beside number 2 a jagged piece of masking tape served as the label, the word "resident" written in block letters. That would be Mona. Never write your name down anywhere you don't have to; that was right up there with never talking to cops. Marissa's flight instinct began howling again. But how many Thanksgivings could she run from in one day? She didn't like to think of herself as a coward. She pushed the button.

Inside, the buzzer trilled angrily. She waited, lifting her right foot to rearrange the tension in her back. The flight tonight would be a nightmare—but one nightmare at a time. She was thinking she ought to have called Caitlyn to make sure she'd be here when, with a metallic clack, the door swung open and a male voice was saying, "Whadja forget your key or someth—The fuck?"

This was her question, too, seeing the man before her. Tattoos covered his wiry arms and bare chest, and he studied her through bifocals attached to a red plastic cord that dangled behind his back. His ponytail and beard were stained with gray, and creases ran every which way over the rough skin of his face, like battered boots treated against water damage. "You ring the wrong buzzer?" he asked, more curious than suspicious, scratching a triangle of white chest hair, his quizzically parted lips revealing a bottom row of teeth that all seemed to have different ideas about which way was up.

"I'm looking for Mona Cavano," she told him.

He gave her a disappointed look. "You a process server? Because legally, you need to declare yourself as a process server, if asked by any, um," he scratched his chest hair uncertainly, "resident of the county."

She smelled, or imagined she smelled, a powerful odor of marijuana wafting off him. "No, I'm not a process server, I'm . . ."

"Thank Christ!" He smiled, leaning against the doorjamb. "I once got ass-nailed by a process server. I knew this guy was after me, and I didn't go home for a week. This was in, say, '88 or so. I see him waiting at my car, I take the bus. He shows up at my buddy's door, I get out the fire escape. Man, we cat-and-moused it all over Minneapolis in the summer of 1988. But then one night I got coldcocked in a bar, and I opened my eyes in the hospital, and guess who I see?" He laughed, pleased, then broke down into coughing. He wiped his mouth with the back of his hand and continued, "Gotta give the sonnafabitch credit, right? He earned his paycheck that week." A shiver raced down his tattoo-carpeted chest. "God almighty, what are we doing out here? How can I help you, sister?"

"I'm Marissa." He nodded at her, unfazed. "Mona's daughter," she added, her voice oddly insistent. "Marissa Cavano."

"Caitlyn's sister?"

"Caitlyn's sister," she confirmed, inexplicably jealous that Caitlyn had been there, met whoever this guy was.

He straightened, lifted his hands behind his head, giving her a view of crooked strings of charcoal armpit hair, and blew through pursed lips to let out an airy whistle. "Caitlyn's sister. Mona's oldest kid. You went to college upstate New York somewhere?" Before she could answer, he said, "Hoo boy."

"Who are you?"

"Folks call me Special K 'cause I used to be a vegetarian." He whistled again. "Well, fuck it," he concluded, "come on in, you can't believe half the things you hear about people, right?" He turned from the door. She tried as best she could to ignore the implications of what he'd just said, and followed him inside.

A domed fluorescent in the entry buzzed and blinked over teal industrial carpeting, apartment doors with vertical lines of deadbolt locks stretched out to a chained fire door. The door to apartment 2 stood half-open, a busted handcart leaning beside it. It was all a little more like Marissa's growing up than she'd anticipated. As Special K pushed the door open, she said, "Maybe I should wait outside. Could you ask my sister to come out so . . ."

"Oh, Caitlyn isn't here."

Fresh flight adrenaline burst into every limb. "She's not?"

"She'll be here any minute."

"When?"

"Oh, any minute."

"Then can you tell my mom I'm . . ."

"Mona just went out, don't worry, she'll be back any—"

"Are you my mom's boyfriend?" She sounded like she was twelve now. But the familiarity of the scene—the mildew smell, the hints of seediness, her mother's unexplained absence, the unaccountable stranger, the fuzziness as to who or where anybody was—it had all become so potent it was like she'd forgotten she'd grown up.

"Your mom and I are . . ." Special K smoothed his

ponytail as he searched for the word. "Compadres," he finally said. "Fellow travelers. We've still got some time on the road yet, so why not spend it together? Ya dig?"

She felt like the passengers you sometimes got, who after the plane pulled away from the gate demanded to be let off: only when it was too late did they realize that something horrible was going to happen. "You can tell her I stopped by."

But Special K shook his head—friendly, conspiratorial. "Your mom'll cut my balls off for letting you in, but she'll pickle them and throw them out in the snow if I let you leave. You know how mothers get. Mona'll be back any minute now." He waved her toward the apartment door with a lopsided, consoling grin. "Come on in, little sister. You'll make it out in one piece. Most everybody does." Those passengers were always wrong, she reminded herself. The planes never crashed—not yet, anyway, in her experience. She went after him into the apartment.

The smell of cat piss tempered slightly by lavender kitty litter struck her first. But her mother was allergic to cats, she thought. The apartment had thin, gray carpeting, walls painted a dull yellow shade, with some faded brown water stains near the ceiling opposite the door. The furniture triggered another pang of déjà vu, not that she recognized any of it, but it had that worn-out and jumbled quality of having been acquired from anywhere it could be found on the cheap: a dented metal card table on a frayed area rug; a pocked, upholstered couch, sun-bleached to colorlessness; a taupe recliner with a mismatched green seat cushion; a boxy little television, flashing muted scenes of a car chase.

Special K picked up from the carpet an ashtray in which a joint was burning and offered it to her. When she shook her head, he took a long hit himself. From where she stood, she could see through an open door into the bedroom: a mattress on the floor, piled with clothing, a cross hammered to the wall above. Her mother was close to sixty, and she still didn't own a bed. This thought was painful enough that Marissa turned her head the other way and surveyed the narrow kitchen. Beside an overflowing plastic trash can was a great black garbage bag, bulging with curves; she could as much as hear the clunk of empty plastic liquor bottles that would follow if she touched the bag with her foot. She turned her back on the kitchen.

Special K had seated himself on the couch, had the joint between his lips, a blue-painted guitar in his lap. He blew some smoke through his nostrils, offered the joint to her again.

"They drug test at my job." Marissa knew it was the only kind of excuse guys like this took seriously.

"Bummer," he said. "You need any ice for that?"

"Ice?" she asked, puzzled, then remembered the cut. "No, I'm fine."

"I should see the other guy, right?" he chuckled. "None of my business, of course." He bent forward to replace the joint in the ashtray, and began strumming, singing. "From the—" A coughing fit interrupted the verse as it got started. The coughs were hoarse, throaty, the kind she associated with mouthfuls of blood. But he smiled good-humoredly when the fit was done, and took another long hit. "Take your coat off and stay a while," he said as he exhaled billows of smoke. Marissa kept her coat on, but sat down next to him, angling her back to the kitchen and bedroom. A window, half-covered with a slat curtain, opened on a snowy patch between the apartment and a rear wall of another building in the complex. "You know 'This Land Is Your Land?'"

"No."

"How about 'The Weight' by the Band?"

"Sorry."

He strummed for a while, then slapped the strings with his palm. "Shit, sister, what do you know?"

This might go on for hours, Marissa realized: her

sitting around waiting for her mother to appear, Special K smoking weed and playing guitar. She should have called Caitlyn; more, she should have anticipated her mother's seemingly supernatural ability to transform any situation, divert any intention, however serious, into absurdity, into farce.

"Look," she said to Special K.

"How come you don't look a thing like Caitlyn?" he asked.

She lowered her eyelids, rolling her eyes behind them. "Take a wild guess."

"Oh, gotcha," he said. "Different dads."

"Smart guess." She cringed—she'd said "smaht," her childhood reaching up into her mouth and crushing her vowels.

"I can't say I'm surprised," Special K answered. "Your mother is a real sexy woman. She's got the kind of sexiness—okay, okay, turn off the death rays."

Marissa dug in, trying to make something of the visit. "Look, how—how is my mom doing?"

Special K considered, still strumming as he blew smoke toward the muted television. "Sister," he began. "I know what you're asking." He took another hit, letting the smoke curl slowly from his nostrils before he went on. "Sister," he repeated, "she's not walking any better than you are. Something's wrong in her knee. And I'm guessing you're familiar with her opinion of doctors. I'll tell you though, Mary."

"Marissa."

"The fact of the matter is, she's been going on like this for twenty years, and she could go on for another twenty. It's a demon, there's no getting around that. But she and that demon settled on terms a long time ago, and so far, nobody's killed the other. I make sure she sleeps on her side and without any cigarettes going."

Marissa used to do that: She used to take the burning cigarette from between her mother's fingers when Mona passed out in bed. "Thanks," she said. "Thanks."

"I can't say I envy you girls. Alky Mom ain't exactly starting life with a pair of aces. But you both grew up tough, and that's not nothing. And I know Mona took you both to church every Sunday. That's not nothing, either."

"No, actually, that would be a lie," she corrected him.

Special K shrugged. "Well, a Sunday or two, at least. You get on in years, you learn not to get so hung up on the details."

"As a matter of fact, most Sundays my mom left us to—"

Special K lifted a hand from the guitar to stop her. "That ain't my cross to bear." He watched her face, already contorted with the old, ever bright anger. "Can I tell ya a little story?" She guessed there was little point saying no. "This was back in the late sixties, say, '72, '73. People think the sixties ended in the sixties, but the truth is they rolled right on for a while. For Special K, at least. I was shacked up with the most beautiful little surfer chick God ever made. Strawberry hair with all the little freckles over her cheeks and nose. We used to run sheets of acid from Vancouver down into Northern California four times a year. There wasn't a border agent she couldn't charm. Other than that, we were surfing, sleeping on the beach, going where the wind took us. It was the Garden of Eden on the Pacific Coast Highway, take it from me. Well, the Lord giveth, and the Lord taketh away. I got jammed up on some possession charges on account of a broken taillight outside Sacramento, and while Esther was coming up to post my bond, bus driver fell asleep and *bang!*" he shouted, loud enough that she jumped. "Drove into the wrong lane. Head-on collision, you believe that shit? Nineteen years old," he said, mournful, confused, like it still confounded him, like it'd happened the day before. "Well," he went on, "paradise gets lost one way or another, don't it? We're all naked before the winds of time and change, and all we can do is find someone to love and hold on to each other tight, ain't that right? So take it from Special K, life's too short to worry about how often your mom took you to church."

"I'm not worried about it," Marissa said matter-of-factly.

But Special K was singing again. "On a hill, far—" And then he was choking with coughs again.

She looked down at her purse at her feet, sitting in a field of Dorito shards and ash. She wasn't getting used to the cat piss odor, either. She stood up. "Is there a vacuum cleaner?" Special K stared up at her. "Fine. Where's the kitty litter?"

He pointed toward the bedroom door, and started strumming what she was pretty sure was a Beatles song. She saw the blue plastic tray in a corner, pebbles dark with urine and dotted with rounds of black shit. She picked the tray up without looking at anything else, went into the kitchen, dumped the contents into the black bag, and hefted it to the door. "Is there any more?" she asked Special K.

"More?"

"Kitty litter."

"Nope. But we ain't seen Screamin' Jay in a week, so it might not make a difference one way or the other."

She returned the empty tray to the bedroom. "Is there a gas station around here?" She doubted there'd be a grocery store nearby, and if there was a CVS, it wouldn't be open today. But she could picture the gas station's row of cleaning products: the spray bottles, sponges, brushes, bleach-coated wipes. She'd put it all on her credit card and spend however many hours it took scrubbing this place until it fucking glistened.

"Nah, stick around!" Special K told her. "You know 'Freebird'?"

"No," she said sharply. "No, don't play that."

He scratched his beard quizzically. "What'd, somebody in Lynyrd Skynyrd stiff you on a bar tab?"

"I just . . ." She felt strange and sickened and guilty to think about Adam, as she'd last seen him: in the rearview mirror, standing by himself on the sidewalk outside the bus station. "I just don't want to hear 'Freebird.'" It seemed the least loyalty she owed him.

"Suit yourself. How about some CSN? I held David Crosby's coke for half their tour in '77. Or '79. He was all right."

The door swung open and slammed with a clatter into the trash bag. "You left this goddamn trash in the—" Mona caught sight of Marissa and stopped abruptly. She wore a gray-purple coat, knee length with faux fur around the collar, and a pair of ridiculous red rubber boots. She'd gained another fifty pounds, at least; the mounds of flesh of her face were struck with fine red veins, her skin otherwise an almost shocking white. The last of her thinning hair had been dyed jet black, and two thick black arcs were tattooed above her eyes in the place of vanished eyebrows. She sneered, her lips bright with cherry red lipstick. "Well, well," she began.

Marissa stood unmoving by the bedroom door; she felt so tiny standing there across from Mona. "Hi, Ma."

The sneer subsided and Mona bounded to her. "Don't move until I got my arms around you." She wrapped Marissa in a fierce hug, her cheek still cold from outside. She smelled like booze and cigarette smoke and Head and Shoulders shampoo, the same as ever. "My oldest," Mona said in Marissa's ear. "My first." She dropped her arms and took a step back, giving Marissa a full examination. "That's no paper cut," she said, eyes on the Band-Aid. "We'll get to that." She reached out and started to unbutton Marissa's coat.

"Jesus, Ma, hold on," Marissa said, unbuttoned the coat for herself.

"Huh," Mona said. The longer Mona stared the smaller Marissa felt, like a shrinking Alice. "Are you getting a little fat?"

"You're one to talk," Marissa said.

Mona smirked. "She always had a lip on her, Ken, you watch out," she said to Special K.

A plastic bag dangled from her hand, the neck of

a capped bottle wrapped in brown paper peeking out. Only her mother could have found an open liquor store on Thanksgiving Day—or maybe it was easier than Marissa imagined. Mona clopped with a noticeable limp into the kitchen, set the bag down, and pulled out the bottle: Smirnoff, the same as ever.

"Could you not, Ma—"

Before Marissa could even finish the question, Mona had spun around, eyebrows jagged between her eyes. "I had twenty years of you telling me what to do, and that was plenty. If you try to give me orders in my house, that little scratch above your eye will be the least of your troubles." Her accent was so thick it filled the Athol apartment with seagull cries, T train whines, the occasional hollers from porches that would follow them down the streets in neighborhoods where they'd out-stayed their welcome: "Those kids should be in school, Cavano!"

"Now, hey, play nice, Big Mama. It's Thanksgiving!" Special K was calling from the couch.

Mona looked at Special K, then looked at Marissa. Surprisingly, she grinned, showing her tobacco-stained teeth. "Did you hear I was living with Bruce Springsteen?"

She returned to the bottle. Marissa sat back on the couch, hearing the snap of the plastic cap twisted from its ring, the glugs of the vodka into the Solo cup, the Sprite liter pulled from the refrigerator, the token splash, the refrigerator door closing, and the first, long slurp. And then Mona stood in the kitchen doorway, cup in her hand. To Marissa she said, "How long'd you stay away from me, five years?" Then, to Special K, "And then she comes waltzing back. Looks like she caught a bump or two climbing that ladder of hers up to Beacon Hill. Well, we'll get to the bottom of her." Mona took a long drink, wiped her lips on her coat sleeve, then took her coat off to reveal a sort of frock dress underneath, white blazed with blue and orange flowers. She tossed the coat in the direction of the bedroom, limped in her boots over to the recliner, sat down heavily. "The cat come back?" she asked Special K.

"No traces," he answered.

"You feed them and care for them and give them all the love in the world until one day they decide they're too good for you and run off. Who does that remind you of?"

"I thought you were allergic to cats," Marissa said.

Mona ignored this. "Well, out with it," she demanded. "Someone used you for a punching bag. Was it this husband of yours I heard so much about?"

"I fell down the stairs, Ma."

"A cop a day out of the academy wouldn't be stupid enough to believe that one. You better try harder. I know you're not here for the pleasure of my company."

"It's Thanksgiving," Marissa parried.

"And it was Thanksgiving last year, and it was Thanksgiving the year before that. If you want to bullshit me, Marissa, you need to start using that famous brain of yours. Keep your eye on this one, Ken. My other daughter got the face and the double Ds, she never had to rub two thoughts together in her life. This one, the day I put her in the crib, you could see the wheels turning."

Special K grinned. "Like mother, like daughter."

"Don't get cute, this isn't the Lifetime channel," Mona said over her cup. But Marissa knew the compliment flattered her; it flattered Marissa, too, more than she would've admitted. Her mother had many (many) faults—but from the time Marissa was old enough to notice, she had admired her mother's guile, her savvy. Perhaps the kindest thing you could've said about their relationship over the years was that they regarded each other as worthy opponents.

"So why are you living in Athol?" Marissa asked. "I thought you swore you'd never live more than ten miles—"

"More than ten miles from where Grandma Sofia's buried, I remember what I said. Not all of us are as youthful as you are, Marissa, it's not so easy for me to get around a city anymore." She scowled. "I tried to explain to you girls what it was like for your grandmother, an Italian woman on her own, making a life for herself in Boston. The Irish don't exactly do one of their jigs when an Italian shows up. But she made something for herself there. I didn't want to turn my back on it. But you girls never cared. Your sister didn't understand and all you wanted—God knows what you ever wanted." She took a long sip of her drink. "Now everything's changed. All the old parishes are dying dead. I could fall down in the street, all anybody'd do is step over my corpse." She finished whatever was left in her cup, shook it at Special K. He got up and took it, giving Marissa a shamefaced grin before dropping his eyes as he went to the kitchen. But she'd done that, too, in her time: She'd poured Mona plenty of drinks, until she vowed never to do it again. "All right, then, detective, if you're done with your questions, let's get back to mine. Did you get kicked out on your ass today or what?"

"Not exactly," Marissa answered, failing to come up with a better evasion.

Mona snorted triumphantly. "In other words, exactly. What have I been telling you your entire life?"

"Never open a bank account?"

"And I was right about that, wasn't I? When half the country lost their mortgages, you can bet they wished they kept their money like I did. So did he find a twenty-year-old who makes more sparkling conversation? Then when you got lippy about it, like you do, he figured out a way to change the subject."

Mona had it all wrong, but somehow it didn't matter; Marissa felt herself reddening, getting defensive. "You don't know shit about it, Ma."

"I know everything about it!" she cackled. "Because I know you. And you can play cuckoo bird with some family of cops in Needham, you can earn your keep at some holier-than-thou college chasing a ball around a field, you can marry into some rich black family with a Back Bay mansion I'm not welcome at. But it'll never change what you are."

In five years, Marissa had grown unaccustomed to her mother's escalations, her hairpin counterattacks, her instinct for blood: She felt like Mona was trying to slice her up and serve her to herself. "Okay, Ma, you tell me, what am I?" She stared at Mona's dark eyes, set in the folds of her face. This was why she'd come, she thought, and no other reason: to ask this question.

Mona leaned forward in her recliner, raised her fake brows. "You're poor white trash by way of Boston. Your mother's a drunk and your father got shivved in

Walpole while he was doing ten years for bank fraud. That's all you'll ever be, so you better learn to live with it, Marissa Sofia."

It was as if some vacuum had opened around her, drawing away everything that was not utter stillness. She believed she could feel the words working their way, inch by inch, into her mind. "Who?" she finally managed.

Mona looked around the floor uncomfortably. "Never mind, I'm an old lady, Marissa, I forgot I never . . ." Then her look was ferocious again. "You stay away from me for five years, after all I done, you expect me to keep track of what you know and what you don't know? Ken, where is my goddamn vodka drink?" she bellowed toward the kitchen, then shook her head, reached over, and put her hand on Marissa's knee. Marissa slapped it away. "Okay, okay, don't be dramatic. What'd you think, your dad was Ted Kennedy?"

"I thought he was . . ." She was surprised to hear herself talk. "I thought he was alive. And—somewhere." The hollowed-out sensation had returned. She'd believed she never thought about him, but now wondered if she hadn't thought about him every day.

"He was a deadbeat who got sent up when you were two and he never got out. That's the whole story right there. You thought whatever you thought and you never listened to me anyway. Besides, I didn't want you to think you were . . . For Christ's sake, Ken! Bring her some water."

Special K appeared, holding a Solo cup of water. Marissa took it, had to grip it with both hands to drink it without dropping it.

"What are you looking so white for?" Mona demanded. "He was a stranger."

"But I thought he had . . ." She thought he had done with his life what she'd done with hers: escaped Mona, escaped Boston.

Special K grabbed his guitar. "You ever hear the record 'American Beauty' by the Grateful Dead? I can play the whole thing from memory."

"Spare us, Mozart," Mona told him.

"At least lemme play her 'Ripple,'" he insisted. Marissa was staring down into the empty cup, the dental white surface flecked with beads of water. This time the coughing started even before the first word. She missed Adam. It was an unexpected sensation, a kind of tug at the bottom of her chest; but they'd been together for all the other ass-kickings the day had handed out, and she would have liked it if he'd been here for this one. She doubted he could've helped, but she believed for whatever reason that he'd get it: what it felt like to be robbed of someone, just like that. Penance—was that why she'd come?

A sound like a robot's death scream filled the room. Special K put the guitar down. "You two keep the gloves on," he said, and he went out to answer the door.

Mona watched Marissa with a sour, unsettled expression. "He knock you around or not?"

"Who, Ma?" Marissa answered dully.

"Your precious husband. Because if he did, Marissa, I can help you with that. Half your cousins are still in Boston, and—"

"What cousins?" Marissa shot back. "Vincent Palleta? Danny Annapolo? Those assholes aren't my cousins."

"They looked out for you like they were your cousins, didn't they?"

"Danny Annapolo tried to feel me up when I was thirteen."

"Like you were so pure when you were thirteen. I know what you were up to," Mona spat back. She took another sip. More mildly, she said, "Anyway, you should've let Danny Annapolo get in your pants. He owns two car dealerships up in Brockton."

"Yeah, I really missed the boat on that one."

"Roll your eyes all you want, but I bet his wife's

never gotten knocked around after Danny stepped out on her."

"I cheated on him, Ma!" she at last erupted. "That's what happened. I cheated on him. He'd never hurt me, he's not . . . He's nice." How had she landed on "nice" again? It only added to the sense of utter uselessness that seemed to have sapped the last of her energy.

Mona studied her for a while. "My first girl," she said at last. She lifted her cup to her lips, then studied that. "You always were your own worst enemy." All at once, it was like the terrifying, indomitable vitality slipped from her body; Mona looked like an old, obese alcoholic, drinking away her last days in a recliner. "What are you doing here, Marissa? Not even I understand it." She brought the cup to her lips.

Marissa's phone was ringing in her purse. She doubted she'd have the strength to talk to whoever might be calling. "What was his name?" she asked Mona.

"Who?" Mona said. "Oh. Him. It doesn't matter one way or another. Make up whatever name makes you happy, Marissa." And now she was sharp and defiant and indomitable again: Was it possible to hate someone, to fear someone, to admire her and love her, in the space of a single conversation? A single thought?

"See? They're getting along great!" Special K was walking in. Caitlyn followed, carrying on her hip her stepdaughter, Jade, a flushed two-year-old with a pacifier in her mouth.

"Aren't you full of surprises," Caitlyn said when she looked at Marissa.

"Hey," Marissa said. The little girl wore a pink, puffy jacket, a wool hat and wool mittens that dangled from strings inside her sleeves. Caitlyn had just an unzipped windbreaker over her purple scrubs. She worked as an aide at a retirement home in Somerville and looked worn out from her day, but even after she'd pulled a double, no one was going to get confused about which of the Cavano sisters was the anointed pretty one: Caitlyn was three inches taller, had straight, dirty blond hair, a girl-next-door button nose, and yes, a double D bra size. "You look good," Marissa said to her sister.

Caitlyn rolled her eyes tiredly. "I bet. C'mon, Jade, stand on your feet." She began lowering the child by the armpits.

"I'll take her," Marissa said. She stood up and the girl fell into her arms, her head against Marissa's shoulder.

"Jade, you remember your aunt Marissa?" Caitlyn asked her. "And Grandma Mona?" Jade looked up, pushed the pacifier out toward Marissa as she considered, rubbed her eyes dramatically, and dropped her head. "They tired her out at Hanley's sister's," Caitlyn said. "She says hello."

Caitlyn's husband, Hanley, followed inside, carrying four large bags from KFC. He was an attractively broad-shouldered guy, olive-skinned, a Bruins beanie pulled down to his eyelids, a set of keys jangling on his belt.

Special K sat back on the couch, picked up his joint. "Can you not?" Caitlyn said. "Around the baby?"

"Oops, oops, oops," he chuckled, snuffing the joint out in the ashtray. "That's just Grandpa's wacky-tabaccy," he said to Jade, sticking out his tongue comically. The child stared back at him blank-faced from Marissa's arms.

"You are so not her grandpa," Caitlyn muttered. She took two of the bags from Hanley. "Ma, can we get this show on the road? They're making Hanley go in tonight."

"Yeah, hello to you, too," Mona answered.

Caitlyn disappeared into the kitchenette. "I told you to have the oven on!"

But Mona was eyeing Marissa with Jade in her arms. "What'd you ever do with all that babysitting money?" she asked Marissa.

This was one Mona would never, ever let go. "Went to college," she answered.

Mona went on eyeing her, as if seeing her holding her niece raised Mona's suspicions about Marissa herself on the question of children; you had to remind yourself sometimes that Mona was not, in fact, clairvoyant.

"For all the good it did you," Mona muttered at length.

Marissa pulled off Jade's mittens, took her hat off her head and stuffed it in the girl's coat pocket. "There ya go, sweetie," she cooed.

"Mah-issa," Jade said.

"Look at that, and even I barely remembered," Mona declared. To Caitlyn, she called, "You better watch out for your stepdaughter around cuckoo bird, Lord knows what she's capable of."

Caitlyn ignored this, asking from the kitchenette, "Why isn't the oven working?"

"It's broken!" Special K called cheerfully, strumming "Jingle Bells."

"Okay, we'll eat it cold," Caitlyn huffed.

Hanley picked up the TV remote from the carpet. "Second half started," he said to no one in particular, changed the channel to a football game and turned the volume up.

Caitlyn emerged from the kitchen with two tubs of chicken as Mona was waving her empty cup at Special K. "Can you take it slow while my kid is here?" Caitlyn half whispered.

"It wasn't my idea for you to come over here," Mona answered. "Anyway, you and your big sister have some catching up to do." Special K took her cup. "Guess what happened to her today."

Caitlyn looked at Marissa. "What?" she asked.

"Barack Obama kicked her ass to the curb. Shoved her down the stairs, only she won't admit it."

"That true?" Caitlyn asked.

"He didn't push me down the stairs," Marissa told her.

Caitlyn watched Marissa's face. They'd never had one of those sister-best-friend relationships, but they'd spent their childhoods in the same foxhole. They knew how to detect fragility, injury in each other. She gave Marissa a sympathetic nod. "I know, Marissa. I know he'd never." Then, to everyone, "All right, let's just eat."

"Ken, bring my bottle and the soda in here," Mona shouted into the kitchen.

"Christ, Ma," said Caitlyn.

"You gonna take the Lord's name in front of the baby? What would her real mother say about that?"

Caitlyn absorbed the blow the way she always did,

tucking her lips into her mouth, hardening her eyes into an aggrieved glare that never translated into words, ending with a fluttering, twirling gesture with her hand: Okay, let's just move on.

Special K carried the vodka in from the kitchen, at least wrapped discreetly once again in its paper bag, whispering to the sisters as he passed, "Better to just let her have it. We don't want her to get on a roll."

So Mona ate with the bottle between her feet; Special K hadn't bothered with the soda. Marissa put Jade on the couch between her and Caitlyn, and Caitlyn gave the girl a bowl of macaroni and cheese to eat with a plastic spork. Hanley lay on the floor in front of them, legs extended, staring at the football game. Special K was up on one arm of the couch, knees pressed together to make a little table of his lap for his food. They passed around the buckets of chicken, ate off the logo-emblazoned napkins, didn't speak as the football and commercials blared, squawked, sang. Occasionally, there'd be a fresh glugging into Mona's Solo cup. Caitlyn pulled a few pieces of chicken off a wing, tried to tempt Jade with them, but Jade pulled her lips into her mouth much the same way Caitlyn did, patted the mac and cheese with her palm.

Marissa didn't have much of an appetite. She'd already eaten Thanksgiving dinner that afternoon—

though, in her opinion, the KFC was even a little better than what the caterer had prepared. But it was all a question of familiarity: She ate KFC once or twice a week growing up. Marissa watched Jade as she diligently spooned the mac and cheese into her mouth. Was there any hope she'd remember this day? And if she did, what would those memories be? An apartment full of people she loved, who loved her, sharing a meal together? Or was she already attuned to the tensions in the room—the diseases, the toxic histories? Maybe at best she'd remember that they'd succeeded in putting all that aside for ten or twenty minutes. Maybe that was the most any family holiday could be: a little contrivance of peace.

Whatever it was, it didn't last long. By the time the television was showing the football game's production crew smiling and waving to their families back home, Mona'd begun muttering to herself. "Five years. Five years, and she comes waltzing back in, like she owns the whole building."

"Cut it out, Ma," Caitlyn said.

"Cut what out? Why? You wouldn't understand. After I killed myself all those years, she turns her back for a bunch of cops and . . ."

"Who cares?" Caitlyn insisted. "She's here now, so let's shut up and enjoy the day."

"Easy for you to say," Mona snapped. She reached forward for the bottle; it slipped from her hand and landed on the carpet, but there was nothing left to spill out. She sat back heavily. "I deserved better. After all I did for her. Turn your back and there's a knife in it. Ask her husband, he knows!"

Caitlyn was giving Marissa a pleading look. And Marissa knew, after all these years, there was no point trying to match Mona grudge for grudge, spite for spite: She might as well try to drown the ocean. But she looked at Jade and she looked at the food and she said, "Ma, where'd you go when you left me and Caitlyn in McDonald's that Thanksgiving?"

"What Thanksgiving? You're crazy."

"No, you left us in McDonald's all day, and finally the cops came to—"

"Come on, Marissa," Caitlyn whispered behind her teeth.

"You told them our aunt was watching us, but we don't have an aunt." She wasn't shouting, but from the way Jade edged away from her on the couch, she knew she might as well be. But she wasn't stopping now. "So where were you? Running numbers or something?"

"Running numbers?" Mona sneered mockingly. "You watch too much TV."

"If you two are going to do this again—" Caitlyn began.

"You think you deserved better?" Marissa seethed. "Guess what, we deserved better, too. So I want to know why the fuck you left us in a McDonald's on Thanksgiving. Where did you go?"

"This ain't no good for no one," Special K advised.

"No, I'll answer her question," Mona announced. "I've never been afraid of . . ." She appeared to try and fail in an effort to sit up, ended up sliding backward with an "Oof!" down into the recliner, the springs whining. "Where was I? I got no idea. I never ran numbers a day in my life, don't even know what that is, officer, but did I do a thing or two to keep my daughters fed as a woman alone? You might thank me for some of the things I did one day. And if you're waiting for an apology that I never let some man put nails in my hands and tell me 'this is your life, now go get me a beer,' you better not hold your breath. But you're a smart girl, you know where I was. I was drinking vodka. And either I forgot or I blacked out. You feel better? You got closure? Now why don't you call up your husband, tell him why you fucked around behind his back."

"Alright, that's it," Caitlyn declared, standing and

yanking Jade up to her feet and then up to her hip. "Hanley?"

After a beat, Hanley turned his head to look at her. "Fourth quarter, babe."

Caitlyn twisted her torso so Jade's face was to the door, then lifted her middle finger to him. "I'll be with your daughter, waiting in the cold," she announced, then pushed open the door and went out.

"Chicks!" Special K cried, with barren good humor.

Marissa turned back to Mona. Her mother took in a low, nasally breath, which she didn't seem to let out; then another, deeper. Her head was bent steeply forward from her neck: She was crying, Marissa realized. When was the last time she had seen her mother cry? Then Mona's body slumped to the left, she took in another grumbling breath through her nose, the arm of the recliner pushing into her side. No, she wasn't crying. She'd passed out. And why not? All the vodka was gone. Special K'd been wrong, she hadn't made peace with her demon: The demon was all that was left.

Marissa looked at Special K. "Can you get her to bed?"

"No, but I'll get a blanket over her," he answered.

It was hard for her to mean it, but she said, "Thanks for taking care of her."

She found Caitlyn standing in front of the building,

Jade asleep in her arms, cheek pressed into the zipper of Caitlyn's windbreaker. Caitlyn stamped her feet back and forth, trying to keep warm.

"Sorry," Marissa said.

"Whatever." Then she grinned a little. "It's just like a sitcom in there, isn't it?"

"Yeah, I couldn't stop laughing."

"Is she worse than ever, what d'you think?"

Worse than ever or as bad as always? What was the difference? "I dunno," Marissa answered. "I guess it was about what I expected." She closed her coat around herself, crossed her arms over her chest. The afternoon light was fading in the sky. Birds swooped before clouds closer to black than gray, settled on the building opposite's roof. "Since when does she have a cat, though? Ma's allergic."

Caitlyn made a *pssh* noise through her lips. "She's not allergic to cats. She just told us that so we'd stop asking when we were kids."

And just like that, Marissa was furious again, ready to go back inside and scream at Mona, conscious or not. "That lying b—"

Caitlyn was tugging one of Jade's mittens up higher on her hand, stamping her feet again. "How do you do that?" Marissa wanted to know. "How do you just . . . let it go with her?"

"I had to do something." She looked at Marissa, and she added matter-of-factly, "I knew I wasn't going to Syracuse, so . . ."

So she'd learned this self-protective forgiveness, forgetfulness: her way of being tough. They'd never talked about it, but Marissa was aware that the two years Caitlyn spent alone with Mona after Marissa went to college, before Caitlyn turned eighteen and got her own place, had been her hardest years. She wished she knew how to apologize for that, justify that—but this wouldn't be the day to try.

"I know I haven't called in a while," Marissa said.

"Don't worry about it," Caitlyn answered.

"How's Hanley?"

"Hanley's Hanley. No surprises. You appreciate that, after . . ." She jerked her head back toward the building. "And he made good money this year doing the landscaping, and until the spring he's getting shifts as a bouncer at a sports place by us. He's a good pro-vider, Marissa." For a moment, Marissa thought Caitlyn was mocking her, or mocking Robbie, but then she realized that no—Caitlyn was telling her because she was proud. She'd married a dependable provider from Somerville, with a good body, who liked to watch football on Sundays. Some line from a college seminar book darted around Marissa's head, something about having all the wrong dreams. But she'd had her chance at that. She could have married Brendan and lived in Needham. Only she wanted . . . "God knows what you ever wanted," she heard Mona saying.

Caitlyn asked her, "You and Robbie really on the outs, like she said?"

"Ma doesn't know the half of it," she admitted. "I got myself pregnant, too."

Caitlyn's eyes widened with surprise, but her mouth stayed even. "And not with . . ."

"Do you remember my boyfriend, in Needham, Brendan O'Shea?"

Not even Caitlyn could manage her reaction to that; her mouth dropped open. "Jesus, Marissa! You go to a reunion or something?"

"He was on a flight I was working."

"Come on, Marissa, you have got to be . . ." She stopped, looked at Marissa for another beat, then back at Jade, brought her hand up to the little girl's cheek. "Can you believe this shit? He's going to let his daughter get frostbite out here."

Marissa waited, but Caitlyn went on pressing her hand to Jade's cheeks, her ears.

"So?" Marissa finally said.

"So, what?"

"So what should I do?"

Caitlyn's eyebrows sharpened above her eyes; briefly, she looked like their mother—she looked, Marissa realized unsettlingly, like her, too. "I went to Massatoilet Community College, you don't need any advice from me." It was old, indelible resentment; or else the boundaries Caitlyn had drawn between herself and Mona were also boundaries between her and Marissa. Marissa didn't blame her sister, either. Maybe Caitlyn was the pretty one and the smart one, too.

Jade lifted her head and looked around uncomprehendingly. "You waking up, honey?" Caitlyn asked her. "Daddy will be out in a minute."

"You're good with her," Marissa said.

"I'm faking it. You're the one with the touch." Caitlyn smiled a little. "You remember that time I was playing out on that frozen ditch, God, out in Quincy, and I broke through the ice and got my pants soaking wet in the middle of winter? I was hysterical, and Ma wasn't home to let us in, so you banged on doors until that Mexican family opened up. You didn't even say a word to them, just dragged me into the bathroom and starting blowing my pants with their hair dryer."

Marissa smiled now, too. "I couldn't say a word. I didn't speak Spanish."

"We did okay, though." She repeated, "We did okay." Marissa wanted to believe this was Caitlyn's way of acknowledging that if Marissa had left her to go to Syracuse, Marissa had helped raise her for sixteen years, too.

"You and Hanley's ex getting along any better?" Marissa asked her.

Caitlyn gave her a whatdoyouthink smirk. "Tanya still goes out to the bars six nights a week. She never wanted to be a M-O-T-H-E-R."

"I wan' popcorn!" Jade said into Caitlyn's shoulder.

"Don't we all, sweetheart," Caitlyn sighed.

Hanley pushed open the door of the building. "Well, who won?" Caitlyn asked him.

"Niners," he said.

"Great." Caitlyn took a step toward Marissa, hugged her with one arm. "Will you have to work on Christmas?"

"Probably," Marissa answered as they parted.

"Me, too. Maybe we can figure something out the day after. Call me and we'll talk about it."

"Caitlyn—" Marissa said, then glanced at Jade, at Hanley, who'd slung his arm around her sister's shoulders. "We did do okay in the end. Didn't we?"

Caitlyn considered this—reached out to squeeze her hand. "We survived her, right? Cavano girls can survive anything."

Hanley had unclipped his keys from his belt. "Let's rock, babe, I'm freezing my dick off."

"Can't have that," Caitlyn said. "All right, let's get this show on the road." They walked side by side down the asphalt path. Jade lifted her head, let out another wail for popcorn, then dropped her face with despair back on Caitlyn's shoulder. Marissa watched them until they were all piled into Hanley's Bronco, and then she watched the vehicle drive down the hill, and up the street.

She stood there for a long time, until the skin of her face was aching from the wind and her teeth had started chattering again. Then she walked back toward the parking lot.

A door to one of the buildings opened, and salsa music drifted across the cold air. The dusk had that sudden and irretrievable quality she associated with coming out of a movie theater to find the day was almost over. Robbie loved going to the movies in the late afternoon. Suddenly, she remembered the missed phone call. She grabbed her phone from her purse: a missed call and a voicemail from an unknown number. She had a good guess who'd called. She was lifting her phone to her ear to listen to the message when the phone rang in her hand: Robbie. She bunched her hair around the back of her head. Cavano girls can survive anything, she reminded herself.

She took a last, long breath, and pushed the button on the screen's face to answer. "Hi," she said.

"Hi, Izzy," Robbie said, his tone very calm. And the Izzy took her by surprise.

"Robbie, I'm—"

"So this is how this will work. I'll do the talking, you'll do the listening, you'll make a decision, and that will be that."

The brusqueness and formality were so unlike what she'd expected, so unlike him; his tone was very— lawyerly. But what else could she do but agree? "Okay, that's fine."

"We need to make some changes, Marissa. Maybe we both have some growing up to do. I'm going to spend the time between now and next fall finishing my movie, and in September, I'm going to start law school at Harvard. My parents will help make that happen."

He'd always spoken of law school with such dread and contempt—everything Roz and Leo imagined for him and he didn't want for himself. But again, all she could do was agree. "Harvard. Okay. In Cambridge?"

"Cambridge isn't Boston, Marissa," he said, short-tempered.

It was, but: "Right, I understand."

"And you're going to quit being a flight attendant.

That doesn't work for us. If we're going to make it, you have to do what's necessary, too. I think at this point, Marissa"—he said her name like it was a slur he'd just decided to start using—"we can both agree you have been pretty fucking selfish. You can go back to waitressing if you want, but it's been ridiculous for you to use money as an excuse to be away all the time. You don't get to do that anymore. If there are money issues, my parents are willing to help on that front, and there is no reason in the world not to accept that."

She'd told him that she would do anything—anything. So why was she crying again as she stood there on the asphalt path, the phone against her ear? Weren't they reconciling? What was she losing in this negotiation? "Robbie, we need to talk about—"

"Nope," he said. "No, we don't. Not for a while, anyway. What we need right now is a fresh start. And whatever you have to do to . . ." He paused. "It's on you to resolve your situation. Do you understand what I mean?"

He meant: You need to have an abortion, and I don't want to hear about it. And he'd never want to hear about it. He might extract a few more pounds of flesh over Brendan, but the abortion would lie buried and unspoken of at the bottom of their marriage. She lowered the phone, wiped her face, and said, "I understand what you mean."

"Okay, then. Like I said, we need a fresh start, Izzy. Maybe that means—well, I'm still figuring out what it means." But whatever it meant, he would decide, and he wasn't going to get boxed in now by giving the specifics. How much coaching, she wondered, had he been given by Roz, by Laila, fuck, maybe Leo, too, the whole family, before making this phone call? Then again, she'd gone scurrying off to her family, too.

"Robbie . . . ," she began, then didn't know what to say to him.

"We can put this behind us, Izzy," he promised, his voice for the first time a little more familiar. "I am willing to put this behind us. You have a lot of apologizing to do, of course." He was back to the lawyerly. "And maybe I have some to do, too," he conceded, and she had an image of Roz standing at his shoulder, giving him a Thumbs-Up sign. "But we can get through this, because we love each other."

She stared straight up into the darkening clouds. Marriage was a matter of adaptation, of survival, like Leo said. You could make arrangements, compromises. You had to. And she still loved him, didn't she? Like it or not, she did. So she had to decide what she could live with, and she had to decide quickly. "All right, Robbie," she said. "I'll quit, we'll move to Cambridge, I'll apologize, for forever if I have to. But I want to have kids." It sickened her how badly she wanted this—how easy it would be for him to say no. "Please, if you promise me that, I'll . . ."

"I don't have to promise you a thing, Marissa. And to be honest, that is the last thing on my mind right now. Maybe after law school, but even then—I mean, the fact you'd bring it up makes me wonder . . ." He paused, then resumed, more calmly, "I've been clear and I've been fair. I still want our marriage to work." He even sounded like he meant it. "So, what do you want?"

What did she want? She stared up at the sky. What did Marissa ever want?

IV

Let's Start
a Band

[1]

Thelonious Monk
at the Hungry Panda

Adam wandered around the bus station for a while. He followed the right turns of the station hall past the long ticket counter, manned by a single agent; past a bright little shop that sold lottery tickets, magazines, soda, chips in palm-sized bags; past the numbered glass doors out to the curb where the buses came and went; past the cream-tiled entryway to a pair of restrooms, Men to the right, Women to the left; past rows of bolted wire chairs, above which a television displayed a screenful of times and destinations; past an alcoved pizza place, neon sign switched off, the counter behind the glass barrier bare; and back to the pair of revolving doors, through which he'd entered. The lines of overhead fluorescents in their plastic husks cast a chalky light that did not reach the bases of the walls. The waiting area had a cloying smell of powdered sugar, the restrooms smelled like bleach.

He really didn't know what to do. He considered continuing with the charade of going to Ann Arbor—riding the bus to Hartford, to Cleveland, to Detroit, finally arriving at his destination ten or fifteen hours later. But then it would just be a different bus station. He hadn't spoken to Johanna's parents in years; all that tethered them now was a shared grief, and even that tether was frayed. They'd probably never forgiven him for not showing up for Johanna's funeral, something for which he had a hard time forgiving himself. He'd meant to go—but he'd needed some drinks to steel himself, and by the time he felt ready, he'd missed his flight by four hours. No, the only reason to go out to Ann Arbor would be some ass-backward sense of loyalty to Marissa, but actually getting on the bus wouldn't get her her money back, wouldn't do anything to make good her gesture. Plus, she'd never know.

The longer Adam made circuits around the station, the emptier it seemed. The presence of other people scattered here and there only seemed to build to a shared solitude. The scowling, pock-nosed agent at the ticket counter, face bent over a magazine; the Mohawked guy in army fatigues, big red headphones on his ears as he sat against the wall near the bathrooms; the woman pacing before the gates, shouting on her cell phone in Russian, a bottle of cough syrup in her hand; the older man with sallow, malign features, eyes screwed up to the display of times and destinations: There was something remote in all these faces, like they appeared in the old sepia portraits you found jumbled in shoeboxes in antiques stores. And even if he could talk to anybody here, what did he have to say?

There was, of course, only one sensible thing for him to do, the same sensible thing he ought to have done all day: find his way back to the airport in Connecticut, then get his ass back to San Francisco. But he'd succeeded so thoroughly in not doing this so far, it was hard to justify doing it now. Anyway, as he imagined climbing the stairs to his one-bedroom in the Outer Mission, he was struck with the same sense of pointlessness as when he pictured stepping off the bus in Ann Arbor—or, for that matter, continuing to walk around this bus station all night. He'd only go to San Francisco out of habit, or maybe obligation, an obligation to who or what he didn't even know. He was like a marionette who'd gotten so tangled up in his own strings, he hadn't noticed that he was the only one left doing the pulling. He worked at a Citibank; he went swimming five times a week. But, why?

He passed the station entrance, where a stooped man

with peculiarly swollen features and thick, hairy brows, dressed in an overcoat on top of layers of sweatshirts, was leaning against the partition of a pay phone. "Excuse me for a second, you got change?" he called when Adam passed, but Adam ignored him. When Adam passed again, the man scowled knowingly at him. On his next trip around, the man was gone. As if in repentance for this—repentance for something, anything— Adam left the envelope of tickets on top of the pay phone. When he came back again ten minutes later, the tickets were gone, too. Maybe someone had attempted to trade them in for cash, or maybe hopped on a bus to try his or her luck in Michigan, or points in between; for Marissa's sake, at least, Adam hoped the tickets would do whoever'd come upon them some good.

As he came around again to the gates, a woman ran past him—blond hair pouring from under a knit cap embroidered with rings of flowers, a black duffel bag swinging at her hip. Adam watched her—through one of the numbered doors, watched her step smilingly, gratefully onto a bus. And how he envied her that feeling of having made it: arriving just where she'd wanted to be. It was such a simple and perfect consonance: the place you wanted and the place you were. Why was he denied it? Why did he deserve to be stuck in a bus station, with nowhere to go?

Adam wasn't stupid. He'd been through rehab twice. He knew what his mind was doing, what decision he'd arrive at when the gears in his head clicked into place. He'd walk around the bus station a while longer, and finally muster enough loneliness and self-pity and estrangement from his sober life that he'd decide to have a drink. Maybe this had been the plan all along, from the moment he'd woken up that morning: find his way to a situation (say, wandering around the Brattleboro bus station alone on Thanksgiving Day) in which having a drink would be the only thing that would make sense, the only thing that would feel honest. Adam was ashamed to be a drunk, but at least he could recognize himself, too, through the prism of that shame. He'd be less lonely when he began drinking, because he'd find himself in the company he knew best: his own drunk self.

"Cope," he said aloud as he passed the pizza place, and the word landed with a farcical pop, like a snapped guitar string. "Nine months and four days!" and the words came out the same way, like a joke told so often it was no longer funny. Through the glass door, he watched as the bus the girl had caught jerked and pulled away from the curb, seemed to hesitate for just a second, and then headed off to wherever.

He got out his phone to call Marissa. He wasn't ready

to give up quite yet; he recognized that he'd want to be able to tell himself, maybe around the third or fourth drink, that he'd done everything he could. He scrolled among his contacts until he found her name: Marissa Cavano. His thumb hovered over her name but then he changed his mind. He worried that if she knew who was calling, she wouldn't answer; or maybe he worried that if she knew who was calling, she would.

Either way, he turned around and went back to the pay phone, dug out a quarter, appreciated the tactile sensation of sliding it into the slot, followed by the little rattle the coin made as it worked its way down the call box, and dialed the number off his phone. Three rings. Four rings. Five. Then: "This is Marissa Cavano. Please leave me a message. If this is Venture Scheduling, my AIN is 7574813." *Beep*, he heard.

The metal handset had some kind of moist film on it. He held it a little away from his mouth and ear as he spoke—quietly, like he didn't want to be overheard. "So, hey, it's Adam. Um . . . I'm still in the bus station, believe it or, um—yeah. I'm not going out to Ann Arbor. I'm really sorry about that. Thing is, I'm thinking of making some pretty, like . . . bad decisions. Sobriety-wise, I mean. And I didn't know who else to call. So . . . Help? Ha ha ha. Anyway, no worries. Hope it goes well with your mom. Okay, thanks, bye."

He hung up, feeling lighter already. That was it, his last, best shot. Now he could surrender to his folly—his fate. His life in San Francisco lacked any toehold of emotion, it had nothing to do with him, really. It was merely his impersonation of a life. He'd fucked it up with his family, who'd be smart enough never to have anything to do with him again. And the last person he had left to call hadn't answered. And Johanna was dead, he hadn't saved her, and the music hadn't saved her. So what else could he do but the only thing he knew he'd do right, every time?

"Time to get fucked up!" he announced. As he turned, he saw waiting behind him for the phone a stout woman with a scarf wrapped around her face up to her eyes. She glared at him, her eyes above the scarf fierce with enmity.

"Sorry!" he shouted, louder than he meant. She edged backward, bobbing her head in little jerks.

Adam hurried over to the bright little shop. "Rocket Man" was playing, which had to be the universe telling him this was the right thing to do: It was a song about drinking and it was a song he'd played drunk so many times he could do it in a blackout. He stepped over to the cooler, with its refrigerated racks of beverages in cans and screw-top bottles. But as his eyes darted over the juices and sodas and energy drinks and varietals of water, top to bottom, he saw they didn't carry beer. A desperate, aggrieved feeling washed over him: He'd decided to have a drink, so why the fuck wasn't he drinking yet? His body had thrown off all pretense of recovery—every inch of bone and sinew cried out for alcohol with such harmonic aching need, it was downright orgasmic. And the fucking shop didn't sell fucking beer! "Take it easy," he told himself aloud, because he was on the verge of tears. "You'll find some." And it was true, too. The primordial alchemy of a divining rod for water, the bloodhound pack on the scent of an escaped con, the most technologically sophisticated tracking systems ever devised to spot nuke-laden bombers before they reached American cities—that shit had nothing on an alcoholic after booze. If there was a bottle of anything in Brattleboro, Vermont, he would find it.

He pushed out the revolving doors, came out onto the street. The sky had darkened into dusk, skeins of snow coiled in the air, a haze hung over the street in which the headlights of approaching cars glowed with wolfish menace. The whole world had turned bleak and fierce, and he knew this wasn't just the weather: The fear and desperation and that old sadness for himself had grown so thick he couldn't see past them. But the sensation thrilled him, too, addled him, with its potency, the clarity of intention it gave him.

He rushed down the sidewalk, on the hunt. "Tryin' to get my load on on Thanksgiving Day again," Adam sang to himself, to the tune of "Stuck Inside of Mobile with the Memphis Blues Again." The jukebox in his head would shut off, too, when he drank.

This was going to be harder than he thought, though. Everything he passed was a fucking antiques store or a kids' clothing store or a bougie home goods store, all of them closed. He felt anxious walking under the street-lights, but when he moved into the dark on the edge of the sidewalk, he worried about getting jumped. But who had ever gotten jumped in Brattleboro? Tchaikovsky strings screamed tragicomically in his head. Serenade in C Major. What a fucking joke.

Had he walked for ten minutes? Twenty? An hour? By the time he found himself in front of the Hungry Panda, a freestanding Chinese restaurant on a stretch of sleepy sidewalk, the arthritis and cold had dug so deep into the fists in his pockets he wasn't sure he'd be able to open them. But beer signs glowed in the windows like the deck lights of a ship to a castaway. Pushing open the door was like stepping through the parting of the pearly gates. If it was meant to be any other way, it would've been closed, he thought as he walked in. Then he thought, If it was meant to be any other way, it would have been some other way.

Globular paper lanterns dangled across the ceiling, mirrors lined the walls, the sides of the booths were painted red and gold, carved in swirls and waves. From somewhere, orchestral Christmas music played feebly. And there was a full bar at the back.

But Adam was prepared to take his time now. He brought his fists to his face, blew on them as he waited at the podium for someone to appear and seat him. A great, blue-lit fish tank stood beside the door, striped and spotted and lacquered fish swimming around in brainless content inside. He tapped on the glass with his knuckle, watching for them to scatter. "Don't do that, please!" a lilting voice said. A hostess had turned up: a plump, sturdy woman with a high forehead and a thin, quick mouth. "Only one?" she asked him.

"Yup, yup, only one," Adam heard himself say; some breach had opened inside himself, and he was peering in from the margins, watching to see what he did next. Unity would come with the first swallow, he knew.

He followed the waitress to a booth, the table set for six. She put the menu down in front of him and disappeared. From his seat, Adam saw that the Christmas music was coming from a synthesizer in a corner, a cheap off-brand you could pick up at Target for eighty bucks, an iPod on the stool behind it plugged into the input jack. "It figures," he said. Probably somebody played the synth on the weekends or something—and Christ, he could just hear it: glossy digital notes played off sheet music, a muzak "Yellow Submarine" interrupted by "Happy Birthday." Yes, it figured.

"God Rest Ye Merry Gentlemen," all strings, anemic and tinny, spread through the restaurant. An Indian family in a booth by the door were the only other customers: a chubby, mustachioed dad, looking bored, a mother in powder-blue scrubs, looking tired, and two heavyset little boys, one playing a video game on a handheld device, *beep-do-deep*, the other watching the fish in the tank like it was the goddamn Super Bowl. Adam turned his head toward the bar. He had a clear view to the stacked shelves of bottles, the alpha through omega of shapes and colors, from the crystalline high-end vodka to the electric blue of Curaçao to the inky black of coffee liqueur, the manly square of the whiskey and the unwieldy elephant trunk of Galliano and the squat sphere of Chambord.

"So we meet again," he said toward them in a James Bond–villain accent. Yup, the gang was all here, reunited at last. He used to spend hours just staring at the shelves of bottles behind the bar, finding such comfort in the abundance: every viscosity, every proof, like a new box of crayons, like a family at a dinner . . .

"You ready order?" The hostess who'd seated him was back, notepad in her hand, pen poised.

"Yeah. Yeah." Awkwardly, he picked up the menu, opened it—suddenly shy, for some reason, like the guy who strides into a brothel, all macho and fuck-swagger, and gets tongue-tied when the pro asks what he wants. "So, uh . . ."

"Need more time?"

"No," he said sharply. "I'll have . . . Let's see . . . I'll have some egg drop soup, and the fried pork dumplings, and a beer, and—"

"What kinda beer?"

He stared, like she'd caught him red-handed. She looked back, bland and disinterested. "You want Chinese beer?"

He nodded. "And moo shu with chicken," he went on, "and a double gin and tonic, and . . . and . . . and General Tso's, extra spicy, and crispy beef. And some . . ." His mouth was dry. "And water. And a Jack and Coke." He tried to smile. "I know that's a lot."

She wasn't looking at him, her eyes were on the pad. "Egg drop soup, fried pork dumpling, moo shu with chicken, General Tso chicken extra spicy, crispy beef, Chinese beer, gin tonic double, and Jack Coke, right?" She spoke in a detached, singsongy voice, like she was chanting an incantation she knew by rote. He nodded. She didn't see. She looked up and he nodded again. It was a ridiculous order, but what did she care? The more, the better, right? he wanted to ask her. She turned and walked away.

A gust of wind tumbled in as the door opened; Adam looked up with a shock of hope. But who could he expect to see? An elderly couple walked in: the man in big, square sunglasses, like he must've just had eye surgery, the woman's face a cold-pinched ruby red, earmuffs on her ears. The hostess hurried over to them. "Hi, Mister, Missus Bernstein, Happy Thanksgiving," she said cheerfully.

"The Little Drummer Boy" began now. Marissa hadn't called him back; Kristen hadn't called to check on him; Jack hadn't, his parents hadn't. It was amazing, how short the list of people who might care where he was had gotten. All his friends—well, he'd fucked over most of them: borrowed money, pawned their instruments, insulted their girlfriends or wives. And the money his parents had spent! For rehab, plus the lessons, camps, teachers over the years. Jack told him they'd taken out a second mortgage to afford Stone Manor. He was an expensive habit! And all a waste. Because now it was all settled. The future was more predictable than anyone liked to admit, because no one ever changed. You were the fish tank you swam in: only so much was possible between those four walls. Johanna was crazy; Adam was an alcoholic. You could rub them together however you wanted, but the outcome would always be the same: the loony bin; the bar. He was never going to be Sufjan Stevens. She was never going to be St. Vincent. It was a miracle they'd even made the one record. It was pretty good, at least. But too bad it hadn't been better.

The beer appeared before him with a clunk. The hostess had maybe forgotten to open it; he didn't check whether it was a twist-off. He watched as she went behind the bar, poured a gin and tonic: *his* gin and tonic. She swirled the ice cubes in the Jack and Coke with a straw. Adam had to piss.

He shoved his way out of the booth, looked around. The hostess, with a sort of hostess-manager-only-waitress-working telepathy, lifted her head and pointed to a doorway to his left. He jogged over, pushed the door open, almost toppled down stairs he hadn't expected. Grabbing the rail, he let his momentum carry him down two at a time. On the landing at the bottom, through a gap between racks of glasses and stacked cardboard boxes of paper towels, he saw a white sliding door with the pictograph for a bathroom. He slid the door open, flicked on the light switch, closed the door behind him, and locked it.

The toilet and sink and electric hand dryer were enough to make the space crowded. He undid his pants, pulled them to his thighs, and pissed. Then he pulled up his pants and looked in the mirror. It was easy to forget how you really looked, how bony and shifty your face must appear to other people. This would be the final relapse: You could see it like it was etched into the creases that wrung his eyes, like it was the only words his trembling, untrustworthy mouth had to say. And there was comfort in knowing that. He'd never again force himself to make the long climb up to sobriety—he'd just let himself sink. Rock bottom was a myth: You never smacked into some unbearable floor of shame that impelled you back up to the arms of good sense. Rock bottom was just whatever point addicts reached before they cleaned up and then, looking back, declared, That was the worst. In truth, you could spend a whole life sinking, if you wanted. And that would be Adam's life—being one of those guys at the bar with the fragile, friendly, grasping look, who got kicked out every night, but was always there the next day. He'd never drive anywhere without stopping for a twelve-pack, trash bags of empties would accumulate wherever he lived, like tumors.

He washed his hands, as certain of this later destiny as he was of the course of the next hours, as if it was annunciated by the choiring angels Johanna believed she heard from the spigot of their bathroom sink. He'd drink here until they cut him off, and when they cut him off, he'd trash this place. Adam was a happy drunk, until he became the opposite. He grinned in the mirror at the thought: ripping the paper lanterns from the ceiling, smashing plates on the floor, grabbing bottles from behind the bar. He'd shove the fish tank over, he'd watch the cascading water hurtle the fish across the floor—flop, gasp, die. He'd jump up and down on the synthesizer, he'd throw chairs to try to break the windows. You could do a lot of damage before the police finally showed up. I'm not scared anymore, he thought as he climbed the stairs, I'm not scared.

His ears were ringing when he sat down again, he couldn't hear the music. The food had arrived: beef and chicken piled in mounds on the plates, oozing to their lips, the table so crowded with dishes it was like he'd ordered for the empty seats, too. And his three drinks: the beer now plucked of its cap, the double gin and tonic, the Jack and Coke. That was all it would take; it was more than enough. He hesitated a while longer, but only because he knew it was already too late. God, he was tired of being himself; God, he was tired of being himself, and being ashamed of it. And at last the simplicity that made the dependency so powerful, for him, finally, incurable: If he had a drink, he would feel better.

His phone dinged its voicemail ding. It wasn't exactly a lightning bolt, it wasn't Johanna with wings descending from the sky. But he figured he should at least check it. On the screen, he read that he had a message from Marissa. But he didn't believe it until he heard her voice, alto-ish, firm: "I'm in the bus station, but I don't see you. If it isn't too late, let me know where you are and I'll pick you up and take you to a meeting. I know you may not believe this, but there are a lot of people counting on you." She was silent for so long he had to look at the phone to see whether the message had ended. "Think about the people who love you, Adam." And *silenzio*.

As Adam tossed the phone across the table, he felt the most clear and perfect hatred he had ever known. It was like a black, polished diamond burning in his palm: He hated Marissa. He hated her for calling him back, he hated her for looking for him at the bus station, hated her for what she'd said in her voicemail: "the people who love you."

In the grip of that hatred, with an anguished wail,

he shoved everything on the table off the table, onto the floor. There followed a tiny symphony of shattering glass and bouncing flatware, the foodstuff slither, and a plate spinning almost to a whistle before its sudden facedown plop, ice cubes tripping over tile, a final diminuendo of a rolling chopstick, and, like applause, the gasps from everyone else in the restaurant. It was worse than the worst case of blue balls; Tantalus himself wouldn't have understood the physical torture of what Adam had just done to himself. He even considered getting on the floor and licking up some of the spilled Jack and Coke. Because no matter what he said to the hostess now—and he'd have to come up with that pretty quickly—there was no server on the planet who'd bring him a drink after this.

And just like that, the hatred drifted away like smoke. Adam blinked around the restaurant, smiling stupidly at the Indian family, at the Bernsteins. He climbed out of the booth, got down on his knees, and started picking up the shards of glass.

When the hostess, rattling off an unbroken monologue in Chinese, walked over with a mop, he took a minute to text Marissa:

Chinese restaurant near the bus station. Hungry Panda. Not too late.

A restaurant table, Christmas music, a waitress who wanted nothing to do with them. "Here we go again," Marissa said as she sat down across from him. He looked worse for wear since she'd first seen him, and he hadn't exactly started the day looking daisy fresh.

"I'm sorry" was the first thing out of his mouth.

"For what? Not getting on the bus? Calling? Whatever happened here?" She pointed to the yellow tee-peed Wet Floors sign, standing at the head of the table like a scarlet letter. But before he could answer, she waved her hand. "Forget it, I don't care." She was all out of judgment—all out of blame, for him, for herself, for anybody. All that mattered to her was that she'd gotten there while he was still sober, which she could tell by now by looking at him: He had the skittish, eager-to-please appearance of someone very carefully doing the right thing, doubting how long he'd be able to pull it off.

"I'll pay you back the eighty bucks sometime," he promised.

"I didn't drag my ass back up to Brattleboro for eighty dollars." Besides, she might have told him, if she had money problems, it was by choice. It was one of so many, many choices in her life. Instead, she asked, "What about Johanna?"

He chewed on his pinkie nail for a minute, then told her, in a plain, flat voice, "She killed herself a couple years ago." Marissa felt herself recoil, like he'd slapped her, but she realized she wasn't surprised. "They switched around her meds, or she stopped taking them or something. But she snuck out of her parents' house and she jumped off a bridge into the Huron River. It was wintertime. She left a note, they didn't find her body for a while. Then they did."

Marissa found herself mired in the same speechlessness she always did, that everyone did, in these moments. "I'm really sorry" was the best she could do.

"Yeah," he said. "Yeah. It's hard because I guess she'd been doing better. Even if better meant living in her parents' basement and watching QVC all day. But I don't think Johanna ever believed she could have a normal life, y'know? Going to work every day, paying rent. She didn't think she was cut out for that. See, Johanna was a . . ." He stared down toward the red lacquered table, as if making an effort to see through it—through the table, through the floor, down through the bones of the Earth, to some final, hard, specific truth about her. They both knew he wasn't going to find it.

"I watched a YouTube video of you guys playing," she told him.

He smiled, a rare, complete smile. "Oh yeah? What song? Where?" She shook her head, not knowing. "Maybe it was when we played Coachella. I know people still watch that video."

It was maybe the first time he'd appeared genuinely happy all day. "You don't miss playing?"

"No, not really," he answered, the smile flatlining. "I mean, I can look back and say that Johanna and I played some good shows, that I wrote some cool songs . . . But all that failure? I don't miss that at all. I don't even mean my career, just the sitting down at the keyboard and knowing ninety-nine times out of a hundred you're going to get it wrong. I'd say I'm pretty relieved that music and trying to reach people with music and all that is somebody else's problem now. And I'm free to just . . ." He trailed off; his angular features settled in an embittered look. "It wasn't healthy. It wasn't sustainable. Playing started putting me in a really bad headspace. I kinda think being good at piano was maybe the worst thing that ever happened to me."

Marissa was glad she reached him sober; and she didn't deny that something like friendship, at some unremarked point, had spread between them. But she'd forgotten how fed up she'd been with him, even before she'd dropped him at the bus station. It was like he could thread any needle with a sense of victimization, even being born with a gift. "That's such a bullshit thing to say," she said.

"That doesn't mean it's not true!" That was exactly what it meant, but she didn't feel like arguing. And maybe he sensed she was out of patience with him, because he asked, "Why did you come get me, then? If it wasn't for the eighty."

It was a good question, and she could have given him a lot of answers: because she'd learned for the umpteenth time today that it was hopeless with her mother, but maybe it wasn't hopeless with him; because she would have done anything to take her mind off the decisions she had to make in her own life; because they were both a couple of strays, in the end, and she'd felt some loyalty on account of that. But what she told him was the truth: "I didn't think about it. I just did it."

He grinned. "You know what your secret is, Marissa? You're nice. You think you're this callous hardass. And maybe you are, kinda. But actually, you're like a really, really nice person."

She lifted her hands so her fingers hid her eyes. She wanted to cry again, or she didn't want to cry; she couldn't tell anymore. When she lowered her hands, she asked, "If I'm so nice, then why'd I cheat?"

He made a face like she'd just asked him the square root of an eight-digit number. "Shit, Marissa," he said with sympathy. His hand started to reach across the table for hers, but then he thought better of it, and smiled instead. "I said you were nice. I didn't say you were boring!"

She looked over his shoulder at the bottles lined on shelves behind the bar. In different company, she would have ordered one of those sickly sweet cocktails with the paper umbrellas—ordered one, ordered five. She was so tempted she thought she just might do it. But she'd known since she was about eight years old she would need to spend her whole life being careful about alcohol. She pictured her mother, crumpled over in the recliner. She imagined Special K, struggling to tuck a blanket under her thighs. She looked at Adam, chin in his hand, drumming away at his cheekbone with his fingers.

"Why don't you go home?" she asked him. "Don't you know how lucky you are, that you can just go home?"

He jerked back, like she'd insulted him. "Like it's so easy."

"It is easy," she insisted. "Just . . . walk in the door."

"Yeah, that's a long walk though," he told her. "That's a long walk . . ."

"Fine, Adam," she said, giving up. "Have it your way."

His eyes shifted down to the table again, up to the door of the restaurant, back down to the table. "What do you want me to say?" he asked her. "Look," he went on, "you remember what you said in your voicemail about . . . Y'know, the 'people who love me.' And yeah, that's great and all, but—my family never gave up on me. Even when they didn't want me around, I knew they hadn't given up. And Christ, I hated them for that. I hated you, too, for a couple seconds, when I knew you were coming." He leaned forward, elbows underneath his chest, eyes still lowered. "You can't imagine how awful it is, when you've given up on yourself, to know someone else hasn't. I did a little AA for a while. I even went to church, if you can believe it, but none of that higher power stuff helped me at all. 'Jesus loves you,' they said. Fucking hope not! Kristen loves me. Jack loves me. That's bad enough."

He looked so lost inside himself. She didn't know what else to say besides, "You can't make it on your own, though. Nobody does." He shook his head, muttering something underneath his breath. "What?"

"I said," he enunciated loudly, "that that was a fucked up thing to say."

"Well, I'm sorry, Adam, if that offends you, but believe it or not, I was trying to be nice. Remember me? *Nice?* Have you ever noticed what you do to anyone who tries to be *nice* to you?" She was swinging her hand in the air at him; he was making a show of ignoring her, so she dropped it to the table. That was a mistake—it was her left hand, already crowned with a black-and-blue welt from the steps. "Fuck!" she groaned.

"You okay?" he asked her.

"I'm great, Adam, I'm fucking fantastic . . ." She rubbed the hand against her pants leg. "Look," she said. "I can take you home, or I can take you to the airport, or I can drop you at a meeting. But I can't sit here with you forever. I've got to . . ." She needed to get back to the Sheraton soon if she was going to work this flight; or she was also maybe fifteen minutes from the Russells' Vermont house, and if she told Robbie she never wanted to see his father again, that might be something, possibly the only thing, he'd agree to. So she had to decide—only she couldn't. But hadn't she already made up her mind? What decision was there? She was going to refuse to quit her job, refuse to be the wife of a lawyer, refuse to live like a millionaire for the rest of her life—why? For what? She didn't feel like looking at Adam anymore, so instead she turned and looked around the restaurant: at the fish tank by the door, the hostess glaring at her and Adam, the elderly couple eating slowly, the synthesizer and the iPod playing "Good King Wenceslas."

"Can I tell you something," she said, turning back to Adam. He nodded. "I want to have this baby. I want to have this baby so fucking bad. And I know it was the stupidest thing I ever did in my entire godforsaken life, but, fuck, Adam, *I* did it. And when I did it, I felt . . ." Are you happy now? she asked herself. You told your sob story, you had your moment, and the whole world is bawling for you. Now go home to your husband. Have your abortion, you think you're the first? There are a lot worse things a marriage can be than an arrangement. Only lucky people get to worry about love, and freedom. The Cavanos aren't lucky. Somewhere in there, the voice in her head had started talking like Mona.

"I mean, you could," he said.

"Could what?"

"Have the baby," he answered casually. He grimaced. "Fuck, are you listening to this 'O Tannenbaum'? The treble is so loud you can't—"

"Hey, Adam?"

"What?"

"Fuck you!" she shouted, letting it all loose. "You mean, stupid, drunk fuck-up! And don't you dare make your palms-up-me-so-sorry gesture, you whiny prick."

His hands were halfway in the air; he placed them flat on the table. "It's a miracle if you can get your dick out to piss without screwing something up, but me, oh, sure, I can just go have a baby! Will you stop telling me to fucking do that? Do you have any idea how terrifying that is for me to think about? What if I can't feed her, Adam?" She realized at some point, she'd started imagining the baby as a girl—there were things you couldn't help. "What do I say to her if she's hungry on Thanksgiving? What do I say to her if we get evicted, and all she can take with her is what she can fit in two shopping bags? What do I say to her about her father, if she never gets to—You're an idiot, Adam. You're a goddamn idiot." Spit had been bursting from her mouth for a while now as she yelled. But his look was surprisingly measured: brows pulled low over his eyes, mouth clenched shut, like a man standing in a rainstorm. It occurred to her that of the times he'd been screamed at, even that day, this was relatively mild. She slumped back into the booth, stared down at the undulations in the grain of the table.

"Sorry," she heard him say.

"How about we make a deal you never have to apologize to me again, and we call it even?"

"Deal," he answered.

"I'm so scared, Adam," she confessed, her voice

quiet, trembling now. "God, I've never been so scared. I didn't care about leaving Boston. I didn't care about college. I cared, but only because . . . I didn't want to be like my mother. That's all I ever wanted in life. That was the only thing I ever set out to do. I know it'll never be good again with me and Robbie, whatever was there got used up, maybe a long time ago. But I can't turn into some mean drunk bitch, dragging my kid around outside the grocery store while I try to sell my food stamps for cash." Tears she didn't even feel, wouldn't have guessed she was capable of, splashed onto the table.

"Hey," she heard him say, his voice gentle. "I've known my share of mean drunk bitches. That's not you, okay? You'd be a great mom!"

She understood what he meant earlier, about the torment of people believing in you more than you believed in yourself. "If I hadn't left you a voicemail, you'd be blacked out on the floor of this shitty Chinese restaurant right now, because you're too frightened of the last people on Earth who love you," she told him, her voice lean and sharp, even as she saw more tears splash onto the lacquer. "I don't need your advice about what makes a great parent."

At length, he said, "Don't give up, Marissa."

She looked at him. She hadn't noticed before how

small he was—his thinness not lean but rather slight, like he was dwindling away in his own skin. "Haven't you?"

He could've said nothing, and let that nothinged silence be the end of their time together—their friendship, if you wanted to call it that. He knew they'd never speak again after today. Speaking would be a reminder they wouldn't want: of a Thanksgiving when they'd had only each other to turn to. In a year, she'd be back at the Russells' house in Vermont; he pictured her standing by the windows in the conservatory, dressed in a cardigan and this same necklace. She wouldn't want pity, nor deserve it, really. (But then, who did?) He had no idea where he would be in a year, which was itself a clue that wherever he'd landed by then, he wouldn't be sober. The odds weren't great for any recovering alcoholic—and like she said, without family, without support, without people . . . Today, he'd ordered drinks, he'd sat down to drink them, come within an inch, a breath, an iPhone ding he could've just as easily never heard. Dumb luck. Next time, the luck would be different. All in all, though, the price of letting their day together end with nothing said was not so very high: an alcoholic relapses, a woman resigns herself to an unhappy marriage. If you didn't know the alcoholic, if you didn't know the woman, you'd never know it happened. You might pass Adam in an airport, you might glimpse Marissa's face in a car window, you would never be able to tell. If it was tragedy, it was tragedy so ordinary it would sink in the world without a ripple.

But even so.

It wouldn't be wrong to say Marissa had saved his life that day, maybe more than once. And he owed her better than to let their friendship (what other word was there?) dwindle to nothing, when there was still so much he wished he could say to her, so much he wanted her to know. He'd probably fail but he owed her his best attempt.

His fingers still ached from the cold, he hadn't warmed up or played a goddamn note in years, the synth was a piece of shit, and there wasn't even an amp. But you've either given up or you haven't. You either play, or you don't.

So Adam took off his coat and he took off his sweatshirt and he walked to the synthesizer with what he hoped looked like dignity, or bravery, or something; he unplugged the iPod, he said a prayer to the face tattooed on his arm—"Just get me through the first chord, man"—and when he played that first chord he felt the sound rising up to his neck to swallow him, but he followed the sound out until he could lead it. It wasn't agony; it wasn't joy; it was keys and purpose, Adam staying within the boundaries of what arthritic, years-out-of-practice fingers on a hundred-dollar restaurant keyboard could do—but trying, eyes closed and with all his might; trying, so she could see that he was trying: darting notes, and then waves and ladders, taking apart every song they'd heard that day and trying to strike keys for every face they'd seen—playing like a poor man's Thelonious Monk, making allies of skips and broken phrases and dissonances, weaving his accidents into grace, because all he wanted to say was that he thought she was brave, and that she had been the hero of his day, and she would be the hero of her child's life, too, if that was what she wanted. He tried to play courageously, and to put courage into the music; he tried to play without succumbing to loss or grief or fear. He tried to play with freedom. Until he was panting, and out of breath, and handsore, and fucked out.

When he lifted his fingers and opened his eyes, the elderly couple had left; the hostess was shaking her head in a scolding way, as if he'd found a whole new way to disappoint her; a busboy in a dirty smock had appeared, leaned against one of the booths, his mouth bent in too many directions at once for Adam to interpret. But Marissa had her hands clasped together in front of her mouth, like she was watching him walk across ice. He heard her pull in a breath, maybe relief, maybe wonder. And then she applauded—two hands clapping in the whole place.

[2]
The Warshaws'
(Take 2)

The driveway was steep, short, led straight up to the garage. Marissa pulled in behind two parked cars; several others were parked along the street at the bottom of the hill. "It looks like they're having people over," Adam said grimly.

It was dark out by now; in the glow of the Sonata's headlights, big, slow snowflakes fell, and to Marissa the view through the windshield was like looking into a snow globe: the windows of the two-story, slate-roofed house gold-yellow beneath the eaves, the porch light lit above the steps of the stoop, a wreath on the door around a brass knocker. "You grew up here?" she asked.

"I know, right?" Adam answered. "Like if you Google Imaged 'suburbia,' this is what you'd see."

He'd misunderstood the wonder in her voice, but

before she could explain, a little boy in a blue snow-suit appeared in the porch light, running around from the back of the house. He was five, maybe six, and as Marissa watched he bounded up the steps, wheeled around, stopped, and stared at the car. "Oh, there's . . . my nephew," said Adam. "We had a little chat this morning."

"What did you have a chat about with a six-year-old?"

He didn't answer. After staring at them another moment, the boy turned and ran into the house, slamming the door behind him. "Great," Adam said under his breath.

She looked at her watch. She wouldn't have time to go up to the dayroom, would need to change back into her uniform in the car, and meet the shuttle in front of the hotel. It would be tight—but she'd made it under tighter circumstances. Even so. "Okay, Adam," she told him. "I'm out of time. Just take a deep breath or whatever and remember—"

The door opened. A heavyset, middle-aged man in a brown parka, jeans, and a Red Sox hat came out, looked at the car, and started walking toward them. He had an uneven gait, slouching shoulders, a scowling face.

"Fuck," said Adam. "That's my brother."

His brother stopped in the beams of the headlights and leaned his head forward, peering through the windshield. The scowl tightened as he walked over to the passenger side door and tapped on Adam's window. Adam lowered it. "Hi, Jack!" he said.

"Have you been drinking or not?" Jack asked.

Adam replied with a sarcastic whistle. "Wow, right, great to see you, too."

"You want to quit fucking around?"

"Jesus, relax, I'm sober." Jack's expression in the window didn't budge. "You want me to take a Breathalyzer, too? I wouldn't be back here if I'd been drinking, okay?" he said, with a little more contrition.

"Yeah, you and your famous tact . . ." Jack leaned his head into the car, looked at Marissa. "And who's she?"

"A friend," Adam said.

"A friend," Jack repeated, skeptical.

"He hasn't been drinking," Marissa told him. "I've been with him all day, he's—"

Jack shook his head in two solid jerks, cutting her off. "Sorry, I don't know you, but ma'am, I don't need to hear the story." He looked at Adam, his arms folded over his chest, his chin pressed against his collar, petulantly. "All right. You're alive, so maybe Mom will stop crying for fifteen minutes. You're sober. That makes me happy, believe it or not. I guess what I want to know is what you're doing sitting parked in the driveway." Adam didn't answer. "It never stops with you, does it?" After a moment, Jack asked, "You still smoke Marb Reds?"

"That's a problem now, too?" Adam asked.

"I want a cigarette, genius," Jack shot back.

"I thought you quit because your cholesterol . . . Yeah, fine, sure." Adam took out the pack. "Only one left, so . . ." He put the cigarette in his mouth, and seemed to feel the look Marissa was giving him; he opened the door and got out.

He leaned back against the car, as if to ensure she couldn't drive away. She heard the lighter click, she could see through the open window as Adam offered the cigarette to Jack. For a while, they just stood there, passing the cigarette back and forth. "What the fuck," Jack finally said. "What the fuck . . ."

"I know, I know," Adam answered—looser, more apologetic than Marissa would have expected.

"You want to tell me what happened with the coffeepot?"

"It just—slipped off the counter."

"Did it? You know for two hours, Mom convinced herself you were coming back with coffee."

"I thought about it!"

"Oh, good for you!" Then, quickly, he added, "Sorry. But it's hard to watch. They never stop giving you the benefit of the doubt. No matter what, you'll always be the chosen one."

"Yeah, right."

"Yeah, Adam," Jack said, "that's right." When Adam offered him back the cigarette, he said, "No, this was a dumb idea, anyway. I'm hanging on by a thread with Lizzy as it is."

"What d'you mean? You guys are great!"

Marissa heard Jack snort. "When was the last time you saw Lizzy, Adam? Two years ago? The world didn't stop while you were getting sober." He paused, then said, "I cheated on her. How about that? Fucking idiot, right? Don't even know what I was thinking. Three kids, forty-five years old, bad knee . . . One afternoon I decide to fuck a . . . twenty-six-year-old dental hygienist." Another pause. "So I'll be in couples therapy for the rest of my life. But anyway, we're—I don't know. Trying. So how about it, Adam? Are you coming inside or not? You feel like doing some trying?" Adam didn't answer. "Okay, then, I won't get anybody's hopes up. I'll tell them somebody got lost. You can do what you want, as usual. Just don't leave the butt out here, Mom'll notice." He walked back up the driveway and went inside.

Adam stood by the car for another minute. Marissa was about to say something when he finally turned and leaned down to the window. "That is mind-blowing!" he cried, eyes wide. "He cheated! Jack never . . ." He stopped, noting Marissa's face. "Right. You gotta go." He grinned, in a knowing way, and, reaching in the window, locked the passenger side door. "Because what if I get back inside and do something stupid?"

She grinned back at him, also knowing, and a little sad. "Imagine that."

He looked at the house, looked back at her. "I feel like I'm nine again and I have to play Chopin in front of a thousand people. What am I supposed to say to them?"

"You don't have to say anything. Just walk in the door. That's all you have to do."

"You don't want to—" He stopped himself. He gave her a look she'd think about for a long time: It passed through many possibilities, like a bird that didn't know where to land. But in the end he lifted his hands into the car, palms pressed together, and bent them toward her, in the manner of a salute—appreciative, admiring— and all he said was, "*Bravissima.*" He added, "Get home safe, Marissa."

And he turned, and he walked up the driveway. At the bottom of the stoop he stopped and put his hands over his eyes, his body taut and poised, and she thought she was going to see him run off across the yard. But instead he walked up the steps the same way she'd seen him walk to the keyboard—with a readiness—and he opened the door, went inside, and closed the door behind him.

She watched for as long as she had time to watch. He didn't appear again—not kicked out, not searching for her. She'd left the engine on, and now she put the car in reverse, and when she reached the bottom of the driveway, she stopped, and put the car in park. She put her hands on her stomach, for the first time without regret. What promise could she make? What assurance could she give? What could she say to her child that would be true? That she would do her best for her—that she would always have a home with her—

Marissa turned on the radio, beautiful soul music she'd never know the name of, drove down the street, a song ending, a song beginning.

Acknowledgments

Many thanks to Susan Golomb. You couldn't ask for a better ally in the foxhole of the writing life. I also want to thank Kate Nintzel, my exemplary editor at William Morrow, whose insight and diligence helped make this book better, all any author can hope for from an editor. Kelly Rudolph, Molly Waxman, and Margaux Weisman also helped see this book out into the world, for which I am very grateful. Alexandra Shelley gave valuable guidance in the early draft days.

I've been blessed with a large and loving family, which, for the record, in no way resembles any of the families portrayed in this work of fiction. My mom and dad, my grandmother, Leah, Jon, Aleigh, Sarah, and Jeff were always there when I needed them. Naomi, when she is old enough to read this, will learn that she was a source of boundless inspiration to her father. My wife, Julie, every day offered faith, patience, and love without which this book could not have been written; that's just one small reason *Start Without Me* is dedicated to her.

In researching this book, I had the privilege of hearing stories of people who have struggled with substance use issues. Too often, these people face stigma, misunderstanding, and severely limited treatment options. Adam is luckier than he'd admit: Most people don't get to go to a Stone Manor. I want to acknowledge the heroic work of the counselors, social workers, psychologists (including my sister, Dr. Sarah Feldman), group leaders, and others who are on the front lines of treatment. They and the people they treat deserve more of our support.